OLD JIM
CANAAN

MARGARET SKINNER

OLD JIM CANAAN

A NOVEL

ALGONQUIN BOOKS OF CHAPEL HILL

1990

With gratitude to Louis D. Rubin, Jr.

Published by Algonquin Books of Chapel Hill
Post Office Box 2225
Chapel Hill, North Carolina 27515-2225
a division of
Workman Publishing Company, Inc.
708 Broadway
New York, New York 10003
Design by Molly Renda.

Library of Congress Cataloging-in-Publication Data
Skinner, Margaret, 1942–
Old Jim Canaan: a novel / by Margaret Skinner.
p. cm.
ISBN 0-945575-37-8: $18.95
1. Irish Americans—Tennessee—Memphis—History—Fiction.
2. Memphis (Tenn.)—History—Fiction. I. Title.
PS3569.K525O44 1990
813'.54—dc20   90-35594 CIP

10 9 8 7 6 5 4 3 2 1

First Printing

In memory of my father,
and for his grandchildren

OLD JIM
CANAAN

The Canaan Family

1843–1920

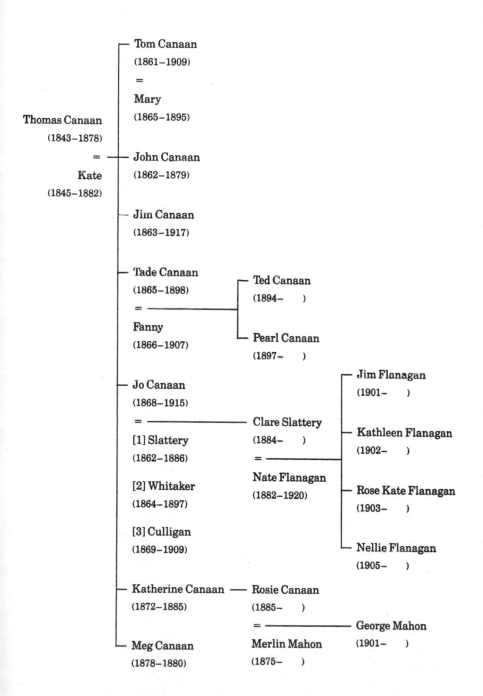

PART I

Second Street

1914, *Jim Flanagan*

Saturday was a laggard. That's what Uncle Jim Canaan called people who were slow to cross the street when his man, Distance Mills, drove him all around Memphis to collect rent. Distance would blow the horn and "the laggards" would scatter. Saturdays always started slow, but ended up leaving in a hurry.

The house sat on the corner of Second Street and Overton Avenue. It was tall and white with a high pitched roof of tiles that were mottled green and rust. The porch ran the front of the house and extended along both sides, the south part warm, the north side shady and still, except when Uncle Jim sat talking with his men about the effects of the prohibition law. Their cigar smoke would heat up the air, hanging around the house like thick fog, mixing in with the words that bunched, pitched, and rumbled in a low riding thunder that stopped suddenly whenever Uncle Jim spoke.

"They'll never enforce it," he would growl. "Damned thing's just a crumb for the reformers."

And I thought of his pronouncements as I sat on the front steps waiting for George. The steps were steep and cut the front porch in half the way Uncle Jim's voice did when it shot through the house stilling the current of family life, the slack in time stiff and breathless as in an old photograph. It was then that my own carefree spirit would take on flesh and bone, the heft of it making talk or even movement seem somehow unsafe.

I felt the rough concrete of the steps. I always sat on the middle step so my sisters couldn't sneak up on me. They were soft-footed like Indians and lightning quick; in the middle, I could see them coming both ways. But thoughts of their eaves-dropping on this Saturday was a waste of worry, since they lay sleeping in the great feather bed like three birds in a nest.

George Mahon was my cousin, but he and I were really blood brothers, or so we said. He and I could be together for a whole day without talking. It was like we knew what each other was thinking and didn't have to say it. The blood that ran through Uncle Jim was inside me and in George. Since we already had some of the same blood, no need to do any cutting.

George was an only child, but wasn't spoiled. That was because he often had to take care of Rosie, his mother. She drank a lot. In the kitchen, whispering as if she were on stage, Viola had said that "Miz Rosie" was a sot and that she had been one since her first highball. George would fetch and carry for Rosie to keep her quiet, since any ruckus she raised stirred the wrath of the Major, Merlin Mahon, who was George's father.

The Major drank his share too, and as Dad would say, with much "attention and deliberation," but he cursed the "vulgarity of drunkenness" and was especially dogmatic when the vice cropped up in a lady. Ladies were "the flowers of the earth deserving of respect and honor." What with Rosie constantly slipping off of the pedestal, I can say that he went a long way in keeping the tenet of his faith.

He was not a military man, but was called Major because he said "harumph" like a crusty old soldier and because he walked like he was in a parade balancing eggs on his square shoulders like epaulettes. My father, who loved a good joke more than anything, pegged him with this name.

4

One night as the three of them ate dinner with us, Rosie became fractious and swept her arm across a huddle of crystal goblets that had tinkled like bells as they fell broken in the puddle of water. Everyone then became quiet. George squirmed in his chair twisting his napkin into a rope. Holding a little silver after-dinner coffee spoon, Mother tapped lightly on her goblet, which had not been broken, a signal that dinner was over. Mother's timing was perfect, that is to say before the Major could become irate. While Dad steered the Major to the parlor for a cigarette, Mama Jo hustled Rosie out of the room. The Major balked, but Dad's grip on his elbow reminded him that words left unsaid wouldn't have to be erased. Whenever he could manage it, Dad jumped over problems like a runner over hurdles. When it came to keeping life smooth, my parents, Nate and Clare Flanagan, were silk; my grandmother, Mama Jo, a strong thread.

Viola came in to clean up the mess. George had been trying to pick up the slivers of glass, but Mother had stopped him. "George, Viola will spread newspaper over it," she said. "It's her special trick." Then she gave him a pat on the back, nodded to Viola, and left the room, her perfume lingering after she was gone.

Viola had taken the pieces of glass from George's hand, then, looking at him and shaking her head said, "I don't know how dey got a peach frum two such persimmons." I agreed about Rosie being the persimmon. But the Major, who was a lawyer, was also an apple, a sort of sour green one, his tartness a welcomed taste.

Now the streetcar stopped at the median. I could barely see George's head passing by the windows, his face wedged between the chests and backs of taller people. George's legs bulged under the black stockings as he crossed Second Street. I glanced down at my own skinny legs that allowed my stockings to ripple in black waves. The stockings stayed put in winter by the bulk of the long underwear, but in spring not even God could keep them up. I pulled up the slack and stuffed it under the bottom band of my knickers, grateful that the Confirmation would bring me a pair of long trousers.

He was carrying a book under his arm. We traded books every Saturday. I had planned on giving him *The Three Musketeers*, but Mother had taken it before I could finish, recalling that it was on "the condemned list." I had only gotten as far as the chapter called "Police Mouse-Trap" when she had put it back in Uncle Jim's room. I wondered how many of his books were condemned and if he had read them.

George walked up five steps, handed me *Ruggles of Red Gap* and sat down. "How much do you think Uncle Jim'll give us?"

"If Nellie does the asking, maybe two bits."

"Let's wait on her then. Must be nice to be a girl."

"It wouldn't," I said. "Mother's been making them walk around with books on their heads. Yesterday Kathleen got almost to the bottom of the stairs balancing two of Uncle Jim's Dumas, a Fielding, and a Thackeray." Mother apparently didn't think that evil would creep out of the Dumas and into the girls' heads during the lessons on posture, although sin, according to all that I had learned in school and from Mama Jo and from Mother herself, lurked around all of us waiting for an invitation. My stockings began creeping down again. "They aren't supposed to stay out in the sun, either. Mother says their faces should look like lilies."

"The way Mama Jo scrubs faces they're lucky to have skin left!" said George.

Viola poked her head out of the door. "Come on up stairs, your Mama Jo want you. She doing what your own mamas ought to be doing. She's got the trousers ready."

Besides being my grandmother, Mama Jo was George's great-aunt. She looked out for us even more than our own mothers, spoiling us in between her Irish aberrations that were usually brought on by one of our "sins against the Lord."

We trudged through the hall and up the stairs pulling ourselves along the heavy mahogany bannister. Mama Jo waited on the sleeping porch, her wicker sewing basket resting beside her as she sat on the chaise lounge. The room was warm with morning sun.

"Stand in these and be quick about it." She got up and handed each of us a pair of long white pants. "While I pin, you take turns saying your prayers for the Confirmation. And while you're of a mind, sing the hymns for the Benediction."

"Mama Jo, it's not for another week," I complained.

"Jim Flanagan, you can make no mistakes in front of the Bishop."

I was tired of the prayers, but the prick of a pin on my leg told me to get on with it. "Tantum ergo sacramentum . . . " My voice cracked as the words, swollen in my mind, came spilling out like water from an overflowing sink.

"Veneremur cernui." George had the same flood of words. Neither of us knew what the words meant, but Sister Edith Ann had done her job well. This satisfied Mama Jo.

"You'll both be soldiers for the Lord," she said.

Mama Jo crouched on the small footstool, the skirt of her black dress sprawling behind her in a fan. I rocked back and forth as I watched the top of her head. She cocked it in the direction that I was supposed to turn, the knob of hair on top pointing like a wide thumb.

"Mama Jo, why do you always wear a black dress?" I asked, hoping to draw her attention away from the hymns.

"Jim, I've buried three husbands, so I'd better keep to my mourning clothes." She kept sticking pins in the pants' leg. I whistled "Tantum ergo," hoping to prevent another reprisal.

George was waiting his turn. "Which one did you like the best, Mama Jo?"

7

"Well, I took care of the first two, John Slattery and Mr. Whitaker." She lowered her eyes at the mention of the dead. "But my third man, John Culligan, God rest his soul, took care of me. I loved him best." She whispered as though John Slattery and Mr. Whitaker could hear themselves being placed second and third in line for her affection.

"John Culligan was a police captain, wasn't he, Mama Jo?" I asked knowing the answer.

"Yes lad, that he was."

She pricked a finger. A drop of red threatened the trousers. "Saint Brigid in heaven, be still! You will stand straight or I'll brandish ya!"

"Brandish" meant she was losing patience, so I decided not to stray from the spot that I was ordered to stand on. I could hear Uncle Jim coming down the hall grumbling and thumping his cane. Uncle Jim announced the purpose of his charge toward the bathroom with his usual directness.

"Calatab! Calatab!" he hollered.

That was one of his medicines. Uncle Jim—he was really my great-uncle—had rheumatism and was crippled over in a bent-like position. He was Mama Jo's brother. She had said that he had acquired the malady from his early days when he worked for the post office delivering mail in all kinds of inclement weather. Strange to think of the political boss of North Memphis ever wearing a uniform or carrying anything heavier than his cane or his Cremo cigar. Uncle Jim was head of the house and I was afraid of him. I shifted my weight as I heard the bathroom door shut.

I don't know why I was afraid of the old man. He rarely spoke to me and sometimes I wondered if he saw me at all. My mother, of course, had no fear of him. He was her uncle. But even though Mama Jo said that Mother was his favorite, she kept a wide berth and talked to him only in the evening and only if he so desired. But I sensed that my father feared him as I did. He only spoke to Uncle Jim if spoken to first, which was seldom. This was a mystery, but I understood that I was not to ask questions about Uncle Jim. I almost never did. But in the silence of myself, I could not escape his presence, the awareness of him the guide of my dreams.

While Mama Jo pinned the hems, three shadows crept in the doorway. The small one, between two taller figures, had curly shadow hair. It was Nellie between Kathleen and Rose Kate. They had finally gotten up and wanted to find out what George and I were doing for Saturday.

George muffled his words. He was getting them riled. They expected it and would have been disappointed had he not gotten the day moving. Forcing my voice down low and gravelly, I whispered back to him pretending some black secret. The girls leaned in, straining to hear. Kathleen's shadow lifted her hair, pulling it in back of her ear. She kept the pathway clear —always ready for an earful. We scowled at them and cast spidery shadows with our fingers that crawled toward them like tarantulas. They hollered and acted scared.

"Oh, come on in," said Mama Jo. She could talk in spite of the row of pins clamped between her lips.

George enlisted Mama Jo into Saturday's scheme. "Don't tell them!" he said.

Mama Jo just grinned a promise, easy enough, since she had no idea what we were up to anyway. We knew our prayers and that was enough. She had told me that the time would come when I would have to take over for her. Fitting her ever increasing list of prayers for the dead and needy into a routine day would have been difficult. On Saturday, next to impossible. She told me to step behind the door and take off the white pants without catching the pins on my shoes or I would have to do it all over again.

The girls filled up the chaise and listened to Mama Jo hum the tune that she always hummed. The tune sounded tinny between the pins as she turned George's hem. She didn't know the words, but the melody was part of her earliest memory and mine. Since they had shared childhood, I wondered if Uncle Jim remembered the words. But I couldn't imagine him singing and didn't ask. When Mama Jo finished, she waddled away, the trousers hanging on her arm.

"We're going to the carnival," piped Nellie. Her curls circled her head in a way that suggested she was God's special girl. "What about you?"

"Maybe," smiled George. "What about it, Jim?"

"For awhile. Then we have something better to do."

Kathleen tried to glare us into telling her what. She looked a bit like Mama Jo when she wrinkled her forehead. She talked like one of Mother's friends that I didn't like very well. "It cannot be all that important," she said.

"Probably not." I knew she was really burning to know.

The three of them followed us into the wide hall, each knowing what came next. The Saturday ritual began with Uncle Jim, the source of all wealth. We argued over who would do the asking even though we knew who it would be.

Kathleen started with logic. "You're the oldest, Jim."

"George's almost as old."

Rose Kate thought George should do the asking.

"You're the oldest girl, Kathleen. You ask him," said George.

We all began talking at once, a chorus of voices bouncing off the high ceiling, filling the hall with confusion. Uncle Jim rapped his cane. He cut the argument with his deep rasping voice.

"Send Nellie in!"

Nellie skipped down the hall, her nightgown trailing behind like an angel's dress.

"Nickelo . . . dimeo," she sang, the o's, like bubbles, bobbling after her. She reached the room, turned the knob and flung open the heavy door with remarkable strength for a small girl, the door banging on the plaster wall. She entered Uncle Jim's domain, collected the money and came back with her small fists loaded with coins. Either Uncle Jim loved Nellie as much as I did—though I'd not admit this to anyone—or the small size of her hands didn't require as much generosity as would Rose Kate's or Kathleen's and certainly not as much as George's or my own.

Since I was oldest, I was bursar. I carefully divided the money, Kathleen counting along with me to ensure my honesty, although I wasn't sure of hers. George graciously accepted a nickel less since the count was uneven. He was always a good sport. Then too, he didn't want to listen to the girls carp about being cheated. He put his share in his pocket and laughed at the girls as they raced to their room to dress, the money smoking in their hot hands.

My clothes were kept in Mama Jo's room where I had slept when I was small. In truth, I don't think they knew where to put me as I grew. Our house was one of the largest in the old Irish neighborhood of Pinch, but the four bedrooms were packed. Since I was one of a kind, it made sense that I would be the nomad. It was May and I slept on the sun porch. At night I could hear spring drifting in the open windows. I went to sleep listening to owls hooting and woke in the morning to the relentless chirping of robins, both sounds often drowned out by the deep horn of a passing riverboat or the sad call of a train. But summer heat would move me to the daybed in the wide hall. I would sleep on it and sometimes under it on the cool floor. I considered this bed my territory all year round and so kept my things under it.

George waited while I got the cigar box out from underneath. I had saved a little extra money for this particular Saturday, since he and I were planning to see the fire-eater. The smells of food sold on the street constantly begged George to spend, so I knew he had not been able to save even a penny. I saved for both of us. But fire was not the only thing on our minds. One way or another, we were determined to actually see what we had only heard about. The Peep Show.

Uncle Jim came out of his room and descended the stairs for his solitary meal. He almost always ate alone. Dining with the whole brood disturbed his routine and inhibited his digestion.

George and I gave him plenty of time to get to the dining room, his progress known by the thud of his cane. Then we went scrambling down. I could see him sitting at one end of the long dark table as we passed by, his face white in the shadowy room. A light sprinkle of rusty freckles dusted his cheeks.

Viola sat the bowl of oatmeal in front of Uncle Jim. "Prunes, Viola," he said in a voice convinced of necessity. "You forgot the prunes."

"Oh no sir, Mr. Jim. You not getting none today. Miz Jo says you relying on prunes too much. She just won't have it, Mr. Jim."

"Jo," he called to my grandmother, who was straightening the hats hanging on the hall tree. "Don't be interfering with a man's prunes. The function of prunes is the eradication of waste. The janitor of the system."

"Such a fuss you are, my brother. You'll be having prunes then. But mind you, they'll rush through you carrying everything off."

"That would be the hope, Sister."

He was unfolding his napkin and glanced up. His eyes met mine and I knew that he wanted to speak to me, but he said nothing. If he spoke, it would most likely be over the matter of our making too much noise on the stairway. George, avoiding the possibility, went on to the kitchen where he would beg toast and fig preserves from Viola.

Uncle Jim stared at the steam that rose from the bowl like a cloud. Then came the unexpected blast. He said to me, "Jim

Flanagan, beware of women. They'll devil you, bark at your heels, waylay you from the blind side, then have the carnassial gall to inform you that their intentions were only meant to protect your good health." The words seemed to tire him. I wished then that health were a present that I could give him. That he would take it and smile.

He spooned a bit of the oatmeal from the edge where it was cooler. The steam glazed his eyes as he slumped back in his chair in a daydream. I did not know what he thought about, but I understood that his often closed eyes were not really in repose.

Mama Jo put her hand on my shoulder. "I want you and George to take that old goat back down to O'Lanahan's before you escape to any carnival. Viola beats her ... I beat her, Moony beats her, but that old nanny still eats up all the grass."

"I thought Uncle Jim wanted goat's milk," I said.

"No, lad. It hasn't helped him any more than that tray of medicine he's got up in his room."

Uncle Jim opened his eyes and looked toward her. The eyes stated clearly that the business of the medicine as well as that of the goat's milk was between them and none of mine.

Mama Jo blessed herself as though it might cure Uncle Jim of his ailments. His eyes followed her fingertips. "Save yourself of the trouble of all that crossing," he told her.

But she paid no attention and mumbled a prayer to go with it.

George and I headed for the shed on the back of the lot. It was part of the garage and stable with the entrances to each part opening on the alley side. Entering the shed, we stooped to avoid the low rafter. The smell of hay lingered in the building even though old Molly had been killed by a streetcar the month before and her stall had been scrubbed out. Moony had the goat cornered in Molly's stall.

"Hurry up, boys," he said. "She fixing to kick. She real mean when she kicks." Moony squatted low and held her tight.

Finding some pieces of old reins, we harnessed the old nanny and pulled her outside. She didn't mind the harness, since she was munching on the forbidden grass. The coarse sprigs gave her extraordinary energy. As we held her, she barreled up and lurched for the picket gate with a force far in excess of her size. Moony hollered, "I done told you she real mean."

The goat raced down Overton and headed east toward Second Street. Running after her at full speed, George and I couldn't catch the dragging rope. The goat traveled on past the vacant lot where the carnival was being set up. I could hear the money jingling in my pocket, but the goat wasn't interested in stopping for games. She turned left on Third Street and didn't even pause long enough for us to bow heads as we passed Saint Brigid's. She was northbound and tireless.

When I finally caught up with the sprinter, I wanted to give her a kick, but thought better of it, since it would be like kicking one of my sisters. I would not let anyone kick Nellie —that I was sure of, although there had been times when I thought of giving Kathleen a swift one.

George came puffing up out of breath. It took Moony several more minutes to catch us. George was a turtle, Moony a snail.

"You boys run like a dose of salts," said Moony. He sat on the curb, his short legs sticking out like two overturned fireplugs. "Rest easy now. Running's not too good for you boys."

Moony Franklin was older than George and I, say twenty, but he was only as high as my shoulders. Viola had said that Moony was probably not a midget, but that if he wasn't he missed a good chance.

We rested by a billboard on the side of a large clapboard building that advertised the Monday night fight. The goat ate a sunflower that drooped over the sidewalk. She finished it and tried nibbling my sleeve. She bleated in disgust as I pushed her away.

George looked up at the boxer on the billboard. "Why do they call that one 'The Spaghetti Kid?'" he asked.

"Because he's a 'Dago,'" said Moony. He seemed pleased with his name calling as if he could turn the tables for once. Boys in Pinch called him "Tar Baby" and "Black Bug." "They eats spaghetti everyday. They don't eats nothin' *but* spaghetti," he said.

George didn't believe it. "Even for breakfast?"

He was looking at me, but I didn't answer. Instead, I thought about how Uncle Jim owned the Phoenix Athletic Club and how I was finally going to see a fight. Dad was not a great fan of the fights, but when I had asked him to take me, Uncle Jim's eyes shot toward him, urging him to say yes. Somehow I felt that I would be older and far wiser having attended. "Monday night's the night. Dad's promised he'd take us both."

"Mama Jo and your mother aren't going to like it," George said, not mentioning his own mother's possible objection. Moony nodded.

But because it was Uncle Jim's club, I knew that Mother and Mama Jo would allow me to go. They would sift disapproval like Viola did flour, letting it get thin and powdery.

We stood up, headed the goat toward O'Lanahan's street, and got moving. Approaching a large tenement, we saw some boys arguing on the sidewalk. George and I both recognized one of them as the bully of Saint Brigid's who respected only one person—Sister Edith Ann. His name was Red Shanley, his nose ran constantly, and he was bigger than any other boy in the eighth grade. He held an old ax handle. They had been down in the Gayoso Bayou killing rats.

"Hurry up," said George. Moony kicked at the goat.

Retreat would have been too obvious. Besides, the presence of the goat killed any chance of an unobtrusive turn. The noisy haranguing ceased as the bully and his testy friends spotted us entering their territory.

"Well, look what we have here!" Shanley snarled like a

dog. His band of shadows followed his lead, mocking and yapping insults.

"If it isn't Mr. Jim Canaan's three nephews."

I looked at Shanley's nose and wished I hadn't. "You need glasses. It's two nephews. What's it to you anyway?"

"What with the goat, the count's three nephews."

"The goat's a girl, stupid." I felt my feet scraping the ground, wishing I'd held my tongue.

"You have to be kin to that goat—she smells like you."

The goat looked upset by the comparison. Her gray beard hung straight down as though she had groomed it. She pawed the sidewalk, sharpening her hooves.

I had never before been in a fight, always managing to talk my way out of any situation. And I knew that being Uncle Jim's great-nephew had a way of keeping me out of trouble. But this didn't seem to matter to Shanley.

"I take it back," said Shanley. He looked straight at Moony. "It *is* three nephews. I figured your uncle would have a *black* one," he said to me.

"You shouldn't say such about Mr. Jim," said Moony. "You won't be living for long now."

"Shut up, black boy. I'm not afraid of Mr. Jim. He's being muscled out. If Mr. Crump don't get him, my uncle Jack Shanley will."

I didn't know why the war had started or what it was about, but suddenly, like it or not, I was leader of one of Uncle Jim's squadrons.

George stayed busy holding the goat. I looked at him. He was thinking hard like me, groping for some plan or words to quell the coming storm. I didn't consider myself a coward, but wasn't all that brave, either. I saw no point in taking a licking from somebody bigger. The odds were just not there. I swallowed hard, but it would not go down.

Shanley's shadows closed in. Moony and George began agitating the goat. I guessed it was the only thing they could think of to give me time to figure a way out. My brain kept stumbling over the problem, finding no path around it. But the goat responded with a kick. She butted knees and rumps. "Bah . . ." she bleated. Shanley's gang scattered around trying to dodge her horns, but she had good aim. Right then I recognized the value of a good goat. She butted one of them right in the jewels. Moony must have felt sorry about this or maybe he was worried about his own. Either way, he caught the goat around the neck and held her.

Then Shanley bristled up, remembering the fight. He bounced around shifting his shoulders and swinging his arms.

I stood flat-footed and wide-eyed, able to see the rim of my cap and feel the stockings finally anchored by the friction of raised hair on my legs. I ducked my head in time to avoid Shanley's punch. I pulled the cap almost over my eyes, not wanting to see what was going to happen, and took a swing. My fist glanced the jaw of Shanley who countered with a left blow that knocked me three feet. Shanley's bunch pushed me back. Out of control, I sailed into Shanley, who lost his footing and fell to the ground, scrambled to his feet, and squared off on my nose. It felt like it was gone.

With blood running down my face, I took a deep breath and swung like a wild man.

"This one's for Uncle Jim."

My knuckles jammed a jaw, a punch that saw Shanley to the dust. I looked down at Shanley, then at my own fist. Shanley was quiet; his friends, slack-jawed. George patted me on the back. "You did it!"

Moony agreed, but he was always practical. "Yeah. Now let's us get out of here."

I had championed Uncle Jim's honor, had stood ground in the face of disaster, but was not above skedaddling when the opportunity came round.

Shanley was never as fierce after that day. Sister Edith Ann thought that the lessening of his aggression was due to the good influence of her stern discipline. She most likely congratulated herself until the real story penetrated the convent.

My nose kept bleeding. As much as it was a nuisance, I was proud of the blood. George was glad to loan me his handkerchief. Special pride inflated him, as if he too had defeated Red Shanley. He yanked the goat.

"C'mon."

Officers Nash and O'Leary saw us and motioned us over.

"Where'd the blood come from, Jim?" said Nash.

"I fell over this goat, sir," I said. I did not want Mother or Mama Jo to know about the fight even if it meant lying. To them a soldier for the Lord was one thing, regular fighting another.

"You'd better come up with a more fitting tale before you face your father and your uncle Jim, not to mention the ladies in your family."

Mr. Cuccia, the hot tamale vendor, was calling to the policemen. Small tears trickled from his eyes from exposure to chili powder. "Hey, officers! You've got yourselves some mean-looking varmints! I'll bet they robbed a bank and the goat's the get-away-man."

O'Leary tried to look serious. "No, Mr. Cuccia. Not the get-away. The ringleader!"

Several customers buying Cuccia's tamales laughed at the suggestion. "Look to the rear, officers! The goat might try another 'stick up.'" His customers laughed harder as Cuccia dished up the fiery stuff covered in corn shucks.

George bought a tamale, but I was too busy dabbing blood to eat.

"Come on," George said. "This old goat smells like the Gayoso Bayou." The odor didn't keep him from swallowing the tamale whole. His throat bobbed as the tamale logged its way down.

"You boys go on home quick," said O'Leary. "I'll take the goat to O'Lanahan's. You've caused enough sweat for one day. Your Uncle Jim knows about the fight." He took off his blue cap, smoothing his hair with his free hand. "You can't keep anything that happens in the Pinch from Mr. Jim."

"No sir. Not from Mr. Jim," echoed Moony.

It seemed that the Pinch had a hundred eyes and ears and that most of them belonged to Uncle Jim. Still, it was hard to think of being watched over or listened to when it was least expected. But this was Saturday and I quickly forgot that my actions were observed.

Officer O'Leary took hold of the reins and pulled the goat forward. Stubbornly pulling back, she seemed reluctant to change partners. Finally he patted her head and she scuttered alongside him. We walked on down the street.

As we neared a streetcar stop, Moony got out a nickel. "I fixing to have my Saturday, boys."

"How's that, Moon?" asked George.

"Going on down to Beale Street, boys. Where the elite meets." He cocked his head, swelled his chest, and grinned with his mouth closed.

"What's it like down there, Moony?" I asked.

"Climbs on and finds out. It wouldn't hurt you boys none to scud down on Beale in the daytime. Of course, you all has to go on home before dark."

"What is 'scud'?" asked George.

"Slip, slide, scuff, or scud. They all the same, boys. It's cheap and it's fine. Fine as wine and free as long as you don't spends none of your money."

Moony rocked back and forth. He rotated his shoulders, snapping his fingers with each hump, wheeling his elbows out and down. I had never before seen the excited Moony, the one arch-

19

ing his back, shaking his fanny, wiggling his great ears. It was hard to let go of Moony, the entertainment being first rate. We got on the streetcar.

He sat down in the back with the Negroes. We sat in the front.

Moony didn't waste any time on his Saturday. He knew some of the passengers around him and started to tell stories. George and I stopped talking and listened.

"Now the Salvation Army, they's a sight. Such caterwauling from white folks you never did see."

"Is that right," said the man beside him.

"The truth," said Moony. "They was standing outside of Mr. Jim's place last night singing louder than the choir at the Beale Street Baptist Church."

"No way, brother," said one of the women.

"The truth," repeated Moony. "They sang 'When the Roll Is Called Up Yonder.' A fat white lady shook the tambourine like this." Moony clapped his hands together like cymbals. "Her belly jiggled like them bells."

"You don't say."

"One of them played the coronet and another one beat the big kettle drum, but the men kept going in and out of Mr. Jim's place. Some of them laughed and some of them didn't pay no mind. Then this big old drunk man stumble out the door and fall headlong into the drum. His legs stuck up like flowers growing out of a pot."

"Is that right," said his friend.

"That's truth." Moony paused to admire his story. "But the Salvations never did stop singing. And they was even louder after the drummer had to quit beating, 'cause he had the loudest voice of all."

On Beale Street, George and I lagged behind Moony. The taps on his shoes clicked as he walked. The street was much like Second Street, except that the haggling and trading were done by black people who were even more persistent than Mrs. Morganstern, our neighbor, carping at old man Sites, who sold vegetables and fruit from his wagon.

Bodies moved down the street with the same easy rhythm of Moony. Flies hovered over the vegetable stands. Little black boys swatted and sang. "Shoo fly. Shoo fly fly."

"Watch this," said Moony.

A fast-talking Negro wearing a white suit and spotless white gloves, his shoes covered with spats, played the shell game on a sidewalk table for some country people.

"That's Slick. Watch him take those jakes."

The country bumpkins were fascinated with the game. They scratched their heads as though the game had given them fleas.

"Couldn't teach those jakes if you wanted to. Slick'll fleece them down to the drawers. But they come on back to Beale Street every time."

A pink pig smoked on a pit of black coals. It wore a necklace of cranberries and spices. It smelled good after I saw that its eyes were closed.

"Mmm," said Moony. He licked his lips and looked as if he could taste what he smelled.

A yellow-skinned gypsy with blue-black hair, her robes red and purple, whispered her secrets from a cart shaded by a big white umbrella hung with necklaces, passion flowers, and cats'-tails. "Aspidistra," I heard her say as she handed the tiny bag to her customer who wore a flower in his lapel. I envied him the chance of knowing the secret held in that mysterious word that he might soon discover. And I wondered what strange benefits might be gotten from the vials filled with small leaves and powders that lined the wooden counter.

"Keep moving," said Moony. "That's Madame Litha. She the gypsy queen what sells graveyard dust. We don't wants none."

I wanted a whiff of it, but Moony was firm in his refusal to get any closer to the exotic Madame.

But he allowed us to stop when a black boy about my age cornered a jake. "Bet I can guess where you got them shoes," said the boy. Moony watched him like a judge.

The man smiled at his wife, a wide lady dressed like a garden. "How much you willing to bet?" he said to the boy.

"Fifteen cents!"

"It's a bet," said the man.

"Where you got them shoes?"

"Where?" said the man, sure of the outcome.

"On you feets!" The boy laughed and held out his hand for the money. Moony nodded his approval.

Then down the middle of Beale came a man who was seven feet tall even without his black top hat, which was a foot high. His elbows bent outward under the black cape like the wings of a great bird.

Moony grabbed us both by the elbows. "Look down, boys. It's the Chicken Man. He can kill you with one eye."

"That's not possible," said George.

"The evil eye. It's the truth." Moony's hold on my arm was so tight his nails dug into my skin. "He voodoo. Eats live chickens."

The Chicken Man's shadow was a giant, its blackness still shading us minutes after he had passed by. Moony breathed in and out and pinched himself. Satisfied that he was unaffected by the voodoo powers, he began snapping his fingers to the rhythm of a three-piece jug band that was playing on the corner. The jugman filled his instrument with air sounding as loud as a tuba. The Negroes sang about Mayor Ed Crump who was running for reelection . . . "Mister Crump don't allow no easy riders here."

Moony answered them, singing in his high pitched voice. "We don't care what Mister Crump don't 'low. We gonna barrelhouse anyhow."

The music makers laughed and kept on singing. One of them

plucked the washtub in time with the jug. Thump . . . thump. Thump thump thump. Then, as George and I passed by, we heard them singing about Uncle Jim.

Mister Crump, he went down . . . down to see Jim Canaan
Mister Crump, he went down . . . down to see Jim Canaan
Mister Crump went down to see Jim Canaan . . .
He say, listen here Jim . . . I'm in command.

George elbowed me. "Do you think Uncle Jim's really on the way out like Shanley said?"

"There's some kind of trouble," I told him. "Mama Jo and Mother and Dad are always talking. But they hush up when we're around." I remembered the rise and fall of their talk. "Mama Jo prays for him all the time."

The singing was spirited, but it seemed sad to me, like music at a funeral. I didn't want Uncle Jim to hear it.

"You boys don't knows nothin' from nothin'," said Moony, steering us to the chili dog stand. Before I could ask something about the "nothin'," he was shoving us up to the counter. I didn't really want to spend my money on food, but something about Beale Street had made me hungry. The chili smelled fine. It was thick and rich. It didn't slide off of the hot dog or drip out of the bun. George finished his before I was halfway through—just as the three-legged dog came down the street. George was upset by the handicap, but the dog was full of pep and had no notion of his grief. George held his stomach and made a sound like the one he'd made when the incense had caused him to throw up in church.

"Look at it this way, George," said Moony. "He don't have to hike a leg."

We stayed on Beale all afternoon, listening to the music and the pop of shoeshine rags. We combed the pawnshops and watched the parade of black men and women, their faces the color of rich dark earth—dressed in colors that shouted

23

—strutting their easy pride up and down the street. They talked in groups, waved and called greetings to friends, and feasted like us.

I smelled and touched and tasted Moony's Saturday. But I knew that I would never feel quite like he did. I would never really learn to "scud."

"You boys best be showing your faces at home," said Moony. "It's getting on toward dark. Don't you tells where you been. Don't you lie, now. Just don't be telling anything you don't have to. I'll be on later to help Viola with the supper." He was snapping his fingers again. "Then I'll be coming on back down here."

We left Moony and caught the streetcar on Third Street. George sat down, took off one of his shoes and rubbed the corn on his toe. I was glad to rest my legs even for a few minutes. As the streetcar started and stopped, the song about Uncle Jim rolled over and over in my mind, a sort of warning that wouldn't quit when finally the plucky sound of a hurdy-gurdy pushed it out.

We got off near the carnival and stood watching as the arc lamps cast an artificial magic over the tents and booths in the growing darkness. The carnival was crowded with people, the alley filled with horses and mules. I could smell crawfish boiling in a pot, its steam carrying pepper in the air. I sneezed.

We looked at each other, both knowing that we should cut a straight path toward home. Without discussion, we bought tickets to the tent show. Inside, our feet sank into sawdust that smelled of clean pine. The carnies, however, were not clean. They were dressed in remnants of costumes, sad and dirty, and I thought about them for a long time after the carnival was over.

George worried over the animals. "Their bones stick out," he said.

"So do mine," I reminded him, but it didn't help. I saw him

fish around in his coat for some of the cookies that he kept in his pockets and I wondered how long he could keep food in his cupped hand without putting it into his own mouth.

The animal trainer announced that his name was Haggar. He wore tight black pants and a dingy white shirt. When he cracked his whip, the dogs jumped up on the backs of the moving ponies. If the dogs were hungry, they didn't complain and seemed devoted to show business. The crowd's favorite dog could stand on his hind legs as the pony circled the ring. At the crack of the whip, the other ponies neighed, the dogs barked, and the trainer bowed, splitting his pants wide open and revealing his holey drawers, an embarrassment that caused him to quickly herd the animals out of the tent. They scattered so fast that George didn't have time to feed them the cookies.

Then Frederick the Great Fire-eater came into the tent, his face yellow, his legs bowed and thin like saplings. The animal hide that draped his chest touched the top of his kneecaps, which were knobby. He looked like a lion tamer.

A woman in a faded gauzy blue dress lit Frederick's torch. She walked around the ring holding it above her head, the flames sending smoke to the tent top. The woman flaunted the fire, waving it around, smiling a yellow smile as sparks floated down around her. The crowd stirred and grew nervous. We both looked toward the flap in case we had to leave in a hurry. George took off his coat, ready to smother the fire if it got started. We both sat on the edge of the splintered bench alert like two Dalmatians.

At first Frederick watched the woman with a smile on his face, but after a few minutes, he walked over and snatched the torch from her hand, reminding me of my sisters. When one of them was getting all of the attention, the others would make sure it didn't last.

Frederick didn't really eat fire. He swallowed, but it came

back up like an upchuck—hot, flashing outward, larger than when it went in. Frederick was skilled at his trade. He didn't sweat. George, however, was red like a firecracker. I was a little warm myself. We both breathed hard when it was over.

Then, as we left the tent, we heard the snake song as we called it.

> *There's a place in France*
> *where women wear no pants.*

The song was jaded and foreign, its melody curiosity, the lyrics guilt. I felt sin crawling inside, but that didn't stop me from following the sound. It came from a tent on the back of the lot behind the kewpie doll booth. I should have tried to win a doll for Nellie, but the music pulled me past the games of chance.

George pointed to the sign with the hand that had been cupped, although I'd not seen him eating the cookies.

MEN ONLY

"Are we?" he asked.

"I might be," I said, feeling the status of advanced age, "since I'm already thirteen." I thought of his juvenile cookies. "You've got another three weeks."

"That's close enough," he said. "I'll just stand up straight."

"You're as tall as me anyway," I reminded him.

We edged up to the entrance. It was noisy inside, the music very loud.

> *There's a place in France . . .*
> *da . . . da . . . da . . . da da da da.*

The music got things stirred up inside me; if it hadn't been dark, embarrassment would have been my middle name. Still, I held my cap in front of my point of shame and stared into the tent. A greasy man saw us, his lips splitting into a jagged grin. He beckoned us toward him, flexing his muscles up and down which made the snake tattooed on his arm seem to slither.

George didn't like this. His big black eyes got bigger. "Hey, we'd better not go in there."

Before we could back off, the man slid out of the tent and was escorting us inside.

"Give a look to the girlies," he laughed. His eyes were shot with red lines, his face grizzled and sallow, his odor distinctly that of onions and sardines. Having guessed my problem, he tried to snatch my cap. I moved away from him and closer to the door. But he didn't follow, since he had become distracted by a woman who was coming into the tent. The horn played and he began to cheer along with the rest of the men.

It was the woman in the blue gauze. She moved around the tent, bumping and grinding her skinny hips. Holding the mysteries of the Orient in her wavering arms, she took over my mind and body. Her thin blond hair wheeled around her head as she turned circles like a top. She was fully in charge here, and did not have to compete with the fire-eater. She would stop now and then to stand posed in an angle, one arm raised above her head, the other pointing down at her ragged black ballet slipper mired in the sawdust. But the men didn't want her to stop. They clapped and I dropped my cap and clapped with them, clapped lightly at first, then louder, until my bonds were loosed. Then I slapped my hands together as hard as I could drive them. George was looking at me with his deep frown, but then his face came to a grin—a transformation like a slow yawn, and for a few minutes he clapped harder than me and like Viola did when she was beating the blankets.

I quit clapping as the blue gauzy lady untied her blue skirt letting it drop in the dust. She was wearing tights the color of

27

skin. The clapping was inside me then. I squirmed as her legs kicked freely, my face warming when she allowed one side of the top of her dress to fall to her waist, my shame rising high with the welling inside me. George was pulling my sleeve, talking about sin, ready to leave hell to the clutter of grown men who sat laughing and clapping and hooting, but before turning my head away, I stared at the bosoms.

"Let's get out of France," said George, still yanking at my jacket. He picked up my cap and handed it to me as we edged out.

The man who had led us in watched us leave, patting his stomach, whinnying a laugh that filled my ears until we got past the crawfish pot.

We walked home with our sin. Sister Edith Ann had said that thinking something was "as bad as doing it." Sister Edith Ann was wrong. Thinking about naked women was not the same sin as seeing one.

We walked slowly as we came near the house. Uncle Jim was unfolding his body from the Ford with some assistance from Distance. He spoke without looking at us.

"George, get in the car. The Major's taking you home. You won't be going to the fights Monday night." His voice didn't approve of the "not going." "He says you've already been."

Then the Major came down the steps with the exacting cadence of a marching man. "George. The car." He came to the bottom step, but couldn't stop. He took small quick steps to correct his mistake. He recovered, held himself quite stiff, and blustered something about being "mad as a dog." But I thought just then that he looked more like a horse or a mule, since his head went up and down on his stiff neck, his eyes round and fixed ahead.

"Your world has boundaries, George Mahon. It does not include Beale Street." He looked at Uncle Jim, who refused to agree. "And street fighting. Today, you and Jim Flanagan have stepped outside the perimeter of propriety."

Neither Uncle Jim nor the Major asked for any explanation, so they got none from George and me, who were glad that Beale Street and the fight with Shanley had gotten their attention and not the girlie show.

I watched them get into the Major's Ford, start up with a jerk, and ride into the night.

Uncle Jim plodded up the ten steps. When he reached the front door, he turned and stared at me. He flicked his cigar and then he spoke. "Clare and Nate and your grandmother —God forbid—know about the fight and about you going down on Beale. They don't know about the other. Nate wants you out in the stable." He drew in on the Cremo. "Work on your left hook." The advice rose from deep inside his chest, a sound that might have come from a well or a cavern. His clear blue eyes were watching mine. Uncle Jim would not tell them what he knew. I was sure of it. I tucked in my shirttail and went on out toward the stable.

In the sky above me, the ocean of lost stars shone across the endless blackness of night. The moon wore a knowing face. I imagined the center of the earth and myself standing under it. I felt small, as I did in my dreams.

As I passed Mother's gardenia bush, its green leaves glossy in the moonlight, I breathed deeply, remembering the perfume of its blossoms from summers past. Then I heard a "Pst . . . pst." Nellie was hiding behind the bush. She wore her blue bathrobe and held three pieces of cardboard in her hand. "Put these in your pants on your fanny," she said. "It won't hurt so much." I took the cardboard, feeling that it was the greatest gift I'd ever received. Before I could thank her, she hugged me and ran back into the house.

Inside the stable I could hear Distance on the other side of the wall. He was in the garage brushing lint from the car seats with his whisk broom. Wsk . . . wsk. Moony was in there with him.

"Betcha he'll git five pops!" said Moony.

29

"Maybe." Distance went on brushing the lint. He seemed reluctant to bet on my punishment. But betting on activities of our family was one of their pastimes and Moony kept pushing.

"Come on, Distance. You wasting time picking lint off a car seat. White folks always wasting your time on things such as that. Take the bet!"

"That boy don't belong down on Beale. You ought to know better than to take him down there. He'll get at least twenty licks on account of it. You jest wait and see."

"That's it!" said Moony. "We done bet!"

I had never gotten more than five wallops before, so Distance's prediction had an unsettling effect on me. Then too, Dad took his time getting to the stable. I waited and began to sweat. He came in carrying the black leather belt in his hand. He looked taller than before.

"Bend over the log pile," he said.

Moony and Distance had quit talking so they could hear the licks.

Dad delivered five stout wallops to my behind. In spite of Nellie's cardboard, each sting smarted with heat. I could hear Distance from behind the wall. "Jest you wait," he said. "Mr. Nate's jest taking a rest."

Moony shushed him. He did not want Dad to know they were betting on my backside.

Dad ran his belt through the loops and buckled it. He seemed to feel like I did when I'd finished taking a test—glad to be done with it whether I'd passed or not. My father did not administer punishment without suffering himself.

"Go clean up and meet me in the parlor." He knew that the dried blood and dirt smudges would upset my mother. He hated for anything to upset her. I waited until he had gotten himself inside and then went in myself.

The stairs creaked as I walked to the bathroom.

My ruddy skin was shiny in the mirror, my nose big and ugly with the swelling. Sandy reddish hair sprung out from my head like broken mattress springs, but the eyes were deep blue and somehow saving of the face. The cool water felt fine, but I wished then that washing away sin were as easy. I was glad to be alone.

I could hear the sound of the carnival from the window, but I was tired and glad to be done with it. I looked out at Second Street below and saw the neighboring houses lit up and looking back at me like the faces of friends. I was not innocent now, but the houses still smiled.

In Mama Jo's room, Rose Kate sat on the bed waiting for me. She pointed to the clean shirt on top of the bureau. Her hazel eyes were almonds beneath her red brown bangs that would not lay flat like she wanted.

"I heard you knocked him for a loop." Her voice trilled as she socked her right fist into her left hand.

Moony must have been telling about it. I knew Mother and Dad hadn't told her. Her curiosity was becoming. She was like a quiver in a breeze, all bristling and alert.

I hadn't had much time to soak in the fight, so her interest both surprised and pleased me, especially since she usually fought me like she did her hair. It wasn't that she got on less well with me than she did with our sisters or the hair. She fought us all equally for she had landed in the middle and was neither adored for her talent and beauty like Nellie nor admired as the perfect lady as was Kathleen. And she held no special place like I did as the oldest and the only son, but I always thought of her as special. In a war, I would want her on my side.

"Well, what really happened? You know Moony. Tell me the facts." She understood that if stories were colors, Moony's were rainbows.

"It wasn't so much. Shanley said a couple of things about

31

Uncle Jim. I don't remember just what." I had never liked evading her and still didn't.

She frowned at the vague answer. I wanted to tell her about Shanley's prediction that Uncle Jim was on the way out, about the snide slurs, about the song. But Uncle Jim's problems were his own business, and while I had a small share in them now, I'd not repeat rumors. I knew this and in a way that I did not know most things.

I wanted her to forget about it. "Let's build some card houses when I come back up."

"You're too old for that now," she said.

"Not really." She was right for the most part, but I was still good for the challenge of a row house or a fire station.

I put on the clean white shirt and went downstairs. I walked slowly and wondered if Dad was still mad. From the corner of my eye, I had seen him grimace when he'd given me the licks, which I thought hurt him more than me.

I went past the life-size painting of Jesus in Agony in the Garden. It was larger than it had been that morning. Jesus knelt by the rock, rested his hands on it, and prayed. His eyes were sorrowfully drawn to the dark sky. I didn't feel sorry about the fight, but I knew Mama Jo would make me go to confession. I would have to "get sorry" or it wouldn't count. Getting sorry about the Peep Show had already happened.

I entered the parlor. Dad sat stiffly on the red velvet settee. "We didn't raise you for street fighting," he said. He sounded convinced of this.

I sat on the matching chair and was equally uncomfortable. Dad's build was athletic, but his shoulders sloped a little. He smoothed the velvet with his hand.

He cleared his throat as though he were about to give a speech that he wasn't sure of, wasn't his own. "The Shanley kid probably had it coming, but fighting doesn't make you a man. I think it's time you knew something about the real world. We'll go on to the Phoenix Monday night. Right now, go and eat your dinner in the kitchen, then apologize to your mother and Mama Jo. And to your Uncle Jim."

I stood up. The muscles cramped in my calves. "Dad, why do the jug bands sing about Uncle Jim?"

He folded his arms and set himself. "It's an election year and the reformers don't like him. They pay the jug bands to campaign."

"Did he do something wrong?"

"Let's just say your uncle Jim *had* to fight." He rubbed the nap on the bias. "He fought his way out of hard times and brought your Mama Jo along with him. Their own father died in the yellow fever and they were left in a bad way. I'll be forever grateful to Uncle Jim for saving Mama Jo because the saving also helped your sweet mother. Some people don't like the way your Uncle Jim's made his money. Now go along. It's not your concern."

"Yes sir." He had no way of knowing that concern was a heavy pack on my back. I carried the burden and walked toward the kitchen wondering if he'd told me the entire truth. I did not doubt the facts that he presented, but I suspected that he left out more than he told like I did Rose Kate and the same as when he had explained about the words "graft and corruption" that I had heard in the Sunday sermon. His definitions were those of games or sports. Not at all like the ones in the dictionary.

In the kitchen, Viola had Moony stirring the spaghetti. We were not Italian, but liked their food better than anything and ate it every Saturday night. Irish stew was tasteless compared to spaghetti.

"You ready to eat, little Jim?" asked Viola.

"Smells good," I said.

"Come on in here and sit yourself down." Viola ruled over the kitchen and also over Moony. If he dared to stop stirring she would flail him with a switch.

The wooden table was well worn, the top scratched dry from

her scrubbing. A jar held a big sunflower that she had picked in the alley. False teeth sat beneath the flower like they had been invited to dinner and were waiting to be served.

"Whose teeth?" I asked.

"They's mine," said Viola. "Mr. Jim bought 'um for me, but they's painful. I can't say just how much." She held her cheek and frowned. Her face was framed in a yellow kerchief, her black eyes large and bright. "Don't you go telling him, though."

Moony kept stirring the spaghetti sauce. "It's ready, Viola."

"You keep stirring, you Moony."

Moony grinned, toothless. "Can't blames me for trying."

Viola brought me a plate piled high with spaghetti, its spicy red sauce steaming.

"I been thinking, Viola," said Moony watching her.

"You not paid to think, Moony," said Viola. "You paid to stir." She fussed over the dishes.

"I been thinking some about these here teeth," he persisted.

"What about the teeth?" she said.

"Often you don't or won't wears them . . . so how's about giving 'um to me!"

She eyed Moony and shook her head. "Uh uh."

She placed a glass of tea in front of me. The little chips of ice floated thinly on top. She looked at me, then rolled her eyes up into her head suggesting that she knew that I knew that Moony hadn't a brain in his head. I smiled at her, but thought that Moony's idea made sense.

"C'mon, Viola," he said. "Let me haves them teeth."

"Well, just you go ahead then, you Moony. You just crazy enough to take somebody's teeth."

When Moony reached for the choppers, Viola's switch came down on his knuckles.

"Not until the stirring's done."

Moony looked disappointed, like the panhandlers that Viola turned down at the back door. She had her rules. She'd make them pick up trash in the yard. "No work, no food," she would say.

Moony stirred faster, sloshing dots of the red sauce onto the stovepipe.

"And stirring fast don't make it cook any quicker," she admonished him.

I finished eating. "Real good, Moony. Viola."

"Don't you want more, little Jim?" Moony wanted to know.

"Have some more, boy. It'll fill out those legs of yours," Viola said. "Make you real stout."

"No thanks."

I left the kitchen. As I entered the dining room, I looked up. The dark plate rail near the ceiling held the Irish steins that surrounded the room. I liked looking at them, since I always found one I had not seen before. Uncle Jim had finished dinner and was in the process of lighting a cigar. Mama Jo fussed about the aroma.

"Mama, it is the same brand that John Culligan smoked," said Mother. "You would miss him even more if Uncle Jim didn't keep his scent going."

Uncle Jim almost smiled. The two of them, Uncle Jim and Captain John Culligan, had kept the house murky with smoke before the Captain died. Watching Uncle Jim, I remembered the great sliding doors of the parlor shutting their conversations away from the rest of the world while their smoke crept out from under the crack, moving slowly through the entry hall, rising up the stairway, and me waiting for the veil of it to come and cover me, filling me with their secrets. Uncle Jim probably missed the Captain even more than Mama Jo did.

Mother sipped coffee from a tiny cup circled with a border of orange, lavender, rose, and yellow flowers. Lovely in her dress of blue tucked organza trimmed with delicate Irish lace, she spoke to me in her usual charming way. "Jim, promise me

35

that you will never do anything so foolish again. You are the only son we have."

"Yes Mother, I really am sorry." I didn't feel I could have gotten out of the fight, but I didn't want to worry her.

Mama Jo pushed her pie plate aside. She taught the girls to leave a little on their plates, but she had not left any. "Jim, you've had your brandishment, but you still haven't made up with the Lord. I'll be going to early mass, so you'd better be going with me."

Uncle Jim puffed impatiently. I took the cue. "I'm sorry, Uncle Jim."

He nodded, waving me out of the room. I hardly got a chance to look at the china plates decorated with American flags. I always ate well from one of those plates, since removal of the food left a good clear view of the flag's colors. As I left the room, I looked back at Uncle Jim who seemed deep in his own thoughts. He looked up, fixing his eyes on me.

"You've kept men from business today," he finally said.

I shrugged my shoulders and wondered what the business was.

The Monarch Saloon

1914, *Moony Franklin*

Since little Jim's already gotten the licking for being down
on Beale, it only fair he should hear about what he missing
out on down there. I ain't calling the boy dumb or nothin' like
that—he ain't—but he have no notion about his own kin. He
think Mr. Jim get all that money from just collecting rent. So
I tells the boy about Saturday night at one of Mr. Jim's places
and how as Lou Barnes sass across the floor there in her red
dress. I tells him that the mens sets down their whiskey on
that long bar and turns and looks. And then how the mens
sitting on the black leather seats stares up at that gal's curves
that fills up the mirrors that go all around the room. Ha!
Then Carrie take a look and move closer to that worthless
man of hers like smoke clinging to them crystal chandeliers.
I tells him these things in such ways that he can see them
hisself. That boy's blue eyes can laugh or cry the way that
voices do. And when I tells the boy about Carrie, I sees that
he watches me real close. Now I don't says I loves that gal,
but he know it anyhow.

My own heel keep a beat as I tells him about Charles
playing the piano. And when I warms into this here story, I
begins singing like Charles and talking like Willie Moss,
Bubba Dee, and other folks that I knows down there at the
Monarch.

37

I wish I was back at old Jim Canaan's
Men and women, they go hand and hand
drinkin' whiskey, sniffin' cocaine
that's why I wish I was back at old Jim Canaan's.

"It a fact," say Willie Moss. "There ain't nothin' in the world like this here place. Charles oughtn't sing about the old place."

"But everybody knows the old song. That's why," say Carrie.

"Charles ought to sing a new song," say Willie Moss. "Mr. Jim done spent $20,000 fixing this here place."

"Ain't that much money in the whole world," say Carrie.

"Mr. Jim's got the green. Got it on gambling and gals."

"No reason to spend it on brown skins," she say.

"Brown skinned sportin' men, that's why." Willie Moss grin real big. He's dandyfied. "This here the finest colored saloon in the South."

Carrie feel the smooth wool of his black pin-striped suit. His pocket hold a handkerchief as bright as Lou Barnes' satin dress. Sweat beads sprouts on his black forehead and I feels the water coming on out of my own head seeing Carrie feeling on him like that. He whisper to Bubba Dee, but I hears him anyhow. "That gal gonna be mine tonight!"

"You crazy. You already got a gal. Looks to be hanging on your arm." Bubba Dee get rid of his jigger of whiskey. "Down this blessed throat!" He look over at Carrie as the whiskey burn down into his chest. But he don't admit he's on fire. Instead, he lean over to Willie Moss and say, "Besides, Mr. Jim sure to send that gal Lou over to one of them sportin' crowd tonight! One of them mens from New York!"

But Willie Moss he pay no mind to Bubba Dee. Willie Moss's just a-squirming beside Carrie. She got a lock on his arm. He's watching Lou's big curves getting dark in the shadows 'cause she climbing the stairs to the gambling den. His eyes

38

follows her red shoes until she's gone. "I'm one of the sportin' crowd tonight!" he say.

I tells little Jim how I listens to Willie Moss and how I wonders how he gots the new suit and how I edges closer. "You the man, Willie Moss! You quite the man tonight," I say.

Willie Moss look at me. "Moony, yo eyes working as hard as yo ears!"

"Sees all. Knows all," I tells him. Then I reaches my elbows up to the bar. I small, so's they tells me, but I don't feels small. Leastways not in the Monarch after my sniff. They is times I pray to be taken out of this here body and put inside a real big man. But even God ain't got ears big enough to hear a real little man. Mr. Jim he can't help none neither, excepting he been giving me my sniffs.

Bubba Dee bangs the counter. S.I. put his hand to his hip. He's tending to the bar. "You don't has to bang, Bubba! I gits to everybody."

"Yeah, sooner or later. Maybe later, eh, S.I.?"

S.I. wipe up a spill of whiskey that threaten to take the gleam off his mahogany bar. I knows about shining myself. "What you want, nigger," say S.I.

"Nigger nothin', gimme another whiskey!"

Willie Moss swallow his. "Set him up, S.I. It's on me. The luck's in me tonight!"

Willie Moss shake loose of Carrie. He slide the big roll of bills from his vest pocket. Carrie's eyes they open real wide.

"Don't be telling about all dis money, Carrie. Not you either Bubba Dee." He look over at me. "You. Little Moon wid the big ears . . . I'll slit you if you open your mouth! I don't wants no gravy train following me tonight!"

Willie Moss know all about the gravy train. Many times I seen him in it. The train it trail after a big winner. They shouts at the winner to bets more, to spends more, and most of all, to shares the winnings. Willie Moss have broke down many a winner. Broke 'um down to nothin'.

Willie Moss down his whiskey. "Gimme another one, barkeep!"

"Don't calls me barkeep," say S.I. "I's the mixologist! This here's the finest colored saloon in the world and we ain't no barkeeps! We's mixologists." S.I. pour him another round.

Johnny Margerum come toward the bar. His tie is knotted just real fine. His mustache is curled up like a smile. He's boss of the saloon. Been busy at the front door. He oblige every man to check his knife or gun before coming on in the Monarch—orders from Mr. Jim.

"S.I., you doing all right? Any trouble?"

"No, boss. Just serving up plenty of whiskey!"

Margerum he see Willie Moss's new duds. "Big game going on upstairs," he say to Willie. "Carrie, keep him company."

Then I tells little Jim that I knows right then that the word's out—Willie Moss done won big at Montgomery Park. Margerum always save the light-skinned gals for the sportin' gentry—always shoo Carrie away from Willie Moss. Always say "Get to hustling, gal." But now Willie Moss got money to spend. The man going to be *escorted* to the crap table for high rollers by *tall* Carrie.

So then she look at Willie Moss. "You don't has to bet. You go on. I meet you . . . later."

But Willie Moss, his mind is on Lou Barnes. He don't listen to Carrie. He's like a belly that's done been fed roast suckling pig so much that he done lost his taste for it, though I myself cannot understands how Willie Moss or any other mans can turn over a taste for sweet Carrie.

"Come on, gal. Let's go up," say Willie Moss.

Bubba Dee slip his shoe off the brass rail and follow. I gets a large glass of whiskey and pats my chest, making sure the coke's still in my pocket. I tags on after them . . . like I'm some-body's little brother.

Upstairs, my eyes is watering and burning until I steps up to one of the crap tables. The ceiling fans above me whirs and chases the smoke.

Lou Barnes is matched up with a dark man dressed in a white suit. He puff on the dice. "Kiss 'um for us, Lou—give us some luck, gal!"

Lou blow on the dice. The feathers on that gal jumps up and down in her air.

I watches Carrie while Willie Moss's eyes wanders all over Lou. I stretches myself and pokes this here chest out. Ain't no use. Carrie, she don't see me.

The man in white roll. "Come seven . . . come eleven."

The ivories bumps turning twelve dots up. "Crapped out again!" say the roller. "Luck's no lady heah!"

Cousin Hog he cull the man's money from the table.

"Staying in, suh?" Cousin Hog slide the money in his pouch without waiting for no answer. That Hog . . . he can always reads a quitter.

"I've fed this table enough!" say the loser.

"I'm ready to roll 'um, Hog." Willie Moss take the man's place beside Lou. Carrie she shrink down.

Lou look at Willie Moss. "You the handsome dandy. Loc'in' lucky to me. Even smell lucky!"

Carrie she pout. Bubba Dee take her by the arm. "Don't worry gal . . . he'll be back. He just sportin' tonight . . . cele-brating . . . never had nothin' to celebrate before."

"I ain't worried none." She lean on him. "There's plenty more jive mens here. I can picks any I want!"

Pick *me*, I says inside of myself and snaps my fingers. *Pick me!* Pick *me!* But Carrie she look right over my head.

Bubba he nod at her. They pushes on through to watch the game. I eases in between them.

Willie Moss he cut up. "Hey you, Juba, don't shakes them things so hard. They eyes'll fall off!"

"I hopes they do. Don't wants more than five eyes lookin' at me." Seems Juba done turned a fiver on his first roll. He sweat and shake them dice with a rhythm that sound like tap dancing. The dice they clicks, hits the table, then rolls to a stop. Five dots up on the table sets Juba to crowing.

"Money is mine, all mine," he holler. All around the table the men are cussin' as Juba pick up the money.

But Juba crap out on his next roll losing half of what he done won. The next couple of rollers catches no luck neither. They's all hollering. "Damn dice. Curse on them bones!"

Lou she grab the dice. "Spit on 'um!"

Cousin Hog tap the table with his wooden hook. "No spitting allowed. You know that, Lou gal." Hog point at the spittoon shining out of the dark corner. Then he say, "Roll them bones."

Willie Moss he rolls the dice on that gal's hand. She hollering, "Rolls 'um. Let 'um come home."

Willie Moss pour sweat. Then he shoot them on the table like hot rocks. But the luck he ain't got. She spin around, come down, and she die.

"Fuck them boxcars!" Willie Moss pound his fist to the table. Lou Barnes put her arms around him.

Then a steady blue beat come from downstairs. The celebrating, singing, and hollering gets mixed up with that piano's low-down bass. Carrie twist and stretch. "I feels like dancing, Bubba Dee. It's W.C.'s song. He sang it here last week for the first time ever. I can't sits still when I hear it." She slide off his arm.

I follows her swaying hips down the steps. I tiptoeing so's to be taller.

"Dance, Carrie," yell S.I. Her dancing is good for trade. Men beats on the bar for shots. "C'mon Carrie," they hollers.

Carrie hike her dress above her knees. She slink around the

room, her long legs taking them long steps. The piano keep the Delta beat.

Charles don't play loud when he sings.

Feelin' tomorrow like I feel today,
I'll pack my trunk, make my get-away.

Charles' fingers runs on the keys. Carrie strut and sway. Her face shine. The crowd they claps and stomps. "Shake it Carrie!" Her tight black dress twist round and round. My heart it is bumping inside.

"Go on Carrie," holler S.I., "you ain't going to heaven nohow."

I tells little Jim how I's standing near the stairs trying to keeps up with Willie Moss's crap shoot and Carrie's dance alls at the same time. My short legs hurts from going up and down them steps. My ears fills with the sound of Saturday night on Beale Street. I claps to the rhythm, my ears they is open to hear who is winning, my eyes they is hurting for Carrie. I wants to put these things in my pocket for later. Then I backs up the stairs. I still watching Carrie from each one of them steps. When I gets to the top, I shuts my eyes away from her, turns my head, then stumbles my way through the crowd to finds Willie Moss.

I fidgets with my bowtie when I sees that Ben Griffin is winning at Hog's table. Griffin he Beale Street's bad man. Willie Moss's handkerchief hang from his pocket like a dark mop. Bubba Dee's forehead it all crisscrossed in a frown.

"What's happening, Bubba Dee?"

When Bubba Dee don't say nothing, I gets worried. "What is it, Bubba?"

Bubba lean down to my big ears. "We needs to get Willie Moss out of dis here game." His voice it way down in his chest. "He done lost it. He tryin' to mooch money to get it back. Ain't got no sense. Hog's gettin' mad with him, 'cause he don't need no more trouble. He already got Ben Griffin at the table!"

Willie Moss sees me. "Gimme some money, Moon. I'll doubles it."

"Sorry, Willie Moss. I just gots a little whiskey money, man."

Cousin Hog he frown hard at Willie Moss. "You finished man. Move on. I done told you!"

"I'm gonna roll 'um one more time! You can't stop me!"

Hog he never beat a man into the crowd. He keep his beatings real neat. He hold his hands together and bring his big brown arms above his head. This is the way it is when he hammer down on Willie Moss's head. Willie Moss then slide to the floor in a heap like a pile of dirt.

Lou toss her head back. "Aw now, the boy need his momma. Sends down for Carrie!" She laugh and slant her eyes toward Ben Griffin.

I feels my head shaking. "Bubba Dee, dat gal Lou ain't scared of the devil as long as the devil's got the dice!"

"That devil Ben Griffin's gots the dice and that ain't all! He gots a gun!"

Myself, I don't believes it. "How'd he gets past the frisk? Mr. Jim he don't allows nothin' like that at the Monarch!"

Bubba Dee shift back and forth like he don't know which way to go. "Ben Griffin's gonna has a gun under one arm. You ought to knows that, Moony. Especially with those big ears of yours. Not to say nothin' about yo eyes."

Bubba and me shakes Willie Moss. He kind of stir a little. Folks keeps stepping over his two long legs.

Griffin's rolling high. He's big over the table. He cut his eyes real sharp to the left and then to the right.

Juba's jumping and shouting. "Gimme, gimme, and gimme some more!"

Griffin's eyes stops cutting. They fixes on Juba. "You ain't gittin' nothin' more tonight! Ben Griffin is here talkin' to ya!" His bushy brows shades his eyes that burns like coals in them dark holes.

Lou hold his straw hat. She spin it around on her finger.

"Ben's going round this table. He gonna clean y'all out tonight!"

Juba fling the dice. He turn his point and keep jumping up and down.

Ben grab his hat from Lou's hand. He's glaring at Juba as he sets it down hard on his own head. "You cheatin' nigger!"

He push through the folks around him. They tries to clears a path, but he knock into any man or woman who get between hisself and Juba. He crash his big fist into Juba's head. Then Juba, he go down and keep Willie Moss company on the floor.

"Hey, Willie Moss!" he laugh. "We takin' a rest, ain't we!" Juba he too drunk to play dead.

Griffin pull him to his feet and send him flying into Cousin Hog. Juba bounce off Hog's chest and fall on top of Willie Moss.

I know trouble she is knocking 'cause Hog yelling at me. He say, "Moony, you fetch Margerum."

But Margerum he reach the top of the stairs before I gets through the crowd. Carrie she right behind him. Margerum he steaming, because no man's never broken the no fighting rule before. I sees his hand is locked on the gun in his coat pocket. And I scoots under Hog and around Margerum and stands myself in front of Carrie.

Margerum push toward Griffin, then look him straight in the eye. "Don't you knowed better than to hit a man in the Monarch?"

Ben Griffin hold hisself real stiff. His white suit hang straight down without even a wrinkle. He glare out from under the brim of his straw hat.

The sound of Charles' piano it keep rumbling on. The hum of voices spread like waves all through the place.

Feelin' tomorrow like I feel today,
I'll pack my trunk, make my get-away.

45

Carrie get scared and hug me when Margerum start moving closer to Griffin. "I done said, don't you knowed better than to hit a man in the Monarch?" Margerum says to him.

Griffin he stand still. I hardly takes air when I sees his chest moving real slow under his coat, but it ain't him what's the cause of it. Carrie she holding on tight and I hoping she ain't going to let go.

"I will hit a man in the Monarch or any other damn place if'n the motherfucker make me mad." His hand slide into his pocket.

But Margerum's ready. He pull the gun and he fire. Griffin's head it jerk hard—he fall to the floor with his hand still caught up in his coat.

Then I feels my own chest with Carrie's arms round it and I breathes in real deep.

Griffin he pulling hisself to his knee howling like a dog. Grabbing on to the crap table, he fire back at Margerum. The crowd, they scatter. Carrie she still holding on. Margerum collapse. The blood on his lapel look like a big red rose. Griffin roar again, then he fall back hitting his head. His hat it roll around the floor like a nickel.

Hog try to raise Margerum. "Call Mr. Jim. Ben Griffin done broke the rule."

S.I. stand over the two dead men just a shakin'. "Hog, what we do now?"

Hog lower Margerum's head to the floor. "Like I done said. Call Mr. Jim."

Little Jim don't say nothin' when I says all this, but his eyes is real big. So I tells him how Distance stop the car and how he come around and open the door for Mr. Jim. The policemens they are waiting for him. They's Tree Top Tall and Coal Oil Johnny.

Coal Oil say, "Mr. Jim, we are going to put both bodies in the alley if you give the okay. We have not written a report

46

yet. As far as Tree Top and me know, they died outside of the Monarch."

Mr. Jim he take off his hat. "Put Griffin in the alley," he say. "Leave Margerum inside. But put down in the report that he was killed by Griffin in the alley. Say that Margerum's body has already been claimed."

"Yes sir, Mr. Jim," say Tree Top. He's real big. "Anything you say, Mr. Jim."

"Keep quiet to the reporters. They'd have the do-gooders down on us."

Then Mr. Jim he point to the big wooden door of the Monarch. "Moony, go call the undertaker. Tell him not to botch the job. Johnny's wife will want him looking nice. And call her." He peel money off of his wad to pay for the box and such. Then he say, "Tell her he died upholding the rules of the Monarch Saloon."

And I tells her. Just like I tells little Jim. But I don't say nothin' else about Carrie. The gal done let go.

The Nonpareil: Jim Canaan

1898

At dawn the fire bell woke him. The ringing stirred his blood. Raising up quickly, his arms and legs aching as though wrapped in a tight wire, he clenched his teeth so that he would not cry out. The pain in his body was meted out with increasing vengeance each year of his life. His legs burned, and as he stood, the voice inside of him kept repeating fire . . . fire.

Jo tried to hand him the cup of coffee as he brushed past her. "Yell at Tade to come on. We've got to check the saloon. Tell the boy to come too."

"The lad ran out when the fire bell started up. Slipped through my fingers, he did."

"For God's sake, Sister. You shouldn't let the boy out alone. The damn Mackerels will chew him to pieces. They're working for O'Haggarty."

Her face filled with terror and he was sorry that he had frightened her. "We'll find him . . . just watch out for him until this God damn war is over. And tell Clare not to go out alone. Never alone. Rosie, either."

"Hurry, hurry." She pushed him toward the door, grabbed the shillelagh from the corner and stuck it in his hand. Tade was rushing to follow.

Outside, Tade made for the wagon, but Jim Canaan motioned him forward. "Faster to walk." He could see smoke rising above the Nonpareil and willfully ordered his muscles screaming inside to carry him toward his saloon.

Tade, leaving his wife, Fanny, and their baby girl, Pearl, at home in St. Louis, had brought his four-year-old son, Ted, down to visit him and their sister, Jo, and brother, Tom, the boy's aunt and uncles, but instead of a family reunion, found himself in the middle of the vice war. Ted was running after the pumper as fast as his little legs could carry him. But he was losing ground as the big white horse clomped steadily toward the fire. Tade ran and scooped the boy up into his powerful arms. "Running after the pumper are you?" He swung him around in a circle, then hoisted the boy on his back. "You little scamp."

Ted's eyes were wide with excitement, the fear of danger not present in his young mind. Catching up, Jim Canaan tousled his nephew's hair, and relieved that he was safe, pressed on to the fire. Before they rounded the corner, he felt the heat and the tightening grip inside of his chest. The flames were lapping the front wall of the Nonpareil. Every last fireman from No. 4 and No. 1 worked to save the building, the pumpers steadily pouring water, the men swarming over the fire with their hoses. His older brother, Tom, once a fireman himself, was helping them.

"The boy's got fire in his blood," yelled Tom when he saw his brothers. "He was chasing the pumper all the way, little as he is."

No. 1's red engine operated the pump that sucked water from the hydrant, forcing it through the hose, a pulsating wet snake, the flames quickly surrendering to the heavy spray of water. Tom shoveled coal into the boiler. "We've beat the devil today, Jim." The hovering gray smoke began to lighten and drift.

Tade lifted Ted up on the seat beside Betty the Dalmatian. His blond hair was wet from the heat. "They've almost put it out, Uncle Jim."

The small voice momentarily eased the hatred he felt, but watching the smoke, his rage quickly began to boil and build

49

up. If O'Haggarty's greed burned his saloon, culling his profits, then by God he could be greedier still. He would wipe out the O'Haggarty gang or die fighting.

Betty was barking and beating her tail against the seat. Ted, jumping up and down, was peering up into the sky, pointing at a great gaggle of geese flying over from the north and squinting as the orange sun rose in the east. Passing overhead, the noise of the squabbling birds grew loud, as if they were debating the direction of travel. The lead goose honked and drew back to the rear for rest, while another bird moved into its place. As the geese made their way southward, following the Mississippi, the honking grew muffled. Jim Canaan strained to hear the last faint sound of it. He felt his feet anchored to the ground, the pain shooting through his legs as he watched the graceful pattern of flight.

He looked up at the boy. He was growing strong and fine, like Tade. There were plans to be made. He drew the attention of the gathering of neighborhood men watching the fire fighters. "Anyone who can hit a nail on the head can have a job, starting this afternoon. I'm rebuilding the Nonpareil and I'll be back in business before the end of the week. Anyone who doubts it, listen now and know that such stink as the O'Haggarty bunch will never come round my place again. I'm taking over. Here I am and here I'll stay!"

"And I'm staying it with you," hollered Tade. "As soon as I can move Fanny and the baby. For good."

"Me too," said Ted, busily counting Betty's spots.

The wide smile felt natural even as it stretched tightly across his face. Tade would be his partner, a wish that he had held for a long time.

Tom looked happy about the announcement. He came over and shook the hands of his brothers. And now their sister Jo would no longer worry over the welfare of Tade's family in St. Louis. They would all be together again.

"Who can paint?" demanded Jim Canaan. "I want a great bird spread across the Nonpareil. In honor of Tade's homecoming." He poked at the charred clapboard of the Nonpareil. "A phoenix. And I want it now." He lit a sweet-smelling cigar and drew in. "See that O'Haggarty's invited to the unveiling!"

At night Jim Canaan could smell them coming. "O'Haggarty's got nothing left but the Mackerels."

"I thought old Pete was selling carp again." The curve of grin on Tade's face glowed in the firelight that flashed from torches outside, his green eyes watering for the fight. He fired the shotgun, splattering darkness. "Rotten fish. Missed him!"

The shadows of firebrands jumped at the backside of Pete's grocery across the alley. The third night of the assault. Jim Canaan estimated the number of raiders, counting seven shadows on the grocery store wall and twelve on Moy's Chinese Laundry as they ran past, heading for cover.

Pete was hollering from his window. "Mother of God, don't leta them burn me down. Jim Canaan, this your fault. Damn you Mick. Damn you, monkey fucker. Mother of God, help me."

"I'm thinking he means motherfucker," says Devlin McBlue.

"Watch your Goddamn language," said Jim Canaan. He had tried to give Pete a gun, but the little Italian sluffed him off. Caught in the war with only two barrels of flour. With it he was snuffing the sparks intended to gut the Nonpareil whenever they fell near his grocery, the blue-black of night overcast in a cloud of his flour and the smoking guns.

Jim Canaan emptied his pockets of the shotgun shells, placing them on the small table beside him, and pulled down the left dog-ear, sliding the double barrel out of the window and adjusting his eyes to the firelight. From the window next to him, his brother Tade again took aim at the footsteps that rustled the leaves and trash behind the saloon. He fired and heard the running steps in the dark. "Pour it on!" yelled Tade to his *brother, shooting both barrels at once, his shoulder jolting with the kick. Picking off one of the enemy, he wanted more. He laughed, reloaded, then fired again.*

"Missed him," Jim Canaan roared. "God damn fiends. Tell me that I won't run the dice when and where I choose. Fire away, Tade." Tade fired, then cocked the right side and fired again, the shots ricocheting off Pete's barrel of fat renderings beside his back door. The fight felt good with Tade by his side.

Jim Canaan picked up the Hadden Horn and threw it out into the alley. "You bunch of no-good sneaking bastards. Loaded dice . . . scared to be seen in daylight." He threw down his shotgun, grabbed the shillelagh, and ran out the front door with McBlue and O'Levy following him.

He heard O'Haggarty's dark voice. "Throw the torches." Through the air streaked a fire pole that traveled in an arc, landing close to the saloon, lighting the night like a giant candle. One of the Mackerels stepped under Pete's window. The Italian quickly reached out and poured a bowl of flour on his head. As the Mackerel brushed the white from his eyes, Jim Canaan came from the side of the Nonpareil and knocked him down with the shillelagh. "Good timing, Pete!" he yelled.

"At least you don't steala from me, Jim Canaan." The Italian waved his fist. He was mad at the Canaans, but hated the Mackerel gang with Latin passion because of their constant thievery.

More shots rang out from the end of the alley. "Shoot that way, Tade." He was pointing and saw Tade's shoulder jerk as he shot at a skulker crawling toward Pete's garbage can. Tade held up his second shot while McBlue kicked the crawler in the head. Pete threw another shovel full of flour from his window, smothering more sparks and the man's head, the ground around him like new-fallen snow in the moonlight.

"They're spread out all over the place. Give them a chance to gang up and they will." He could feel sweat running down his ribs. "Lay low, Pete," he yelled. He motioned O'Levy and McBlue

back toward the saloon. "Damn Dago's going to get his lights put out. Spunky little devil." Pete excelled at torch snuffing. He had put out a dozen fires in three nights, quickly dishing out the flour, then ducking back inside. He saw Pete's silhouette coughing up the rancid odors of fat and singed flour. Tade was also gasping for clean air. He himself was able to stomach such things.

The Mackerels retreated, licking their wounds. He knew they were good for another round. "Go on back in. When they come back around, we'll catch them in a crossfire." He ordered the three Finney brothers, John, James, and Joseph, to work their way around to the front of Pete's grocery. "Tell Pete he's lucky to be alive. That we're taking over his store, until we're rid of the vermin in the alley. Then he can go back to selling his garlic."

"One's coming around back on your side, Tade," yelled Devlin McBlue.

Tade smiled and again cocked both barrels. He stood up, angling the shotgun toward the street where it emptied into the alley. Sighting the figure in the darkness, he aimed and pulled the trigger. Kawoom. The man's torch was blown out of his hand, but he got off a pistol shot as he ran screaming. The shot whistled by Tade's ear before smashing a bottle of bourbon behind him, sending out the smell of sour mash.

Distance said, "Mr. Jim, that one was mighty close to killing at least one of us."

"Put all the whiskey down behind the bar, Distance," said Jim Canaan. "No need in wasting it. And bring me a shot before they start up again."

Bennie O'Levy and Devlin McBlue guarded the front door. O'Levy motioned to the Finneys, who edged out. They were all three dressed in black.

Across the alley, Pete again dumped a shovel full of flour on the grass, snubbing the sparks that lit below his window, then knocked the head of a Mackerel who had tried to grab his shovel blade.

Devlin McBlue shouted that the Finneys had rounded the corner. The constant skirmishing and rapid footsteps sounded from the alley and down the street beyond.

Distance set a shot of whiskey on the table in the middle of Jim Canaan's shells. "Shoot it, Mr. Jim," he said.

"Heads up!" Jim Canaan downed his whiskey and yelled, "Hold your fire on the right until the Finneys get inside."

Days before, Ola had warned him that O'Haggarty was making a stand. He had been surprised that the move was such a long time coming. Business had been good, most of it sucked away from O'Haggarty. In the Iron Clad where Ola lived, information spread rapidly. It went out of the men and into the girls and then circulated. Ola collected and saved it for him. She had been nervously pacing the floor when he entered her room. She had rushed toward him, wrapping herself in his arms, pouring out the warning, and pleading with him to take care of himself and not to die. He remembered the warmth of her body against him. Ola with the hair of sunshine.

He heard the Italian protesting. "Nota in my store."

"Keep the flour dry, Pete!" shouted Tade.

A volley of shots rang out, shaving the clapboard off the grocery. Pete spit hell in Italian.

"Take up a gun, Distance," said Tade. "We could use some more firepower."

"Wouldn't mind taking pot shots, Mr. Tade. But I ain't no killer." He began taking down the bottles four at a time.

"Just keep us supplied, Distance," said Jim Canaan. "What about you?" he shouted to the stranger who had come in earlier for a drink. The man had quickly gotten out of the way when the fight started, and now sat very erect in the corner, observing the action.

"Firearms would prove unstable in my hands of limited experience," replied the man in a precise tone, his lips forming each word. "I'll keep a record of the dead, if you wish," he said. "The name's Merlin Mahon. Student of law." His feet were planted squarely out in front of him. "It occurs to me that you might benefit from my advice in the future . . . if you live through the night."

"These flimsy bastards. Tried to burn me out. If any of them are still drawing breath in the morning, they'll wish they were dead. Sons of bitches."

"If words could kill, the opposition would have expired an hour ago," said Merlin Mahon. His hair was parted down the middle, the line of demarcation exact. He wore a dark suit with a vest and kept his hat on the chair next to him.

Jim Canaan enjoyed the pattern of Mahon's words and the general way he conducted himself. Different from the usual sort of drop in. Highly different. "Well, if you are brave enough to sit and watch, go ahead and have a bottle on the house. We're too damn busy to join you."

"Thank you, Mr. Canaan." Distance handed him a bottle, which he declined. "But a short glass will do quite nicely. I am devoted to moderation in all things."

Just then shots pelted the shelves behind the bar, the shards of glass sprayed across the back counter.

"Best be ducking on back here with me, Mr. Merlin," said Distance from behind the bar.

Merlin Mahon raised his glass in a silent toast, then quickly took shelter.

Jim Canaan watched the deliberate way in which he moved, the confident air, the way he balanced the glass so that not a drop was spilled even though he was moving quickly. He was a survivor not given to the hysteria of the usual customer when trouble started. An idea trickled into his mind. Somehow, he decided, Merlin Mahon would marry his niece Rosie.

And he thought of Nate. Tonight, when every man was

needed, he had hoped that Nate would show up without an invitation.

Tom Canaan came in with reinforcements—John Culligan with a dozen policemen, and a group of firemen headed by Duffy. Tade fired again as the Mackerels crept back into the alley. "I can see that Tade's got the sharp eye, Jim," said Tom Canaan.

"The little brother with the sharp eye is more help than the big one with the silver tongue."

"Better late," said Tom. "Where's my gun?"

"It's fists we need," said Jim Canaan. "You can't kill rats in the dark. Let 'um come out to play in the alley and we'll bare knuckle the bastards to hell and back. Drink up!"

"Get your billies out, men," said Captain Culligan. "Rout the devils."

"O'Haggarty's mine!" said Jim Canaan.

He could hear clusters of Mackerels gathering in the alley with silent torches. When he saw the match struck and put to a torch, Jim Canaan shouted at his men to follow him. "Hell fire!" He moved out the door waving the shillelagh. The Finneys were waiting at Pete's window and jumped out one by one as Jim Canaan and the men poured into the alley and started pounding heads. A match was thrown into Pete's renderings, a blaze of hell that shot up high in the sky. He shoveled desperation and shouted orders to Jesus and Mary. "If a ever you look down, do ita now!"

The streak of fire lit up O'Haggarty's scarlet face. Two of his men stood in front guarding him from the fists that were flying.

"Let me have him, Jim," said Tom. "No, me," hollered Tade. "Throw him in the fire."

Without a word, Jim Canaan plowed through the fistfights all around him. He went straight for O'Haggarty, his elbow clipping the jaw of one of the guards, the shillelagh cracking the shoulder of another. With the same one-two punch, he cracked O'Haggarty's jaw with his left hook and struck him down with his weapon. "You're through in this town, O'Haggarty. Get out."

With their boss on the ground, the Mackerels began to back off, Duffy, Culligan, and the men chasing them with clubs and hatchets.

All in a night's work, he thought, as the smoke cleared.

Some of O'Haggarty's stragglers were captured by the Finneys, some by Culligan's policemen. The culprits were bound and gagged. "You know what to do with them," said Jim Canaan. The Finneys and the patrolmen waited for orders. "You don't have to be particularly neat about it, either." He motioned toward the two men who had been killed. "Burn the bodies. It'll be a lesson to any man who decides to take up with the likes of O'Haggarty."

Merlin Mahon was standing a few feet away, listening. He stepped forward. "In case someone in the police department turns on you, you'd do well to bury them outside the city. The investigations in the county are less than stringent."

The four Mackerels were salivating and sweating blood as they squirmed under the tight ropes. Then their mouths were gagged with dirty rags, their eyes bulging. They were led away by McBlue, O'Levy, and the Finneys.

Pete was standing out front waiting for a word with him. "I never thoughta the night would end, Jim Canaan." The flour covered his swarthy skin and dusted his eyelashes. "For God's sakes, don't fight no more."

"The fire's out, Pete," he said. "Business as usual. O'Haggarty won't be back."

When had he gotten over the killing? It had been such a gradual thing. He remembered that at first he had suffered, that he had not slept as he could not sleep now. But he remembered nothing of what he had felt. He did not want to remember.

57

He insisted on painting the bird with more vivid colors, after Tade was ambushed on the train for St. Louis. Shot down without a warning. Ted witnessed the murder of his father. He talked about the "dots of red" that were spattered on his father's face and how "he didn't move." Fanny blamed Jim Canaan for Tade's death, saying that the riffraff was just getting even. She was right in some ways, but she could not understand that Tade was in with him . . . had wanted in.

Although he hurt with the loss of his brother, the sight of the bird soothed him. The phoenix was a memorial.

Mr. Crump

1909–1910, *Merlin Mahon*

The Mississippi River provided jobs for the indigent and entertainment for the desperate and in general was the heartbeat
that kept things stirred up in Memphis, but the odor from the
Wolf River's tail end as it wagged its way into the "Father of
Waters" was more than I could stomach. In spite of foul air,
foolish citizens spent holidays celebrating on the bluffs over-
looking the Mississippi. Ladies spread lavish picnics on checkered cloths while covering their noses, and lovers, undaunted
by the smell, strolled under umbrellas. And on any Saturday in summer it was usual to witness preachers baptizing
God's children, their eyes wide with terror of drowning. I didn't
blame them for being afraid of the swirling water, brown with
mischief and deceit. I would not willingly duck my head under
the damnable waters, not even for God. But there was a pull
about the river and I sometimes thought that it had power
unrelated to its physical force. As proof of its sorcery, many
sure-footed river men mysteriously fell in and drowned, sobri-
ety notwithstanding.

The river took cotton away from Memphis and brought dollars back. It also brought in men with rough hides tanned
from days in the sun, hands blistered from manual labor I
shudder to think of, and clothes soaked in oil. They got off
the boats wearing heavy brogans that were weapons used to

even up fights. They clamored to the saloons and brothels to raise hell, shouting words learned from the devil. They killed one another for sport, increasing the city's fame as the murder capital of the world. The Mississippi would never be entirely tamed, but Memphis was waiting, however noisily, to be quieted down.

The great bridge across the river had given the city confidence. It showed that men could confront something powerful and live to tell about it. Some of them, anyhow. Like the river men, many of the workers who helped construct the bridge over the Mississippi died in its waters. They would show up downstream, floating big and ugly on the muddy water.

The dead workers were not revered like the men who had died in the Civil War, though the workers fought the river just as hard as the Confederates fought the Yankees, and contributed more to progress. I thought of the Frisco Bridge as a kind of monument to them.

Music flowed in Memphis like debris in the river. Many kinds of music met in the city—formal introduction not a requirement as most of it was unprofessional and lowborn. Italians sang *Rigoletto* from fruit and vegetable stands and between arias promoted the sale of "cantaloupes" and "cucumbers" in broken English. "Cantaloupe" was difficult for them to say, particularly after a night of wine-swilling when their eyes would take on the color of fermented grapes. Irish tenors serenaded the old Irish ladies at the Lyceum—Jo Culligan never missed a performance of John McCormick's, mawkish as it was. The Germans furnished musicians and teachers and organized the Mai Feste; one of them was Kathleen's piano teacher, Mrs. Barmeister, who I must admit lent dignity to a city almost devoid of it. And on the street corners black guitar strummers sang their sad lives so that other sympathetic souls might share their misery and say, "Yea brother." All of this music bombarded my ears.

This was only the beginning. Tunes came up from the Delta cotton fields. Agrarian noise I called it. There was no escape from it. Some of the songs were aggressively sexual, but the singers generally garbled the words so that the illicit meanings rarely raised eyebrows.

K-C girls can shake it mighty fine
Those K-C girls they shake it mighty fine
But they don't make jelly like that ol' high brown
Mempho gal of mine

Some of the Delta tunes got mixed in with the wild screeching sounds of lovers' laments that floated down from the mountains of East Tennessee, brought to town by boxcar musicians playing harps, banjos, and fiddles—anything they could finger, including dirty combs—who at least confined their murders to family members or friends of long standing. Their music was a mutt.

Bringing home her jelly in a jar
My Sarah Jane she traveled very far
Down the path and through the woods
She stumbled into Johnny Good
He spilled her jelly from the jar

Unfortunately, this was not the extent of it. Tunes leaked out of the churches like water from buckets riddled with holes. The purveyors of this music were the most dedicated, I am sorry to say. Just walking down the street for a constitutional, I would meet the rolling thunder of the white Baptists, whose unschooled piano players got tunes pumped out with the mash of the pedal, which they used unsparingly. And the others— my own Gregorian chant, for instance—mysterious as darkness. Add to that the rugged tunes of the tough Methodists —faithful keepers of the flame first spread by circuit riders, who rode their horses to death. And the pristine singing of the

61

Episcopalians who didn't like the Pope. And the calls of the rabbis—sounds pulled from the throats of their ancient dead. All of it interminable, like the talk of women.

Music swelled up in the churches of the Negroes, who sang like bands of rowdy angels. Viola was the worst of them. She bellowed like Moggy when he howled at the moon. She believed that in order for the Lord to hear and understand, her voice had to reach the clouds where her words could be carried by the wind up to that "great Jubilee in the sky." Whatever that was.

To my mind, the constant assault on the ears of the citizenry prevented the development of intellectual life in Memphis. With all the noise, who could read or think? Of course, I must remember that half of the clods who had taken up residence in the city could not read or write and so shall admit that music could provide a banal spiritualism for them, but a solid base of ideas found in literature is the essential prerequisite for the disciplined life, the life in which a higher class of men move forward. But literature was almost entirely lacking in the city of jocularity and tuneful persuasions. I read de Tocqueville during that time when I was preparing to study law. De Tocqueville didn't like Memphis. His distaste centered on the mud, the cruelty, the ruffians. He did not stay long enough to find out about the literature. Intelligent visitors shared his abhorrence. But I was telling about the river and have wandered like it does.

Memphis, like the river, was changing course, and men such as Jim Canaan and his brother Tom were powerless to stop it. Tom Canaan ran the politics of the First Ward and Jim Canaan controlled vice. The pair of them seemed indestructible, even to me, who understood the vulnerability of mortal man better than most. Mr. Crump had been walking toward power for several years. The progressives, preachers, and the do-gooders were shouting and walking with him. Now it was his turn.

W. C. Handy wrote it for Mr. Crump and although the tune was less primitive than most, in my opinion the lyrics provided a rather strange and ambiguous campaign song.

> *Mr. Crump don't 'low no easy riders here.*
> *Mr. Crump don't 'low no easy riders here.*
> *We don't care what Mr. Crump don't 'low,*
> *We gon'to bar'l-house anyhow—*
> *Mr. Crump can go and catch hisself some air!*

On Second Street, the campaign had already affected the spirit of the house. When I came in to see him a few days before election day, Jim Canaan was placing bills in a suitcase. He told me, "Merlin, Tom wants me to play it safe. He said the Red Snapper's going to win and that he's bound to shut me down later if I don't help him now."

"Tom's the student of politics," I said to him. "It's all that occupies his head. You're right to listen." I was grieved to hear that he was knuckling under, for I had the deepest regard for him and cared not a lick that his reputation was black. He was a verity, disciplined in the old way. The most honorable man that I knew. He either told the truth or said nothing. In other words, I trusted him even though he was on the wrong side of the law.

He closed the lid of the suitcase. He locked it, then nodded to Distance, who carried it down the stairs. Distance walked down first to block any possible fall. I followed them.

On the porch, Jo was sitting on the wicker sofa dressed in her usual widow's black. Captain Culligan had been dead for a month. In my opinion, she had killed off all of her husbands with religion and her obsession with cleanliness. Displayed in the coffin, all three of them had glowed with radiant pink skin. My son George was sitting there swinging his feet, and looked rather pale considering the proximity of his great-aunt next to him. Jim Flanagan, beside him, looked a little peaked himself, but I knew that Jo would soon alter their condition, her attention to their welfare only temporarily delayed by talk of the election.

Across from them, Nate and Clare sat on the wicker chairs. Clare was reading the newspaper aloud. I was relatively sure that her mother could not read.

Jo's nose for Jim Canaan's business interrupted the news. "Where on earth are you going with that suitcase, Brother?"

"The Nonpareil, Sister."

To escape from *you*, I wanted to say to her, but manners dictated otherwise. I had learned to hold my tongue from Nate, who dodged the calamity of confrontation with great dexterity.

Nate got up, shook my hand, and then acknowledged Jim Canaan with a strange half-bow. Clare stood and brushed her hand over her uncle's back. He touched her shoulder, then she sat back down.

Nate was a hale and personable man, deserving of the beauteous Clare, but not of the money she stood to inherit from her uncle. As Jim Canaan's attorney, I urged him to make his will, hoping to guide him in the fair division of his properties. He ignored my advice in this matter. But I had not given up and considered ways that might show him that Nate, given the opportunity, would prove an inept administrator.

Jo's voice kicked at my thoughts. She addressed her brother. "Since when have you been needing a change of clothes for the saloon?"

"It's money, Jo. For E. H. Crump."

"You'd help the man get elected?" She stood up to fight about it. "He's said that he'd shut you down . . . that he'd nail up your doors and put you out of business."

"The Nonpareil don't have no doors, Miz Jo," said Distance, reminding her that the saloon was open twenty-four hours a day including Sunday, which was against the law.

"It's a game," said Jim Canaan. "Crump says he'll put the

lid on to keep the do-goods happy. Then, a couple of weeks after the election, we'll open up full steam again. He's said that you can't stop what you don't see. And you can't see what you won't look at." He stabbed the porch planks with his shillelagh. "He'll look the other way." He looked as though he wanted to spit. "Damnation! It's either play ball with Crump or put up with a parade of Baptists."

"But all that money. Just look at those lumps bulging! Heaven help us. We could prosper every poor Irishman in the parish with it!" She had the list in her head. "O'Lanahan could use a new suit. Mrs. O'Grady's little house needs new roofing. And her old mother needs teeth . . ."

"Jo, we already help most of them."

"Yes, and it's a fine thing. And the only way for saving you." She waved her hand in the air as though she might catch her words. Constrainedly, she was looking at Jim and at George. She did not want them to know that the destination of their Uncle Jim's soul was dependent on her prayerful solicitations. She fingered the small gold cross that she wore at her throat.

"It's your friends that need saving . . . from the slack belly," said Jim Canaan. "But even those poor devils would understand the need to put out a fire that would burn down the house." He glanced at the swollen suitcase. "Tom wants me to play it safe. He said that the Red Snapper's going to win and that he'll shut me down later if I don't help him now." I knew that he repeated this in order to convince himself of the merit of his stance.

Then Jo got started. This was the only time that I ever saw the woman cry. Her righteousness poured forth in a flood of tears. Frankly, I had never before seen such a volume of water emerge from a human body. That her brother was wasting money on Mr. Crump when she could be sliding it under the teacups of her penniless friends, then wink at her accomplice —usually little Jim, whom she had chosen to inherit her concept of charity—was more than she could bear. Given the source of her money and the conflict that the source had with her cherished church, I found the whole enterprise laughable. Oh, I attended Saint Brigid's myself, but only because it was a discipline and a way that I might guide my own son toward an ethical life. For my purpose, the Catholic church was less problematic than the rest of them, and the entertainment stellar.

Interestingly, little Jim possessed a directness that eluded his grandmother. When she left money under the cup on one of their recent visitations, he had asked her, "Mama Jo, why don't you just give it to her?" The boy had more sense than his grandmother could tolerate. She was not prone to the upper levels of mental life. As he told it, her reply was "Oh no, you must leave her that little bit of pride." I could picture her whispering and holding a short fat finger to her lips, the sleeves of her dress covering her knuckles. The face would be stern, then after shaking her head, the soft flesh of her face quivering, her eyes would slant upward in a conspiratorial smile. The ritual of her facial expressions was unforgettable, though I have tried heartily to do so.

Jim Canaan hated seeing his sister cry, but as always his proclamation stood firm. "I've given my word. And that's the way it's to be," he told her.

She dried her face and then bandaged the bottom of his shillelagh, but still it made a thumping sound as he walked across the porch toward the steps.

Overtaken with emotion, Distance, who hadn't yet heard about the Emancipation Proclamation, was shaking his head, obviously disturbed by the woman's tears. "Mr. Crump putting on the dog with the colored folks, Miz Jo. That's for sure. He even giving free food."

"What will he do for them after he's elected, Distance? A hot dog won't keep them filled for long."

"No, Miz Jo, not even for an hour I'll bet. But then some folks like the attention. They don't think past the attention."

"They line up for whatever is free and who in the hell can blame them," said Jim Canaan. "For fifteen years Tom and I have doled out free drinks for votes at the Nonpareil. Crump's doing the same giveaway. He's learned it from us." Jim Canaan's blue eyes were very bright under the black hat. "There's no joy in the mayor's race, but at least we can celebrate Tom's reelection as committeeman of the First Ward. He wouldn't lose if he was a hundred and had the breath of a mule. The man causes a smile when he walks into a room." He almost smiled himself when he said this. Instead, he motioned to Distance, raising two stiff gnarled fingers. Distance took a Cremo from his shirt pocket and stuck it into the crimped V.

Nate struck a match and held it to the cigar. As he puffed and blew smoke, Jim Canaan wanted his sister and the rest of them to understand what was coming.

"Crump says he doesn't think prohibition will work. Men are going to slug whiskey and he knows it. He's going to let the law slide. The saloon owners are behind the Crump bandwagon. They can't stand out front where the do-gooders can see. Crump's got to have their votes, too." He drew in on the cigar. "Tom says we've got to play the game."

> *Mr. Crump he went down, down to see Jim Canaan*
> *Mr. Crump he went down, down to see Jim Canaan*
> *Mr. Crump went down to see Jim Canaan*
> *He said, "Listen here Jim, I'm in command."*

Distance brought the car around. We climbed in and drove the few short blocks to the Nonpareil. Nate had declined to go. Nate's lack of enthusiasm came from his own father, who had a tight hold on him. Old Emmett Flanagan owned a saloon down in the south part of town and watched politics from his own door, but he thought that Jim Canaan's organization rifled the sanctity of the ballot box. He had counseled Nate to steer clear of direct involvement because he thought there would be a fire and that Nate would get burned. That Nate could live in Jim Canaan's house and yet remain neutral was beyond me.

My own interest in all of this was twofold. I admired Jim Canaan and offered him legal advice even before my marriage to Rosie. Frankly, and without any shame whatever, I was determined to inherit some of his money and wanted to ensure that there would be some left to enjoy. After all, I had endured the vice of Rosie, his niece, a woman whose drinking had shaken my faith in the delicacy of womanhood. I was steadfast and duty-bound to reform her. And pending reformation, I had resolved to hold her upright no matter how much of my own strength the job required.

I assisted in the removal of his men from jail whenever the request was made of me and, in general, gave whatever advice I could muster to keep them out of it.

But Nate insisted that insurance was his vocation and that no other was right for him. I felt that he was enjoying Jim Canaan's tune without bothering to learn the lyrics.

Distance pulled in front of the Nonpareil. As always, a pile of broken chairs sat outside of the entrance like the makings of a bonfire. "The hooligans must have gotten out of hand again," said Jim Canaan. "Have the stuff carted away before the election."

Crump and his men were waiting in a black Ford parked in front of the saloon. The offensive colors of the giant bird painted on the building cast a garish rainbow across the hood of Crump's car. As much as I admired him, Jim Canaan's taste in art was peculiar. As Crump's man walked toward him, Jim Canaan swallowed the lump in his throat and with it, I thought, the inclination to fight.

Crump sat watching from his car, his red hair springing out

from under his black bowler. He laughed like a hyena, then snickered in rivulets.

> *Mr. Crump say, now look here Jim Canaan*
> *Goin' to chase yo' ass right out the Promised Land*
> *Close your store, shut your barroom down*
> *Won't be no more fightin' and gamblin' in this town*

Jim Canaan breathed in, then nodded to Distance, who got out of the car and handed the suitcase to the man, who took it without a word. The Red Snapper was still watching from the car. He tipped his hat, got comfortable in his seat, and drove off with the heist.

"Have the place cleaned up, Distance. I want it looking nice on election day. We'll have a celebration after Tom wins." He said this and shifted his shoulders, buoying himself, the straightening an effort to show that he had not lost, not yet.

Tom walked by without a wave. Didn't stop, or even look up. He was walking toward home and very slowly.

"Go tote him home, Distance."

"Yes, sir, Mr. Jim."

We went on in. The floor had been swept clean of the wreckage and mayhem of his sordid clientele, the surviving chairs piled on top of the tables, and the disgusting spittoons emptied. The election officials had already placed the ballot boxes on tables opposite the bar. Moony washed glasses, placing them on towels to dry. They appeared clean and properly sanitized.

"Good morning, Mr. Jim," he said cheerfully. "Good morning, Mr. Merlin. Miz Jo sent me on down to help out before the elections."

"And to do a bit of reporting, Moony?" I said to him.

"Miz Jo like to know what happening, Mr. Merlin. Miz Clare won't lets her come on down and satisfy herself."

From behind the counter, the boy looked unreasonably tall.

Then I realized he was standing on something, but curiosity brought him down when Distance came in frowning.

"Mr. Jim! Mr. Tom's taken real sick," said Distance. "You'd better go on and look after him, Mr. Jim."

"What's he complain of?"

"Thinks he's got a bad cold, Mr. Jim. And he's real hot."

"He'll beat it. You can be sure. I'll see to him later. Let the man rest, for God's sake," he said. "My sister'll wash the fever out of him. He won't have the chance to warm the bed. That's a sure bet."

"I'll takes the bet, Mr. Jim," said Moony.

Moony would bet on the sun, moon, and stars disappearing from the constellations. Anything that might possibly bring him money. Jim Canaan understood this and allowed the bet.

"Trying for the elevated shoes again, Moony?" He motioned the boy for his glass of whiskey and bade me to join him. Moony poured bourbon and slid the glasses toward us. "You're only as small as you feel, boy," said Jim Canaan.

Bright: what sounded like a good disposition was a killer. Bright's disease attacked Tom and laid him low. Not knowing that he lay dead less than four blocks from the polling place, his friends cast their votes for him. Those who gathered to celebrate the political victory stayed to mourn him at his wake. For Jim Canaan, his brother's death would mark the end of an era.

Mr. Crump don't 'low it, ain't gonna have it here.

Mr. Crump won the election, was sworn in on a crisp January morning, and immediately declared that the progressive years had begun. Even though his margin of victory was only seventy-nine votes, his supporters predicted that his tenure would be a long one. Mr. Crump was elevated to his position as mayor with votes mysteriously cast by dead men—some of them expired for a decade—who had risen for the occasion. Since the dead had voted for the opposition as well, the court challenges sputtered and soon ended.

The Shelby representatives in the state legislature had every opportunity for legalizing the saloons and doing away with the alliance between favored law violators and those in authority. However, Crump wanted no change in existing conditions, as they gave him a political club to hold over gamblers and saloon keepers and thus hold them in line with his machine. It quickly became clear that "Boss" Crump either gave or withheld permission for whatever was or was not done. Political progression, as I saw it, could not develop under a dictatorship, and so in many ways, Mr. Crump was setting Memphis back just as the Yellow Jack had done. The town yawned while Mr. Crump looked down.

Halley's Comet had been sighted when Mr. Crump came to power, its tail conspicuously brilliant in the deep inky blue of the early morning sky. Distance referred to it as a "comic," but the malapropism was less than humorous for Jim Canaan. For him, the comet was the sign of a new time, an era in which he would not be welcome. But the old times did not die easy.

> *We don't care what Mr. Crump don't 'low*
> *We gon'to bar'l-house anyhow!*

Sunday

1914, *Jim Flanagan*

My sisters and I went to early mass with Mama Jo. Not many people were there. Several old Italian and Irish women were scattered about the church. Some said the rosary. Some lit vigil lights in memory of dead husbands and loved ones. Mama Jo was one of these.

Rose Kate, Kathleen, Nellie, and I genuflected and filed into the pew on the fifth row. It had a small bronze plaque engraved with our family name. It said "The Flanagan Family. December 23, 1905." Mama Jo had said that Uncle Jim had given the money for the pew. His name was not on the plaque. And it came to me then, after what Moony had told, that Monsignor Canfield, who expounded "vehemently"—a word he used in each of his Sunday sermons—against nameless "pleasure palaces," would disallow the name "Canaan" if it were placed there with the engraver's pen. I formed Uncle Jim's name on the plaque with my finger as if I could make up for the omission.

Mama Jo lit three candles that flickered with the other shadowy flames on the darkened walls. The plunk of her coins echoed as she dropped them into the brass offering box. She knelt before the statue of Mary and prayed a long time. I wondered if she said more prayers for John Culligan than she did for the other two.

When she returned to our pew, she looked at me. Her eyes said, "Now." I walked past the Stations of the Cross toward the back of Saint Brigid's, stood behind Mary Leary who was nearly a saint, and fidgeted, since I knew she wouldn't be in there long. The Seventh Station of the Cross—When Jesus Falls the Second Time—hung above my head. It was etched into the small arched niche in the stone wall. The suffering figure of Jesus made me wish that Mary Leary had done something awful and that she would sustain a long lecture while I got my heart to stop beating so hard, but she stepped out of the confessional, her shoes creaking as she carried Grace between her hands, folded like a steeple, back to her pew where she would grow in love to serve the Lord.

I was watching her so hard that I flinched when someone tapped me on the shoulder. I turned around and saw the Major standing behind me in line for confession. He stood rod straight as always, but his eyes were warm brown, his expression a pause between humor and seriousness. "Jim," he said, "Go easy on yourself. Just showing up is enough." Then he motioned me forward.

I couldn't imagine the Major committing a sin, unless it was one of a little conceit, but he was a man who kept habits faithfully and made his appearance in the confessional weekly.

I ducked into the dark closet and knelt down. I could hear Father Pat breathing through the screen. I could see that his head was bowed and that he held it up with his hand.

"I confess to almighty God, to Blessed Mary, ever virgin, to blessed Michael the Archangel . . ." I prayed. Then I began the list of my sins. I had gotten angry with my sisters. And I had lied to Viola saying that I had eaten the liver. In truth, Kathleen had taken it outside and given it to a grateful dog. I thought about how much I had actually liked Kathleen that day. When it came to the fight, I tried to get sorry. And I was

73

sorry about upsetting Mother and Mama Jo. I stammered over the Peep Show and in such a quiet voice that Father Pat could not hear about it.

He sat up straight in the darkness. "Speak up, son."

After he got an earful, he gave me a hard time. "Lusting after women will land you in Hell," he said. "The Jesuits will knock some sense into you."

I didn't ask what he meant about the Jesuits. I just wanted to get out of the dark box. I accepted my penance, then poked at the green velvet curtain, trying to find the way out, getting caught up in its folds before I finally escaped.

Only a few candles were lit at low masses and the church was drab because of it. The choir did not sing, so the low mass should have been shorter than the later high mass. But it wasn't an even trade on this Sunday. While the mass was short and colorless, the sermon was long and dull. Monsignor Canfield got going on charity; he covered the virtue by reading the letters of Paul to the Corinthians. Possibly he didn't see well through his pince-nez. He read very slowly, his rough voice chopping at the words like a hatchet.

Since I had no trouble with that particular virtue, I daydreamed, glad that I did not have to serve mass. Being an altar boy meant paying attention, keeping both eyes open, not falling asleep, although George and I had both done this on several occasions. I could hear the heaviness of the words, but kept to my own thoughts. I wondered if I would do again what I had done, for I had met pleasure, a face hard to ignore. But I did not want to go back to confession, so I sat on my feelings and tried to keep my daydreams white.

I thought of my past sins, which now seemed like small pets. I remembered the day when I had led Nellie astray. She had dressed up in Mother's finery, but had trouble keeping the shoes on her feet; she had looked for a smaller pair in Kathleen's closet where she had discovered shoes stuffed with coins.

The Ten Commandments had somehow faded from my memory then—I told her that it was all right to *steal* that which had already been *stolen*. Since neither Nellie nor I was altogether greedy, we had only taken a little at a time. I smiled thinking of the day that Kathleen had finally gotten caught, even though it had meant an end to the mother lode.

Mr. Larkin passed the wicker basket for offerings. He did not have the style that Dad did. Dad would have said, "No buttons, Mrs. McGillicuddy," his long arms extending the basket. "Benson, no pennies please." I imagined that the take was greater when Dad's charm did the collecting.

When mass was over, I walked home behind Mama Jo and the girls. My sins were forgiven, but still I felt the loss of innocence and wished that I were pure again.

"Catch up, Jim," said Mama Jo. "Flapjacks are waiting."

As soon as we got in the house, Viola tried to hurry us to the table. She had on the black velvet hat that had been Mother's, and held a spatula in her hand. A clean crisp apron covered her dark purple dress.

Mama Jo approved that Viola was ready for church. "Viola, you go on now. You don't want to be late. Scoot along now."

Viola sighed. "Miz Jo, you know how many cakes this boy eats."

"Yes, and I haven't forgotten how to make them. You've set the table?"

"Yes ma'am. The syrup's in the pitcher, the butter's in one too."

Viola took off the apron, carefully folded it, and placed it on a shelf in the pantry. She lifted the dress and rolled her stockings up above her knees. She snugged them, straightening the seams, then rolled them back down until they again rested just below her knees. She retied the laces of her shoes in neat bows. The shoes were shiny black, except for scuffs on the sides that held the polish like rough moles.

"Bye-and-bye," she sang, her skirt moving gracefully as she swayed.

Mama Jo hummed with her as she stirred the batter. Her apron was dotted with pink roses and blue hibiscus. She stopped and turned up the cuffs of her sleeves.

Viola took up her big black purse. She picked a paper fan from inside, waving it in front of her face. She swished it a little at Mama Jo.

"Stop fanning, Viola Jones. Run on to church."

"All right, then. I'm ready to go."

"Blessed Sunday," said Mama Jo.

"Yes ma'am, Miz Jo. Bless Sunday."

The screen whacked the door frame as she left. "That Moony's supposed to fix this here spring," she said in a grump. But soon we could hear her singing as she passed along the side of the house.

"Blessed Sunday," said Mama Jo.

The girls wanted to cook, but Mama Jo wouldn't hear of it. "Keep your dresses pretty. Ladies don't work in the kitchen."

Mama Jo was a lady, or so it seemed to me, but she didn't count herself among them. Being a lady was her ideal and the thing that she wanted the girls to be. But I thought that if they were like her, they would be just fine.

Mama Jo ladled the batter onto the hot skillet, the buttery iron sizzling as she made the small circles, their tiny bubbles forming on top. When she flipped them over, the cooked sides were the color of tigers. "Jim, I know you're hungry. You go first."

Being her only grandson got me certain privileges. "If you say so," I said taking my plate. Rose Kate and Kathleen glowered at me as I put one of my flapjacks on Nellie's plate and continued staring while I buttered Nellie's and my own. They reminded me of the dogs that wandered through the streets, crouching along curbs and alleys near the vendors, waiting like lions for spilled food. Nellie was watching them as she took small bites. My sisters' eyes were on my flapjacks which, I confess, I ate slowly, deliberately smacking and licking my lips, until they got stacks of their own and making them mad was no longer possible.

We stuffed down the flapjacks. I was then only worried about burping at the table or splitting my pants like the fire-eater. My sins were covered with butter and drowned in molasses.

While Rose Kate and Kathleen ate, I carried our dishes to the kitchen. Nellie would have helped, but she was full and couldn't move. Mother and Dad came in dressed and ready for church. They looked elegant—Mother wearing a cream-colored gabardine dress, Dad in his black suit.

"You can go ahead and read the paper, Jim," said Dad. "But keep it straight." He had great hope that I would one day read something in it besides the comics. He himself liked to read it in a certain order. He read the comics first, since a good laugh started his day off right and made it possible for him to "read the political news." Although he was particular about the sequence of his reading, he discarded the spent sections at random. At the end of any Sunday, the paper covered the floor like a rug.

He liked to tease Mother and Mama Jo about the suffragettes. "Mama Jo, if you would take to the streets with placards, you might get the vote," he said. He smiled as though such a thing were possible.

"They would surely roll over," she said of her dead husbands. "They would want to know what the men are drinking these days that they'd be so weak as to let the women pick the bosses."

"I don't believe that for a minute, Jo," said Dad. "All three of your husbands knew who the boss was."

Mother laughed as she retied the bow in Nellie's hair. "I don't think we need to worry about the vote just yet."

Rose Kate frowned and stiffened. "Well, I would march with them. Anytime. And I will."

"Well, our little suffragette," said Dad.

Mother looked at Rose Kate as though she had never seen her before. "Since when did you become interested in voting, dear?"

Rose Kate sat up straight. She was eleven years old, caught between twelve-year-old Kathleen and Nellie, who was nine. She'd learned how to fight. "I've read the paper with Dad," said Rose Kate.

He nodded that yes, she had.

Mother looked at him, her eyebrows arched up high in a question. From her expression, I guessed that the paper was serving Uncle Jim's reputation for breakfast and that it was coming out raw.

Dad was looking directly at Mother. "Rose Kate only reads the front page after *I* do," he said, answering her eyes. "And she doesn't read the editorial section."

Mother was visibly relieved. She said, "Jim, take your uncle Jim a cup of coffee."

"Yes ma'am," I said. I didn't want to take it, because I would have to knock on his door and take the chance of disturbing him, but Mama Jo interrupted and saved me.

"Not just yet, Jim," she said. "He had to go out in the middle of the night on business. I'm sure the poor man's still asleep."

Mother and Dad looked at each other and then at Mama Jo. I wondered if they knew about the murders in the Monarch Saloon and what they would think if they did know.

After Mother and Dad left for church, a man dressed in a navy blue suit came up the steps with a Bible in his hand. His big frame was a husky portrait through the oval glass that rattled when he knocked on it. As I opened the door, his hard eyes stared down at me.

"The Witnesses are at hand." He paused after each word.

"Christ will destroy wickedness on the earth. He will fight Armageddon. I am here to witness." This part rolled off of his tongue with the swiftness of running water. His voice was compelling, but what really got my attention was his black shoe sliding into the opening of the door like a snake.

"My mother and father are at church," I said. "Mass won't be over for an hour."

"Mass!" With the mention of the word, the Witness withdrew his shoe, pivoted, then ran down the steps, dropping the holy book which flipped over and over, spilling out little white notes, book marks, and yellowed newspaper clippings before landing on the sidewalk.

Mama Jo heard the commotion and came into the hall. "Who was that man?"

"Some kind of witness," I told her.

"You must have scared him with your horns."

"Horns?"

"The Jehovah's Witnesses preach that Catholics have horns." We watched him grabbing at his papers flying like confetti in the light spring wind. She smiled as I felt my head.

I went on in the living room with the stack of Sunday paper and sat down, but before I found the funnies noticed Rose Kate sitting quietly by the window in a chair so uncomfortable that no one ever sat in it. She was eavesdropping on Uncle Jim and the Finney brothers, who were outside on the north side of the porch.

"You're listening," I said accusingly.

She held her finger up to her lips and dedicated a stare to me. Tattling was not one of my weaknesses and besides, I did not really want her in trouble. Putting the paper on the floor, I went over and tugged at her arm. She stubbornly refused to give up her listening post. Through the lace curtain, I could hear Uncle Jim.

"He backed out last year. He'll likely do the same again."

"That's the very reason we could mop up, Mr. Jim," said John Finney. "Everyone will expect him to bow out at the last minute. But if he swam and won—the dark horse—we'd make a killing."

Rose Kate whispered, "They're talking about Dad. They think he's afraid of the river."

"Aren't you?" I asked, feeling my own fear of it.

"Certainly not. And neither is Dad. They'll see." Her jaw was set, her fists clenched on the lap of her pale yellow dress.

Laughter from outside pushed my thoughts of Uncle Jim's conversation away. I let go of Rose Kate's arm and looked out the window. Dad was hopping down the street on one foot like a rabbit. He held his arms out front as though he were driving a car. Neighbors who were also coming from church stopped to watch. Mother's face was red under the hat with peacock feathers, but she continued to walk elegantly down the street as if nothing unusual were happening.

"Dad, what is it?" I called from the window.

"Monsignor said that the next step might be toward death." He was out of breath. "I don't want to take it."

In the afternoon, after Uncle Jim had finished his Sunday dinner, the family, including the Mahons, sat around the table eating roast beef, new potatoes, and green beans.

When the Major brought up the subject of the swimming race, Rose Kate looked hard at me.

He said, "There remains insidious talk that you will participate, Nate."

"I hadn't given it much thought," said Dad, sipping his tea.

Rose Kate could stand no more talk of it. "My father is going to win!" she said, out of turn. I fully expected her fist to bang the table.

Her outburst surprised Dad. He was not at all ready to commit to the race and mounded his beans with his fork.

"The decision is not up to you, Rose Kate," said Mother.

"Young ladies do not take charge of the conversation. And your father makes up his own mind about such matters."

This was not altogether true. Dad always counted on my mother's advice and spoke to her about whatever he planned to do.

Mama Jo was passing the rolls and butter. "Your father has plenty of water in the tub, Rose Kate," said Mama Jo. "He needs none of that muddy river."

"Matters concerning the tub veritably plague you, Jo," said the Major in disgust. "It's always the tub with you."

Dad passed the green beans to Mama Jo seated on his left. "Cleanliness is a fine thing, Major. Jo's the expert."

The Major ate his beef and refrained from saying what he wanted.

Rosie seemed confused over the conversation. "Why would you take a bath in dirty water, Nate?"

The Major mumbled something into his napkin and traded sighs with George. From the parlor, where he was smoking, Uncle Jim exhorted in a loud voice, "He'll get in the river if it damn well suits him. He needs no help from the rest of you!" This put an end to the subject and a light chatter surfaced and skipped around the table.

Later, Al Owen came to the door. He came every Sunday. I heard the bell and let him in. "Mama Jo will be down in a few minutes," I told him.

Uncle Jim always left money in a vase on the mantle in his room to take care of Owen's expectation. Owen and Mama Jo were intermediaries between Uncle Jim and the priests at Saint Brigid's. Mama Jo would take the money and deliver it to Owen, left waiting in the parlor. But first, she would inspect the funds. If the amount was less than she deemed just, she would remind Uncle Jim of his perilous state in the Lord's kingdom; he would grumble and give more.

The money came from the kinds of places that Monsignor

Canfield condemned. He talked about the dark business of sin, yet the church stood first in line to receive the benefits of it.

I worried that Uncle Jim didn't go to church, which was a mortal sin meaning Hell. But Mama Jo said that he would go to heaven. She was firm. "He will be there with me. I'm seeing to it. But you should pray for him just the same. He's got trouble with politics on top of his trouble with the Lord."

Without the hawking of street vendors and the busy trade in stores, Sunday dragged along in a peaceful fashion. Saturday was the laggard; Sunday the satisfied penitent. The cherished boredom of the day served as a hospice, giving rest and renewing spirit. It was a fat day filled with leisurely eating and reading. While my sisters played noisily in the playhouse, the adults chatted with neighbors and friends on the front porch.

Mr. Waddell stopped by and joined in the conversation. Waddell was a convert to Catholicism. Dad had said that Waddell converted so he could court Mama Jo. She had blushed.

Mr. Waddell brought flowers to her in spring. In winter he brought chocolates. Once the chocolates had come in a parquet box that my sisters had fought over, but Mama Jo had given the box to me, since I had not asked for it.

Mama Jo brought Mr. Waddell a small glass of Harvey's Bristol Cream. She kept the cream hidden because it was his favorite; she was afraid that prohibition would be enforced and that she wouldn't be able to get more.

I always listened to Mr. Waddell tell stories in his deep baritone voice, its resonance punctuated by his gestures. I could have listened a lifetime. He didn't tell humorous tales about real people like Dad did, or stories of martyrs like Mama Jo did. The Waddell stories were really those of O. Henry, but he told them as though they were his own. The one I loved best was *Sixes and Sevens*.

I eventually read the O. Henry stories myself, since Mr.

Waddell would get caught up in stories within stories, so much so that he could not get to the end.

In the evening, a spring thunderstorm blew over the river. The rain needled the roof and pelted the windows, the lamp-posts, trees, and cobblestones distortions through the water-course. The old house moaned as it protected us from the slash of wind and from lightning bolts that steadily riveted the sky with jagged silver.

"Noah's Ark, Jim," said Dad. "We won't be sending the dove out on this Sunday." It did seem that we would soon float. "Help me light the chandeliers. If the electricity goes off, Nellie will be scared to death."

He was the only person tall enough to reach the gas knob without a stepstool, and as I followed him into the dining room, I hoped that I'd grow to his height. I watched as he turned on the jet. I held the glass domes as he circled the chandelier, striking and touching a match to each of the twelve lights.

Mother came in with a batch of candles. "I hope we don't have to use these," she said. "I'm always afraid one will be left burning."

Then, after a crack of thunder, the electric lights blinked and died. The candle flames above us lit the faces of Mother and Dad, both handsome in the soft light. Mother slipped her arm through his, then through mine, and we continued through the house lighting the gaslights. In this way, the rain, even with its possiblity of peril, sealed us away from the rest of the world, the complete peace of the moment a present to lock inside and remember, because it would not last.

With Nellie wedged in the middle, the girls were sitting elbow to elbow on the same step of the stairway when we got to the entry hall. Rose Kate was telling Nellie, who was quivering, not to worry about the lightning, but was inter-rupted in mid-sentence.

"Good God, sister," Uncle Jim thundered from above. "Save me from your merciless dousings. Out with you!"

Mama Jo walked heavily down the stairs carrying a bucket of holy water. She flicked it toward the girls with her fingers. They knew instantly to bless themselves when they felt the drops. Then she shot a handful toward Mother, Dad, and me.

Dad put up his hands as if surrendering. "Clare, get my slicker. Your mother's invited the rain inside." He loved teasing Mama Jo. She enjoyed it for the most part, but this night she was clearly disgruntled.

"My own brother locks me out when all I want to do is give him the Lord's protection."

"Then he wouldn't let you sprinkle him," said Dad.

"No, and what with this wicked storm, you'd think he'd be grateful for the blessing."

Mama Jo put the bucket down beside the front door, then nodded to me. I went in the parlor with her as I did every Sunday night. The wind died, the rain slowing to a patter. I opened the window so that we could hear it better. She sat in her green leather chair. I sat on the ottoman beside her stockinged feet. The night air waved the lace curtains, making shivers on my skin. I thought she must be cold and brought her the afghan, its pattern a zigzag of pink, mauve, and brown. Kathleen and Rose Kate came in and shared the velvet settee. They traced its curved arms with their fingers. Then Mama Jo showed them how to rotate their feet so that their ankles would stay slender. Her own were thick.

Nellie stayed in the living room with Mother and Dad, since Mama Jo's stories made her have nightmares. But not coming face to face with the words was not as frightening to her, so sometimes she listened at the doorway. Just when the stories got really interesting, she would skip away. What Nellie imagined was worse than what Mama Jo actually told.

Mama Jo's blue eyes were wide open like a child's at Christmas and oddly matched with her ruddy, worn face. She looked through the doorway at the full-length portrait of Captain Culligan gazing down from the dining room wall. One of the buttons on his uniform was not fastened. He held his dark blue hat in his hand. The band under the starched winged collar of his white shirt was embroidered with M.P., which, I was told, stood for "Memphis Police."

Captain Culligan had upheld the law. He was Uncle Jim's brother-in-law and dear friend. Uncle Jim broke the law. The whole thing was like a pile of socks—lining them up was easy enough, finding mates all but impossible. I tried to get comfortable.

Then Mama Jo looked at each of us; at me, then at Kathleen, then Rose Kate. She finally began.

"A crazy man thought his wife unfaithful because she had become nervous and cold," she said.

Her eyes shone under the light of the chandelier.

"When she came to more peaceful ways, it got into him that she had confessed her sin and that the confession had given her the calm. When he demanded to know what her grievous sin had been, she, of course, refused to tell him."

Mama Jo settled into the chair. It creaked softly.

"He had been drinking heavily. The barleycorn had taken over his soul and he was no longer able to reason. He grabbed the poor woman's shoulders and hit her, knocking her to the ground. He then raced from the house in a state of fury."

She looked at us again, then smoothed her skirt.

"He entered Saint Peter's at dusk and chanced the confessional was occupied by Father Mike, his wife's confessor. 'My wife Katie just confessed a terrible sin, Father. Tell me what sin it was? Was it adultery?'

"'My dear son, you are not a Catholic or you would know that I am God's representative on earth,' Father Mike said. 'As such, I pledged upon the reception of Holy Orders never to divulge what is given me in the name of the Savior.'"

Mama Jo looked at the girls. "Now, don't worry over the words.

"The husband said, 'Don't give me that damn crap, tell me her sin.'

"'I beg of you, get hold of yourself,' Father Mike told him. 'This is God's house and you are blasphemous!'

"Infuriated, the man took his whiskey breath and fled into the streets. Father Mike remained in the confessional several more minutes as the situation had left him shaken. He implored the Lord to grant the man peace of soul and relief from rage."

Mama Jo rearranged herself.

"After recitation of vespers, Father Mike dined with Monsignor Blancett and related the incident.

"'Father Mike, you are surely a wonderful counselor, but be careful of this madman,' the Monsignor told him.

"Later Father Mike entered the church to make sure everything was in readiness for early mass. In the sacristy, he hung the red vestments sewn for him by a devoted parishioner. Among the flickering vigil lights Father Mike prayed for the dead. As he sank into his prayers, a voice interrupted his meditation.

"'You'll tell my Katie's sin or you'll never live to say more of your papist pap!'

"Father Mike turned to witness the gray eyes brimming fury." Mama Jo's eyes were blood red and squinting. Her voice deepened. "'My dear man, that I cannot do.'"

Rose Kate came and sat on the corner of the ottoman. Kathleen then sat on the floor and held Mama Jo's feet.

"Father Mike felt that the Lord had planned all things and in as much He had made every man's future. Father Mike turned his back on Katie's seething spouse.

"As Father Mike knelt asking the Lord's forgiveness for the sins of the living, the transgressor delivered him a blow, leaving his black-robed body headless, spilling the dear martyr's blood over the white altar linen. The murderous ax rang like a bell as it hit the floor, signaling the flight of the fugitive into the darkness of Hell."

Mama Jo let out all of her breath, slumped her shoulders and grew limp. She watched us all, her soldiers for the Lord. With satisfaction, she folded her arms across her plump stomach and leaned back to rest. Kathleen slid her hand into Mama Jo's. Rose Kate leaned on my knee. Time stood mute in the dark corners—and in the silence, we heard the patent leather shoes scurrying away like mice.

The Phoenix

1914, *Jim Flanagan*

Monday was thick and hard to swallow, like Viola's oatmeal. At school, Sister Edith Ann caught Shanley with someone else's pencil. Her lessons on integrity and fortitude had been wasted on him, and since the Confirmation was only a few days away, her irritation was warm like the afternoon. She set the arithmetic aside and had us all recite the catechism lessons, even though it was only Shanley who had committed the sin.

Starched white linen rigidly framed her clean face while it hid her ears. As she listened, she walked around her desk, the billowing of her robe softening her strides. Her hands were tucked safely into the billows, except when she took up the ruler—then, our answers, pushed out by the need to escape it, were gray monotones that went around the room like eternity.

Shanley, of course, responded slower than most and got pummeled often. But Sister Edith Ann didn't trust that the cracks to his head would save him from Hell. She kept talking about his sin, her words cutting the air like one of Monsignor Canfield's sermons on the "animality of man." She said, "You start out stealing pencils, then it's nickels and dimes, and before you know it, you're in the penitentiary!" Her words burned and Shanley's face turned red because of it. I almost felt sorry for him.

I got through the day by thinking about boxing. I tried not to talk about it, since George would not be going. But he wasn't all that envious. He was still congratulating himself on not getting any licks for spending Saturday on Beale. The Major had only barked.

Later, I did the homework in a hasty scribble, then knotted my tie and tucked my cap into my pocket. Rose Kate wanted to talk about boxing, since she had heard Mother and Mama Jo complaining to Dad about my going to the Phoenix. She thought that they were silly to worry, and would have gone herself if it were possible. I knew that her desire to go was the same as her wanting to know how to waylay me and our sisters.

But I paid little attention to her, since my excitement left no time for idle conversation. At dinner, not even the flag on the china plate interfered with my thoughts of the Phoenix.

I said goodnight to Mother. She was not as pretty with the frown. She looked as though she had lost something. Mama Jo shared her expression.

Dad and I walked down Second Street toward the Phoenix, which was in an alley off Winchester near Front Street. He was very tall and leaned forward as we walked, the brim of his hat out front and pointing the way. The air was crisp and felt new.

With most of the daily commerce ended, the neighborhood had a different flavor. Plucked chickens usually hanging in the storefronts of Jewish groceries had been put away or sold. The candy store and the spaghetti factory were closed. The factory was tall and thin. As we passed by the big window, I could see the spaghetti hanging down through holes in the second and third floors like hair waiting to be cut.

The Chinese laundry was still open—the smoothing irons were heating on a small stove. I could hear knuckles rubbing on the washboards, but less of the strange harried dialect came from the queued Chinamen, as business slowed after dark. But the saloons, every one of them, bustled with thirsty trade, since the prohibition law was not enforced.

On Winchester, we passed the phoenix, a work of paintbrush art that was painted on the side of the Nonpareil. The bird proudly spread wings across the whole building, which was half a block long. The iridescent colors and intricate design were beautiful, the most beautiful work of art that I had ever seen. As I watched it, I remembered that in Confirmation the Holy Ghost would touch me with a tongue of fire, making knowledge and understanding of the faith possible. The power of the bird seemed alive, a portrait of the Holy Ghost.

"Uncle Jim had it painted years ago," said Dad. "That's one of his oldest places."

I wondered if that was why the saloon had no doors. I could see brown bottles inside on the wooden tables, which were scrubbed dry like Viola's. Men were leaning on them scratching their underarms and talking, both the scratching and the talk having a certain vigor, but still they seemed settled in a way that I was not. They looked as though they could make up their minds to something without wasting time on regrets.

A woman in a tight pink dress was draped over a man's shoulders. Moony's word—"hustlin'"—walked into my mind. I thought that the woman would get money from the man and that Uncle Jim would take part of it. The money I'd spent on Saturday—the money my sisters had spent—might have come from her.

"Looks like they had a brawling good time last night," said Dad. He was stepping over pieces of broken chairs.

I wondered if anyone had been killed in the Nonpareil, and if any of the men drinking there at that moment would be dead in the morning.

A light wind scattered paper along the street. The gutter was lined with bottles. A Negro boy carried a case like it was a tray. He was picking up the bottles.

Near Front, the sidewalk became crowded. The alley closed around us as we pushed in with other men toward the yellow light that hung above the door of the Phoenix. The dark coats blended in shadows. I looked up to see the last strip of daylight fading above the tops of the buildings as smoke drifted from the door. Water crept from my eyes as the smoke wrapped me.

Doc Hollie stood inside the door. His lips moved like those of the man who had sold tickets at the carnival. "Lemme tell ya what's happening here next week." Doc never paused to blow his smoke. He just let it fan out with his words.

"Battling Nelson . . . next week against Lang. Don't miss it! Hey Nate! Who's this?" He didn't wait for an answer. "Has to be your son!" He sucked a puff, his first break in the flow of smoke and talk. "Well, boy. Your name's Jim, isn't it! Named after your Uncle Jim." The ash end of his cigar was an inch long. "Your Uncle Jim brought the fight game back to Memphis in 1902. That was the year." The ashes dropped on his chest, but he didn't notice. "Look down on the first row. He's waiting for you." He winked at Dad. "Fine boy you've got, Nate. First fight I'll bet."

Then he said to Dad, "This week, Nate. We'll talk about the river race—got to get these matches fought now." His eyes glistened with excitement. "In a couple of days," he was swallowing smoke, "we'll talk about Old Man River."

"Sure, Doc." Dad sounded less than enthusiastic.

"Aren't you afraid of the Mississippi, Dad?" I said to my father in a low voice.

"I'm not afraid of water, Jim. If a man could swim through life, he would find it smooth. It's the obstacles on land, things you bump into—things that seem impossible to get around or over—that are fearful." His hazel eyes clouded in the smoke.

The sawdust was packed down firm under my feet. It was brown with tobacco. Whiskey smells and stale air got mixed up with the smoke and the sweat. I tried not to cough. I didn't want Dad to think I didn't like the Phoenix, because in truth I did.

Men that I knew in the neighborhood were lined up on the benches. Mr. Bluestein, the butcher, talked with Mr. Cuccia, the tamale man, who was waving his arms excitedly. It was the first time I'd seen them together, and the first time I'd seen either of them without an apron. I thought that Mr. Cuccia would like Mr. Bluestein's corned beef, but couldn't imagine Bluestein chancing a tamale.

Men kept piling in, crawling over each other to find a place on the benches. They were like the parishioners at Saint Brigid's who didn't have family pews; they would search for an empty space, then hump over the ones sitting like guards near the aisle. The guards never would scoot over.

On the first row Uncle Jim was hunched in his usual arthritic slump, but somehow his hat stayed straight like that of a well man. Distance sat beside him, trying hard to imitate his boss's posture just as he tried to imitate everything about "Mr. Jim." He had Uncle Jim's voice down now after practicing over twenty years. Some people couldn't tell he wasn't Uncle Jim when their backs were turned. Distance talked black most of the time, but when he wanted, he talked white.

Distance grinned at me. "Little Jim!" He held Uncle Jim's cane in the air. "Come on over here, Mr. Nate!"

Uncle Jim nodded and waved us over. I sat by Distance. The benches in back of us rose like steps up to the ceiling.

"You owe me five," said the man behind us. Wagers all around kept the air hot. "Pay me now, or it's no more bets!"

Distance looked at me. "They argue before the fight even starts. Wait till after. Then they really fight!"

His face was wide and plump with eyes showing a wisdom that his position did not mention.

"Do you bet, Distance?" I asked.

"Oh yeah, boy. I'm a little low tonight."

Most likely he'd lost another bet to Moony.

A big Negro entered the ring. The men around us looked up to measure him; the betting got heavier. The man was like a big black tree in dark trousers, with skin as glossy as mud. His eyes watered like mine.

Doc Hollie waved the crowd quiet from the corner of the ring. "This man is built like a black Hercules. Anybody thinks he can whip Hercules stands to win five dollars!"

"That nigger don't know nothing about boxing." Distance shook his head. "He's just for the brawl. Don't you pay no attention, Jim. The real fight's later."

But I did pay attention. I saw things that I never could wake to forget.

A bunch of men lined up near the ring waiting for a crack at the money. The takers were mostly roustabouts who worked the river. They were clustered near the aisle. They pushed and shoved each other, sparring on shoulders, shaking and jumping, cocky with hope, smiling to win, cursing their grandmothers for any sweetness they still felt, uprooting the devil to help them win the five spot.

Dad said, "They'd do anything for a buck, Jim, then knock down the door of the nearest saloon to spend it. Sooner or later boys like Red Shanley will walk into this. But your own life—thank the Lord as your Mama Jo would say—will take the high road."

He seemed sure that I was destined for great things; my own opinion about the future was ill formed and unsteady.

The first challenger rolled under the ropes and came up swinging wild. The big black brawler played with him for a few minutes, then clobbered him across the back of the head knocking him silly. The challenger's neck hung on the lower rope like a dog looking out over a fence.

The crowd laughed and bet on the next round. One by one,

the black brawler knocked the heads that came at him. Sweat slid from his body, but his face held anger as the line of punchers kept coming. The last of his unlucky challengers got pounded bloody by his big fists, but I was glad he could still stand after fighting what seemed like an army of roustabouts. He had earned his money. He got no hurrahs.

Next came the bout between Egghead Patty and Eddy Crutchfield. The Major, I thought, had wanted to change his mind and take George to the Phoenix, because he had asked me who was on the card. Of course, I'd done my homework and responded without hesitation, reeling the list names off in the correct order, which included these two locals, who were not well known. The Major had smirked at the mention of Egghead Patty and said, "Obviously, a man of great intellect." He kept George at home and his resolve intact. This match, as it turned out, was brief. Patty went down for the count in the first round.

When the main event started, the crowd was ready. They spit and bet and hollered. Mr. Cuccia had his shirttail out. Mr. Bluestein held his hat in one hand and clapped at it with the other. The hat was becoming flat with the battering. They were both excited, because the "Spaghetti Kid" was from the Pinch. His opponent was from the rival city of New Orleans.

"They're featherweights, little Jim," said Distance. "Haggarty done beat the Kid last time. Tonight the Kid's got to get even."

The boxers came down the aisle. All of the men were looking toward them, but the boxers looked straight ahead and did not break stride. It was a processional like in church. The crowd cheered for the Kid when he climbed into the ring. His hair was slicked down flat with oil that shone from the light that glared under its green shade hanging above the ring. The light was a streak. The kid was slim and wiry and wore red trunks. His ears were larger than Moony's.

The visitor from New Orleans was roundly booed. I joined in even though I didn't have anything against him personally. He wore black trunks.

Although the Kid was pumped up for the fight, the New Orleans man outfought him in what proved to be a disappointing match. No blood was shed. A substantial amount of money was lost.

Uncle Jim was thoroughly disgruntled. "Crump's tellin' the city dads that we have too many dusky skins fighting down here, but God knows the white boys don't pull their own weight. The crowd's not happy. We might as well have put Jim and the Shanley kid in the ring."

Dad looked at him. "The times are changing, Uncle Jim," he said. "So is the town."

Uncle Jim wasn't listening. "These new politicians take up with the reformers," he said. "They don't give a damn what real men want. They'd throw every bottle of whiskey in the Mississippi if they could get their hands on it. The lilies."

"Tennessee's passed the prohibition law. Sooner or later they'll get around to enforcing it," said Dad. "One thing men don't want is raids, Uncle Jim. Sooner or later, there *will* be raids. I don't know of any man wanting to land in the calaboose."

A smile strained Uncle Jim's lips. The smile stayed, but he kept his lips closed. His fair skin and gray hair, still hinting a sandy red, seemed misplaced on his bent old body, the decrepit body of a man—I had begun to learn—who had fought for the control of vice in the bawdy river town since before the turn of the century.

"I'll rankle the lily livers," he said. "I'll bring in the liquor myself." Uncle Jim lit his Cremo. "I'm negotiating to buy a sixty-four-foot stern-wheel steamer from a German in Illinois. I'll have her loaded to the hilt with booze! We'll have lookouts all around the Blue Goose and the Nonpareil. And I'm having steel doors put in at the Monarch. The sportin' crowd can roll dice all night. It'll be business as usual." He inhaled like other men didn't. The smoke stayed inside of him a long time. "I'll be damned if I'll be put out of business by the foot-washin' Baptists and the shoutin' Methodists!" The smoke came out of him like a gust of wind.

This was the most I'd ever heard him talk. Those men around us were listening to him. They nodded to each other each time he spoke.

"What's going to happen to boxing, Mr. Jim?" asked Mr. Cuccia.

The answer was sitting on the tip of his tongue. It came jumping out. "All this stir about niggers in the fight game started with Johnson beating Burns over in Australia. I could have told them he'd win. Jim Corbett said Burns shouldn't have given a black man the chance to win the world championship. But what was Burns to do? Hide under the bed?"

Uncle Jim wiped his forehead with his linen handkerchief. "Johnson won fair and square, but he couldn't be satisfied just being champion of the world. Had to start going around with white women. Had to butt heads with the fans and stir things up." He signaled to Distance, who offered cigars to the men standing near.

"They were mad enough with him for winning, but they are fired up for hell about his acting up."

"Yes sir." Distance stood behind him and held the cane while Uncle Jim relit his Cremo. "That's one bad nigger."

I couldn't picture Distance with a white woman, nor any of the other Negroes that I knew. I didn't think they could have pictured it, either, nor did I think they thought about it at all.

The next event began with Doc Hollie hollering out the names of the fighters through his megaphone. He had to yell louder this time, since most of the men were in groups talking over the Kid's bad showing in between gulps of whiskey.

They didn't seem ready for the next event and were slow to take their seats.

"In the white trunks—Joe Jones." Doc pointed at Jones as if the fans couldn't see the satiny white trunks. "In the opposite corner wearing black trunks—Leonard Jones." Doc smiled like he'd put one over on us. "The Jones boys are brothers."

The announcement got the attention of the fans. It was like brotherhood was an added attraction.

The brothers didn't know it then, but trouble was riding their backs. The betting got heavy. I would have bet on Leonard since he was biggest, but as it turned out I would have picked wrong, for Joe Jones was the meanest, toughest man —white or black—I've ever seen.

The fight started out with the brothers sparring, but not landing any punches. They were practicing footwork, barely buffing each other's gloves. And I think that the fight would have gone on this way until the last bell, if it hadn't been for the man who threw the rotten turnip. It was the turnip that got Joe Jones to turn on his brother.

The man who did the throwing sat on the other side of the ring opposite me. He wore a grin like a coal shuttle, wide with sharp edges. His eyes never fixed onto just one thing, but kept rolling around his head like marbles. Since he had no neck, his head sat on his shoulders.

The man threw the turnip hard. I heard it splat. Men thought it was funny and laughed. I felt guilty when it hit Jones on the ear. Distance folded his arms and muttered something.

"I'm sorry," I said.

"What you sorry for, little Jim? I didn't see you throw no turnip."

"He shouldn't have done it. That's all." I was sorry that the insult was cheap and low-down, sorry that the men had laughed.

The turnip struck something raw in Joe Jones. He swung hard at his brother, but missed. This infuriated him and he began throwing short hard punches. Leonard's head jerked back twice and his eyes looked dazed as the punches kept coming. The men liked Joe's anger.

"Sons of a nigger whore!" the turnip man shouted. "Black bastards!"

Dad winced and looked over at me. I knew that he wished now that I had not heard the scurrilous stuff, and that we had skipped this part of the "real life" he had wanted me to see.

Anger was swelling in Joe Jones's face. Leonard's face was swollen from his brother's fists.

The brothers were not equal. Oh, I think that Leonard could move well enough. But he didn't have the killer instinct. Also, he seemed stunned that his brother would hit him so hard.

Leonard tried talking to his brother. "What you doing, Joe Jones. This here's Leonard talking."

But Joe Jones heard nothing that his brother said. He kept going at Leonard. His eyes were hard in a brood, his jaw set, his lips knitted tight together.

Leonard Jones tried to back up to get out of range of the fists that kept coming. But his brother chased him around the ring. His eyes were wild, like he was chasing something that no one else could see. The noise of the crowd was deafening.

The turnip man had gotten things started. Now other rotten things landed in the ring. Old potatoes. And onions. Uncle Jim didn't like it. "What do they think this is, a damn vegetable stand?" He snatched his cane from Distance. "Stop the fight!" Not even his voice could penetrate the din. As he spoke, the noise of the crowd banged the walls and vibrated in my ears. His effort was too late. The bell rang, but Joe Jones didn't hear it. Leonard tried to back into his corner, but Joe Jones hit him hard, and Leonard's head swiveled on his neck as he slid to the floor.

The Jones brothers shared the same trainer, who was pouring water on Leonard and talking to Joe at the same time. "Come on . . . get up, Leonard." He held the bucket, letting the first drops trickle down on the mahogany forehead that had not moved. He took the towel from his shoulder and put it around Joe Jones' neck. "Back off, man. You want to kill him?"

Joe Jones let the towel ride on his shoulders. His eyes looked over the head of his trainer to the green-shaded light. He shook his head, then looked down at his brother, still motionless.

"Hey, Leonard." I couldn't hear Joe Jones, but I could see his lips move.

"Distance, do you think he's all right?" I asked.

"I don't know, little Jim. He ain't moving. That fly's just circling on him like a buzzard."

Doc Hollie climbed into the ring. The doctor followed him. Hollie lifted the rope and stuck out his hand to help with the black bag, but the doctor kept hold of it. Doc looked different without the cigar in his mouth, his lips and cheeks flattened on his face. He got down on his knees with the doctor, who was listening for Leonard's heartbeat. Uncle Jim stood and held his cane up for silence.

The yelling ceased, if only for a few minutes. The men had been let loose and now it wasn't possible to contain them. The cease-fire was soon replaced by a low steady hum that thickened and spread through the barn, growing louder than before. The faces of the men around us were masks, twisted and leering, their mouths gaping. I felt my own mouth, which was open. Dad held his forehead, shading his eyes, and wouldn't look at me. I was one of the obstacles that he could neither face nor move around. The Major had made the right decision in not bringing George. And I knew that Dad wished he had not brought me to witness the brutality and ugliness that on this night had leapt out of the men. Uncle Jim sat in silence.

The doctor looked up at the trainer, then at Joe Jones. He shook his head, closed Leonard's eyes, and placed a towel over his face. Joe Jones knelt beside his brother and cried. I had never before seen a man cry.

Distance whispered, "He's dead, little Jim. That's what they came to see and that's what they seen."

And suddenly the sound of Joe Jones' voice slashed through the hurly-burly, the wail of it a wildness that churned my guts and forever touched my soul.

PART II

The Web

1904, *Merlin Mahon*

When the spider feels the urge to fly, it summarily climbs to the top of a branch, bravely faces the wind, raises its abdomen, and fortuitously spins out several threads into the breeze. From this bridge comes the construction of the temporary scaffolding and finally the spiral that ultimately forms the orb web.

It was in the fall, several years ago, when he told me. I stood with him as he surveyed the broken chairs in front of the Nonpareil. In spite of my advice, he kept this disgraceful piece of real estate the same as some people keep rude pets. Distance was standing between us.

"Mr. Jim, they will be rowdy after a time. This place never closes. Some of them just never know when to go on home. Yesterday, I found one man asleep on a table in the card room. He was curled up like a pig's tail."

"The longer they stay, the more the take, Distance."

"I know, Mr. Jim. That's why you don't have no doors on the place. I know." Distance believed in doors. Believed in shutting them.

"You're like my mother, Distance. She wouldn't have liked the place either. But she died from working like a slave."

"I know about it, Mr. Jim." Distance moved his tongue around his front teeth to remove the shreds of tobacco. He chewed on his cigar, which was not lit. He had worked for the Canaans for more than a dozen years, most of that time spent with "Mr. Jim."

Jim Canaan leaned on his shillelagh without a hint of dependence, but it was true that he needed it. It was a traditional weapon of the Irish, so the carrying of it did not suggest his weakness. The cudgel, hand-carved of aged blackthorn, had been etched by a vine while it lived, the design a raised scar that twisted round it.

Jim Canaan jabbed at the chair rungs with the shillelagh and sent them rolling along the sidewalk. "Have this mess cleaned up, Distance. And hurry it up . . . if the rabbi walks down this way, he'll fall over this mess just to sue me." I had warned him of the litigious nature of the Jewish citizenry, whose innate intelligence guided them toward realistic expectations from the American system of justice.

"I'll be telling them inside now, Mr. Jim." Distance enjoyed the dispensation of orders. His station afforded authority over the men working in the saloon and limited his responsibility for any physical labor, for which he was grateful. He went in to communicate the dictates of his boss.

Jim Canaan straightened his striped coat, feeling the wad of legal tender stuck in his right lower pocket and the .45 tucked inside his pants on his left side. The suit was a fine cut of black wool; considering his poor posture, it hung well, a credit to his Chinese tailor.

It was then that he began expostulating about his acquisitions. I wondered why he insisted in delivering this information to me, since he usually said little. Later, I would understand that he was then looking for someone, perhaps a family member, to help him hold on to his organization. It seems that he was having trouble with some of his lieutenants. I think that he picked me because I had always displayed self-discipline. Also, he knew that I would love Rosie, even before

I did. He was a romantic, if that is possible to believe. I formed this opinion when I saw the many books that he owned.

In truth, I think he probably would have chosen Nate as his right-hand man, since he and Clare were engaged and she was very close to her uncle, but he saw something in Nate's character that caused him to think twice. In my opinion, Nate would have proven unsuitable for such a task. As for myself, I was already reading for the bar, and while I mean no disapproval, Jim Canaan's type of work was, in general, foreign to my nature. However, I felt quite comfortable joining him in an advisory capacity.

"I bought the place in 1890 from Mrs. Anna Betts," he said to me. "She was scared off by the Yellow Jack. Only came back down to Memphis to sell out." He pulled his ear lobe down as if to stretch it. Accenting the last word in each sentence, he enunciated clearly even though his voice was rough. "She was nervous and talked very loud. My ears still ring when I think of her voice. She made me promise that I would run a good family place with a grocery store, saloon, and restaurant. She wanted me to keep the lodging house upstairs." He gave a half-smile. "Said that men needed a wholesome place to stay."

He looked admiringly at the hideous phoenix that was painted on the side of the Nonpareil. "I tried it her way until I found that there were better ways of making money. Jo and Clare are living a grand life from the profits I've made here."

I then reminded him that Rosie, as well as his niece, Pearl, and his nephew, Ted, had also enjoyed the fruits of his prosperity. He agreed. "In many ways, it has been a good family place," he admitted.

"Yes sir, Mr. Jim. They is that. Doing well, that is. That's a fact." Distance had resumed his position. He wore a black suit and a black bowler hat; his shoes shined like black stars. His bow, tied at the top of his starched white shirt, looked like ribbon on a present. But it was his hat that creased the mind. The hat, its tiny red feather cocked and tucked inside the hatband, was small, but sat magically on top of his large head. His face was round like the crown.

"Mr. Jim, when are you going to bring Mr. Tade's boy on down from St. Louis to help you? You spent a lot of money on that boy." His voice sounded much like Jim Canaan's, an emulation of sorts. Of course, to see Distance was to know him, his face being the blackest in Memphis.

"When I can wean him away from that mother of his. Tade would have wanted him with us. And I want him . . . to take Tade's place. But he's just a boy now. I'll send for Ted when he's ready."

Jim Canaan felt the gold timepiece in his vest, but did not take it out of his watchpocket—as if he wanted time, but not the knowledge of its passing. Again, he glanced up at the phoenix, the ugly rainbow of its wings spread and ready for an awkward flight. He bit the end off the cigar and spat into the gutter. His eyes were flat when I lit the match.

Ted was his nephew, the son of his younger brother Tade. According to Jim Canaan, Tade had been "ambushed" in a train robbery. He had refused more than the one-word description of the incident. Nate held that the killing was in retaliation for Jim Canaan's victory in the vice war. He had remarked that the price of war grows higher as it draws near. His comment appeared ill conceived, but I determined that he was merely practicing the art of conversation and declined to ferret out his concept.

That Jim Canaan was not a happy man, I could say for sure. It was said that he had fallen in love and that he had never stopped loving the woman. So it seems to me, that as a consequence, he had tried to fill the hollow of this unrequited love, not so much with money as with the fight to get it. He had little use for the money himself. He gave Jo chunks of it. She spent it on lace and finery for Clare and Rosie, but mostly she helped the miserable wretches of North Memphis, though I must say she was not particularly generous to those who were not Irish.

"Mrs. Slattery's roof leaks," she would moan. "O'Lanahan needs shoes."

He seemed to enjoy being both the chief provider for the family and the mentor of Pinch, and I knew that he was proud of the house on Second Street, but it was the war that he came to love, the near calamity of waging it the closest thing to his heart. I believe that it was the fight itself that kept him alive, the fight that moved his joints despite the pain, the fight that relieved him of constantly thinking of *her*.

He was determined that his saloon would be the best and so named it the Nonpareil.

It was his brother Tom who had the Nonpareil designated as the polling place for the First Ward, which distinguished it from the other saloons, including his own, which had no name. (This was because he refused to interrupt partisan discussions long enough to give it a proper moniker.)

And so Jim Canaan's early success was due, in part, to his brother's popularity and political acumen, but mostly it was because Jim himself was well known all over North Memphis from his years as mail carrier. To the people, he was reliable like time and essential as their liaison to Tom, who tended to their needs in exchange for political loyalty.

But the main reason that the men spent money there at the Nonpareil—spent it until they came to the bottom of their pockets—was because Jim Canaan gave them what they wanted. Women, whiskey, and gambling. The back room games lasted all night, pausing only briefly for brawls or killings, the frequency of which stained the floors dark red from the whiskey and the blood.

Profits came fast, allowing him to take over the whole block at Winchester and Front where he opened the only place he ever named after himself: Jim Canaan's Dance Hall. It was a rowdy party organized, overseen, and somehow controlled by one Jim Canaan, who could not dance, and who at the age of forty-one could not stand up or sit down without the help of his shillelagh.

And because he loved a good fight, he brought boxing back to Memphis when he opened the Phoenix.

I had first come to know him in the Nonpareil. The first occasion was the night that the Mackerel gang, under the direction of the late Aloysius O'Haggarty, tried to burn him out. Jim Canaan knew that I was studying the law and often asked me legal questions. Frankly, his curiosity surprised me, since the law was something that he broke daily.

I was there in the Phoenix when Doc Hollie, promoter of swimming races in the Mississippi, and of fast horses, baseball sluggers, and wrestlers, paid him a visit. He approached Jim at the bar. "Heard about the Phoenix, Jim."

"We're fighting Monday night at eight. Set your watch."

"I'm here to offer my services. I'm the man who can manage it for you. I can have every man in Memphis there on Monday night." Doc was dapper and sure of himself. He was the first man to jump off the Frisco Bridge and live to brag about it. His smile was wide, his eyes bright lights through his horn-rimmed spectacles. Hollie obviously possessed an intelligence not found in most of the scruff that Jim Canaan had to elicit. I thought him wise to take Doc Hollie into his fold.

"The fight game's something that I've always wanted to have a hand in, Jim."

"You're all wet, Doc." Jim Canaan gave a rare smile in my direction when he said this. "But I think we can do business as long as it's on dry land."

Doc seldom drank, but ordered a glass of beer to celebrate

the dot of humor. "Here's to the ring." He sipped the beer. "We've got to advertise, Jim. Talk it up."

"You're the manager, Doc. Bring the men on in."

Very little of Doc's talent was required in attracting the men. They were starved for boxing and crowded the Phoenix that Monday night, but it was Doc who kept them coming. He had a good eye for matching fighters and as a frequent referee developed the reputation for fair calls at the Phoenix.

The fights ended about midnight, but the card parties and womanizing would last until dawn. That was the part of the fight game that Doc did not like. "Boxing is an art, Jim," he would say. "This all-night carousing puts an ugly mole on it."

"You like the money, Doc. Now don't you?"

"Can't complain about it. But boxing's a grand sport."

"It's a sport better than any other," said Jim Canaan, "but the men get worked up watching it. They want to keep it going, so I give them the way to do it."

Occasionally the neighbors would complain about the rowdiness. A paddy wagon would pull up in front to pick up the girls, but the arrests were really advertisements, since the parade of women wearing sheer dresses was witnessed by potential customers standing on the sidewalk. The arresting officers would act as though they were at a party; in truth, they were as much a part of Canaan's organization as his own lieutenants.

The women worked in the lodging rooms upstairs. Jack Shanley was the lieutenant who kept them in line. By badgering and babying, knowing when to use the right tactic, he was both master and servant to the women; their loyalty to him was well known.

Then the organization began spreading outside of the Pinch like a spider spinning its web backwards.

When he was a mail carrier, Jim Canaan had heard Robert

Church, political leader of Negroes, talking in Busby's store. "Mr. Busby, a smart white man could clean up on Beale Street." Busby was content with his dry goods business; its button and thread sales kept his wife and children clothed and put pork on the table. But Church's information was not wasted. When Jim Canaan had acquired as much property in the Pinch as he wanted, he bought a saloon on Beale. It was a no-name dive, but its patrons called it Old Jim Canaan's. A bluesman named Robert Wilkins sang a song about it.

> *I wish I was back at old Jim Canaan's*
> *I'd bring my baby back to old Jim Canaan's*
> *Men and women they go hand and hand*
> *I wish I was back at old Jim Canaan's.*

Then came the Monarch Saloon. Jim Canaan bought and refurbished the Beale Street nightspot, making it the "finest colored saloon in the South." His intention was to attract the sporting gentry who came to Memphis's Montgomery Park during the racing season. Negroes were the chief patrons at the Monarch, but white men were allowed to visit on Thursday nights. His investment was farsighted, although I myself never entered the place; my tastes were not so pedestrian.

He then opened the Blue Goose in North Memphis where he ran Policy, a profitable venture that also allowed him to increase his holdings of cathouses on Desoto Street, one of them run by Tick Houston, who employed the most famous madame in the red-light district, the octoroon Lou Barnes.

His monies were ever increasing when he bought Sites' farm at a bargain price. Sites was deeply in debt to him from continual loses at craps and poker. Jim Canaan allowed Sites to continue farming the property, but never set foot on it himself. He called it the Holy Land, since it was the only property he owned that wasn't tied to whiskey, gambling, and women.

My own comparative nature selected the house on Second Street as the biblical well, since it was there that his family drank his milk and honey.

When I learned of his love for this harlot whom he had known since he was very young, and that his love had caused him great anguish, I found his position incongruous. His undying love for this Ola was unfulfilled because of the very prostitution that made him rich. But Jim Canaan spent little time considering the irony. The degradation of the women was not a worry to him. He simply felt that if God could desert a girl like Ola Hedermann, those other women could not count for much.

As he confided in me, he was not sure when his business became more sour than sweet, but he suspected that it began with his reliance on Jack Shanley. He had not wanted to hire Shanley, but bowed to the wishes of his sister Jo.

"Jack's marked for street life unless you help him, Jim," she had groaned in her leftover Irish accent.

"Another of her damnable charity cases," he said to me.

"Poor Jack. Homeless Jack," she would say to him. But as he told me, "Shanley was a rank piece of mackerel."

If he had thrown Jack out in the beginning, as one would throw out a stale fish, Jim Canaan's waters would have been far smoother, and the turbulence in my own life might never have happened.

At first their relationship was pleasurable enough. Shanley had wanted to learn. He listened well. "Sure, Mr. Jim. Whatever you say, Mr. Jim." In those days, he had worn a nubby suit that hit just shy of his ankles and missed covering his wrists. His shoes were brogans, heavy and rough and bigger than his feet, though, as Jim Canaan told me, "They were big enough." At best, he was a sleeve Irish.

But slowly Jim Canaan had curved to Jack, counting on him to carry out his orders, whether it involved training young boys to pick up for Policy or maintaining order among the women. Shanley gradually became his best man. Shanley never failed him; he was good at intimidating—threats a specialty, grimacing his natural expression.

Good to share talk of business, good to hear Shanley's observations. After all, he, Jim Canaan, couldn't be expected to see everything, to know all. Shanley become the trusted one —the one he chose to pontificate with on the side porch. Shanley was as handy as a Cremo and plenty smart. His "Yes sir, Mr. Jim" became "You know what I was thinking, Mr. Jim?" His innovations included using boys who were less than eight years old to pick up and deliver numbers for Policy, although I shuddered to think that I might have a son on such a mission. Unlike the older boys, who were suspect, the little urchins appeared to carry only brown bags of candy. With their pay, the boys purchased not candy, but cocaine. It was cheaper than candy and after the sniff, they could keep pennies in the little tin cocaine boxes. Needless to say, I disapproved of this method of saving.

And it was Shanley who invented the seniority system for the women. The oldest woman, Ida Belle, became the mother of the pack, with the next three in line the designated elder sisters. The older women kept the younger ones in tow, gave out advice, and took their surrogate roles seriously, since Shanley had a way of making everything seem important.

"Ida Belle," he would say, "it's you they all want to be like." He would hug her and pinch her cheeks, which she loved. Other men pinched different parts of her.

It was Shanley who started the contest between the bartenders. Whoever took in the most money in one night—Monday night, for instance—got a bonus. It was unlikely that the bartenders at one location would win all six nights, but if it happened, the prize was fifty dollars. The possibility kept them pushing drinks. Monday nights the barmen at the Phoenix were sure to win, Tuesday nights, the Nonpareil; on Thursdays and Saturdays, it was the Monarch; Fridays, the Blue Goose.

With the spread of his properties, Jim Canaan's enemies became as thick as his friends. Shanley kept him informed as to who his enemies were. But what Shanley never realized was that hatred was sometimes a facade that hid brotherhood. Take Pat Ryan, for instance. Ryan had recognized the futility of driving a dray early on; he had turned his luck into money as a gambler, made it big, then formed his own organization and began to wage war for control of the gambling franchises. Ryan had some success, but Jim Canaan did not, at first, feel threatened. I should mention that in Memphis people were conditioned to accept lawlessness, and Jim Canaan was enjoying his place of honor among kingpins. Also, he still thought of Pat as a friend from the old days when their common enemy had been the Yellow Jack. He let Shanley worry over Big Pat's activities. Besides, his reliance on Jack Shanley left him more time to think of his magdalen—the Bavarian, Ola Hedermann.

Jim Canaan said that Big Pat's man, Chauncy Dooley, "was a spread-tail peacock." Dooley and his band of mulligans, some of whom wore checkered pants—abhorrent costumes —continually fleeced the small dives and crap houses. As coordinator of Big Pat's squeeze, Dooley was hated by the small gambling house owners. One of them, Little Al Mulrooney, would mimic him when it was safe to do so. Little Al would strut and hold his hands on his backside with his fingers stuck out like feathers on a turkey's rump.

Some of the owners of the small saloons and gambling spots came to Jim Canaan for protection. Jim humored them, but took no action until the ugly death of Dago Falvezzi, which was credited to the Ryan gang, commanded his attention. Jim Canaan had fought against the Italian gambling interests himself, but when Falvezzi turned up dead in the streets, his ears cut off and laying like cups beside him, Jim Canaan tightened his operation and got ready to fight Ryan.

Jim Canaan savored the memory of the incident that broke Ryan's business of intimidation. Late one night, Dooley and his boys spotted Distance walking home. One of the mulligans hollered at him. "You black cocksucker. Some night you'll be laid out stiff and black in the alley. A black polecat cocksucker." These men were given to ribald talk, not an exception—the rule.

Dooley interruped. "Get it right. A *dead* black polecat cocksucker."

Distance walked back to the house on Second Street and slept in the car, which was parked in the garage. He had been afraid to walk on home, since his route would have taken him past several of the back alleys that Dooley had mentioned. Besides, he wanted "Mr. Jim" to know about the threat first thing in the morning.

The idea of Distance's harassment burled Jim Canaan's gizzards and knotted his throat. He chose Shanley to "do a number on Dooley," an expression I found wanton, but nonetheless unequaled in its preciseness.

"Little John" Finney and Chubby Leary were chosen to assist in the operation. Leary wanted to kill Dooley right off, but in Shanley's estimation, killing was too easy.

The great comeuppance occurred one night after the Monday night fight, just after the card party had begun, when Dooley was exiting the Phoenix. Ryan men attended the fights, but did not play Canaan poker.

Finney and Leary followed Dooley, who was preening himself as he walked—straightening his tie, dusting his black hat, smoothing his eyebrows with a wet finger, a disgusting habit, but quite normal when considering the perpetrator. After expeditiously catching him on the blind side, Finney dragged Dooley into the Winchester alley behind the refuse cans, where Leary continued to batter him. Under Jack Shanley's direction, Finney and Leary took off Dooley's trousers, a degradation in itself, then painted his private parts black with an artist's brush. Jim Canaan said that Distance especially appreciated this part of the story. I found this mischief a retaliation beyond blunt. In other words, perfect.

I must remark that Jack Shanley was a creative thinker, a most clever fellow. And he now wore well-tailored suits; his shoes fit and were kept in good repair. His hair was neatly trimmed. However, Shanley began making decisions without consultation; in other words, he grew too big for his breeches.

At Montgomery Park, at the peak of the racing season, Jack Shanley sprawled back in his seat to watch a balloon ascension. Behind him sat Big Pat Ryan enjoying himself in the sunshine. Shanley pulled out a cigar—he'd switched to King Edwards—and began puffing like a steam boiler. With his red eyebrows shaped like the tops of triangles, Shanley looked like the devil sitting there in the smoke, and as it rose, Big Pat coughed, sputtered, and mumbled nasty phrases about tobacco.

"Full of crap, that's what." His mode of speech naturally contained a preponderance of expletives. His eyes were glassy.

Jack Shanley was as intent on his fire-making as a prehistoric man and didn't hear Big Pat. When finally the crude words seeped through the smoke, Shanley's face turned red like his hair, the vexation noticed and enjoyed by Pat.

"Nice day for the balloon. Eh, Shanley?"

"And for King Edward," said Shanley calmly, though he was boiling mad from the insults.

"Why, Shanley, I can't see the balloon for the fire you've got blazing. Shall I call the boys down at No. 4?"

"If you see smoke, don't call it fire, Big Pat," said Shanley.

"Well now, Shanley. I believe that I can see smoke, but I think it's soon to *become* a fire." Then Big Pat started into a coughing spell. "You'll put that stogy out or my man will put your lights out."

"You mean that son of a bitch Dooley?" Shanley laughed him right in the face and avoided coughing his own smoke. "The Black Cock?"

Big Pat blustered, then grabbed the King Edward from Shanley's mouth and threw it on the ground. "I came to watch a balloon, not a God damn burning stogy."

Shanley watched his cigar as it rolled down the steps, then pulled out a pistol. Big Pat's eyes got wide. Of course Shanley could not shoot him in public, so he shot the balloon instead, which piqued Big Pat more than his own murder could have.

The men who attended these events were easily amused and had, of course, gulped gallons of whiskey on this occasion. Excitement was running high. They started shooting at the balloon as though it were a dove. With bullets ringing like bells, Big Pat clapped his big hands over his ears and watched as the balloon deflated. He looked sad, like a child when his birthday is over.

Shanley tired of the sport and started to leave.

"Wait just a minute," yelled Big Pat.

"Wait for what? The game's over." Shanley kept on walking.

The crowd kept shooting, bullets kept flying, and in the confusion of the celebration, Big Pat lay dead, caught in the cross fire. Or so Shanley said.

Jim Canaan did not take the news of Big Pat's death well, a fact that was hard for Jack Shanley to understand. But then, some men could never feel anything for an enemy. Jim Canaan was different. He liked knowing his. "Better to see the lion in the street than to pass by the snake in the bush," he said to me.

For weeks Jim Canaan wore a black armband when he made the rounds to check on his establishments. On one of the days, Tom asked Jim to stop by at five o'clock sharp. "Captain John Culligan has asked to speak to the two of us."

Talking with Culligan wasn't unusual, so Jim wondered why the day was special. After all, the three of them drank a pint of ale almost every afternoon.

Captain Culligan sat on a stool, his shirt starched, his badge shining. "I'm wanting the pleasure of a reply," he said.

"Well then. Please be asking the question," laughed Tom.

Captain Culligan smiled, but still the question did not come. He offered Cremo cigars to the Canaans, then lit them. He seemed bent on wasting as much time as possible before delivering his message. "It's Jo," he finally said. "I'm wanting to marry her. First and foremost. Above everything."

"Well of course you do," said Tom. "But one thing I'm not sure of. Are you requiring a dowry or a casket?"

I found this prognostication the equivalent of divine guidance. Unfortunately, Culligan ignored the heavenly advice. The three of them laughed, then Culligan drank his mug of ale without taking a breath.

"Tom's right. Jo's buried two of them already," said Jim Canaan.

"I'm knowing that. I was at both funerals, wasn't I?" Culligan ordered another ale. "I've buried one myself."

"And I," said Tom taking a swallow. He had married Mary McPartland. She was killed five years later by a runaway horse. No children were born to them.

Though they asked me to join them, I declined and continued to sit aside, since this was a business for which I had no stomach. It was then that Jo came in for groceries—she hadn't yet learned that ladies do not present themselves to saloon patrons. The three men took no notice of her because a commotion outside had turned all heads in the saloon toward the window.

"You're just a nigger in disguise," called a man outside.

The Indian grunted. "Argh." The saloon patrons, still clutching their glasses, collected around the window.

"It's Creeping Bear," said Tom. "Old Millard should just mind his own business. That old Indian doesn't bother anybody, except when he's drunk."

"Jo, you need to be at home," said Tom. "Jim, why don't you take her on?"

"And miss the fight? Go on with ya!" she said. As I have intimated, this woman was no lady.

Jim Canaan could see that she was determined to stay. He looked toward Captain Culligan, who just shrugged. I could have told them she was hopelessly nosey, but then, on this occasion, I was curious myself.

Creeping Bear wore a blanket over his shoulders like a shawl. His hair was braided and hung down his back thick and straight. He carried a tomahawk in his belt, which was studded with beads. Creeping Bear turned and walked by Millard as though he were a sentry guarding the saloon. He said nothing, but stared at Millard with his black eyes. He paced five steps, then reversed and took five steps in the other direction.

"You're as black as the ace of spades. From Africa, that's where!" Millard croaked like a frog.

"Argh," muttered Creeping Bear.

Millard reached for the blanket, caught a red stripe, and gave it a tug.

In one motion, Creeping Bear pulled his tomahawk and swung hard, cleanly trimming off the crown of Millard's head.

Tom hollered to Moony, a tiny black child who worked at the saloon. "Bring a bucket, boy!"

He picked up a chair and dashed out with little Moony on his heels. He sat Millard in the chair, while the boy set the bucket in front to catch the flow of blood.

"My God, Millard. Why in hell's name did you antagonize the Indian?"

Millard gave a sickly grin. "Now I believe he's an Injun,

118

all right. I have a stabbing headache to prove it." He fell over. Jim Canaan saw great humor in this statement, which also provided me with a chuckle.

Tom felt Millard's heart. "Still beating." He picked up Millard's hat and placed it on his head while two nags pulled the ambulance in front of the saloon. Tom and the ambulance driver loaded Millard, who was bleeding like the Red Sea.

Jim and Captain Culligan were talking to Creeping Bear, who understood little of what was said. They were trying to tell him that he would have to be incarcerated because of the many witnesses. If it had been up to Captain Culligan and Jim Canaan, the Indian would have been given a bowl of stew and a pint of ale. Creeping Bear went peacefully, but only after he'd wiped off his tomahawk. He didn't want Millard's blood desecrating his weapon.

Jo took Jim by the arm. "Millard is deserving of what he got, though I'm sorry to the Lord for saying it." She was never ready for condemnation without bringing the Almighty into it, though why I cannot say. Such patterns never ripple the mind and are as illogical as the rosary.

"Let's go home," said Jim. "Captain Culligan's joining us for dinner."

John Culligan then took Jo's arm and led her toward the door. She walked smoothly, her steps unusually light for a sizeable woman.

Jim Canaan already had the alliance of the police department, but the marriage of his sister to one of its captains would add to the strength of his organization. The side effect, and just as important, was the good sense of his future brother-in-law.

"Watch out for Jack Shanley," Captain Culligan warned. "I can spot a herring in the pickle barrel. He's a spoiler, Jim. Could be poison to you."

It should be noted that Captain John Culligan was the

prophet. Things came to a head over Shanley's desire to worship at the altar of Ola. Jim Canaan's face was purple when he told of this . . .

"We'll not be needing the services of one Jack Shanley," Jim Canaan said to him. "You're a big fish now, Shanley." Jim Canaan wiped his face with the linen handkerchief when he spoke of Shanley. "You've learned a trade. You can find your way beyond this mud town."

"Maybe I find the mud to my liking, Jim."

"Mr. Jim."

"Mr. Jim, then."

"Cut in on some other territory. You won't get a slice of mine."

"Since you've got the police in your pocket, it seems that way."

But Jack Shanley hung on for some time after. He must have hoped that his former boss would die or that he would be killed by one of Pat Ryan's men or one of the newer rivals such as Will Smiddy. Shanley bided his time, but when he finally went, he took something that would stick it to Jim Canaan. Jack Shanley could not have Ola, so he took Rosie.

She was swept away by him. Unknown to Jim Canaan or to Jo, their niece's childish thoughts of romance had all centered on Shanley. In the dark of night, she left the house and with him boarded the City of New Orleans—destination Chicago—which was the same train that had carried Ola south to Louisiana a few days before. But Jim Canaan had found them out while the plan was still fresh. He knew that I, Merlin Mahon, in spite of a disciplined mind and body, and aside from logical aspirations that didn't yet include wedlock, was enraptured with Rosie's curly black hair and beautiful bright black eyes. At the first word of the dilemma, I volunteered to rescue her.

·   ·   ·

After four years of courtship, Jo, full of superstition and fearful that she would harm him, finally wed the Captain. She wore a white taffeta dress on her third wedding day, a luxury that she could not afford for the previous ceremonies. It was the first of three occasions that she wore white.

During her years of general lollygagging and handholding with Captain Culligan, two weddings had taken place. First, Clare's and Nate's, then Rosie's and mine.

At the Culligan wedding, George and Jim, hardy products of love, squirmed between Clare and Nate and Rosie and myself. The simplicity of the wedding, the unerring good taste, was due to the beauteous Clare's direction. I was sure that Jo had nothing whatever to do with the planning. It was a restful and pleasant day, one of the few family celebrations where I would have pride in both my wife and my son, for she had not yet found the bottle, though her introduction to it came soon after. On this day she was still the black-eyed Susan who had won me with a glance.

Jim Canaan was there at his sister's wedding; the church fathers had not yet declared him a black sheep. Considering the unholy street wars that had taken place in the Pinch, the declaration had probably been delayed only because of the strong support of Tom, who championed all rights of God and man, particularly those of his brother, and because of the works of charity performed by Jo. Both Tom and his sister were loved by the clergy—though it was money from the businesses of Jim Canaan that kept them and the church afloat.

He seemed at peace during the wedding, until he looked at the statue of the Virgin Mary, a delicate, graceful work of stone. Then his face became grim.

Soliloquy: Ola Hedermann

1900

Surrounding her, the cage of vultures clawed her flesh, tearing at her bones, sucking the marrow from them, when at last the great bird of paradise flapped its wide wings, the rush of wind sending them away into the night. Then in celebration of freedom—a soaring that lifted her spirit from the earth, a bird on the wing—she moved toward him . . . her hair, lighter than sun and rippling, her arms outstretched to him, in a dress blue as sky . . . his own body was supple in the air, floating high, gliding easy; he was a feather. With their fingers touching, his arms encircling her waist, he kissed her, his lips clean like spring air, his face fair and soft as morning. A wafting cloud flowed smooth around them.

Cool air brushed her skin with a whisper of hope that sent her higher in dreaminess as he held her gently, her dress lapping his legs with the faint sound of waves.

"There's a certain girl I want to see, Mr. Jim." The voice from the hall awakened her. She tried to slide back into the dream, but it was lost to the scratch of the voice. She rose, and crimping her eye, looked through the keyhole. Jim's hand was holding the shillelagh very tight. She could not see their faces, only the hand, and then, when his body shifted, the red suspenders of Jack Shanley. His pin-striped coat was folded over his arm. His hat hung on his fist.

She could then see Shanley's face in the top of the keyhole. He was glaring at Jim, the red mop of hair slicked down flat on his head, his lips tightly knitted. In a loud steady voice, he repeated, "There's a certain girl I want." The hall seemed filled with his large body, the stillness of the moment frightening.

"And who would she be?" Jim answered him in a voice hard as stone, the tenseness in her neck dissolving in his words. The strength of the reply put a stop to Shanley's request. He said nothing, and began backing down the hall.

"I've never shot a man in the back," said Jim. "Let your toes point your way out of here."

The men all knew that she belonged to Jim Canaan. Their life together did not satisfy him, but at least no one else would have her. He came often to the Iron Clad with presents and money for her and to see about her welfare. Shanley had stepped over the bounds of good sense. Jim had paid old Jolly, the proprietor, to make sure that she didn't have to put up with roustabouts. Or the likes of Shanley.

She knew that Shanley was his confidant, but what he could not have known was how she had made Jim forget his pain. How she had been his only girl ever. How they would lay inside satin sheets that he had bought for her, her legs against his skin, her breasts soft on his chest, her fingers holding his shoulders, touching his face. And how the first time that he had been with her, he could not perform. His was an unripe fig. She had not laughed, had played the timid virgin, and in time, he triumphed, carrying them both into the land of euphoria, where only love lived. For his own part, he let her forget the men. He never said one word about them. And there had been many.

She saw his lieutenant's eyes shooting darts at his back. Shanley's old loyalty had worn out. He was a mongrel waiting to catch the bone.

She blinked her eyes and stood up. Jim was knocking quietly on her door. She opened it and saw Shanley at the end of the *hall, wearing desire like a coat. He did not understand that she was not just a body from which Jim Canaan took pleasure. She was heart and mind. She pitied the man who knew so little.*

Jim had wanted to give her a real home, but she reminded him that his own sister would not be able to rest easy in the company of a fallen woman. "Give it up, Jim. I've made a wrong turn and there's no way you can right it," she had told him.

But Shanley's skulking convinced Jim that it was time for her to seek a life in another city—that in Memphis, there would always be polecats stalking her as prey. Once a fallen woman . . . always.

"I'll send you to New Orleans and into a new life," he said.

"And you'll come?"

"Later. But now the snakes are crawling from the bushes. There'll be a fight."

"Yes."

"Then you know the enemy."

"Ever since he asked old Jolly if he could have an appointment with me. When Jolly refused, he flew into a rage." She laughed at the idea of Shanley. "And, of course, I heard you outside my door a few minutes ago."

"In New Orleans, we might begin something new," he said, smiling at her. "You're young and still the most beautiful . . ." She felt his face warm with the wanting of something that he had been denied. He held her tightly. She, safe in his arms, remembered the first time that she knew he cared for her.

He was a letter carrier dressed in a dark gray uniform. She met him each day pretending that she was expecting a letter. On this day, she was looking for the first sight of him. Standing outside, she saw him from two blocks away as he worked his way toward the building, a four-storied brick that claimed almost the whole block. The men called it the Iron Clad. It reigned over the smaller bawdy houses like a queen over her ladies in waiting, but there was no royalty inside.

She looked at the sky hoping that he would not know she was anxiously waiting for him. Above her the windows were alive with despair. The sun bounced off of Mary's window, hung with a green oilcloth that kept the day away. It was always night inside Mary's room. She hated sunshine. Faded curtains and filmy sheaths covered Ida Belle's and Fannie's windows. Three stories up, burlap, shredded in tendrils, flapped out of Bertha's like a wild dancer. She was pitiable, old and unfit for this or any other type of work, but Jolly allowed her to stay. She had no other place to go.

On the fourth floor, Flotine's curtain reminded Ola of the skirt that she had worn as a girl. It was blue, red, and black. She often wished that the Yellow Jack had buried her, clothed as she was in her innocence, alongside her mother and her father. But whenever she saw Jim, a promise poured from his blue eyes and filled her with hope.

Mr. Jolly owned the Iron Clad. He had taken her in as an orphan to fetch and carry for the working ladies, providing her with food and with a bed that she had shared with one of his women; every night she had waited in the lobby until the woman had scatted her last customer, always very late. A quick shake of her shoulders would tell that her tired legs could leave the row of hard chairs and stretch out in the harlot bed for at least a few hours. When she became older, the sweet talk of a man who came nightly led her into the oldest of professions and gained her a bed of her own, the mattress coiled in bitter lost dreams.

He was looking through the satchel. "No, Ola. Maybe tomorrow."

It was not a letter that she waited for—it was the hope that he would help her escape from Memphis and the miserable life. "He's promised to take me from this house," she lied, smoothing a wisp of hair from her face. "He's coming from New Orleans to get me."

He was fumbling with the letters and looked as though he might be moving on. She was determined that he would not leave just then. "Jim, come to my room. I have a letter to send Joe. Please come take it now," she said.

Inside, she led Jim down the hall, opened her door and invited him to enter. She hoped that he would notice the scent of lavender—that he would be drawn to it.

She picked up the envelope on which she had written the fictitious name and address. When she touched his arm, he slowly took the letter from her hand, and at the same time was staring at her, suddenly whispering that she was slender and lovely and that he would smell the lavender long after he was gone.

Then he handed her his handkerchief. "I remember your lips as they really are," he said to her. The handkerchief was crisp and white.

She looked in the mirror and saw her own turquoise eyes, the powdered pale face, the rouge on her cheeks and the painted red lips. She rubbed her cheeks lightly, and then the mouth hard, the blood red staining his white cloth.

He was gazing at the mirror, his eyes seeing beauty that was not possible for any woman to possess—but it was hers as long as he stayed in her room. From behind her, as he watched, he reached around and touched the faint pink lips. She knew that the feelings that were stirring inside her were the same as his own, but neither of them could say the words. He had a deep look of sadness.

She wanted to tell him that the man named Joe did not exist, but she could not reveal to him that she had lied. She walked outside with him, and seeing the fair skin, the sandy hair, and his face set with the frown, handsome with youth, said good-bye and smiled for the first time in a long while—a wry unpainted smile—and felt the grievous loss of time. Watching him walk away, she cried, the tears running down her clean fresh face.

The commonality between them was more than the marriage bond could have been. They were unable to focus on Jesus, but had no trouble believing in the devil. They had seen him. He was called Yellow Jack. Jim watched as she boarded the City of New Orleans with a letter of credit and the address of a respectable boardinghouse.

"You'll write, Jim." She called to him.

He said she looked young in her traveling suit of brown flecked tweed. She had washed and brushed her blond hair until it was luminous, for she wanted him to remember and follow her, when his obligations to his family were complete. She would wait for him, until that day.

He waved through clouds of smoke and early morning fog, leaning on his shillelagh and waving back with his left hand, until she thought her heart would break.

Mahjong

1914, *Jim Flanagan*

Mother had invited the ladies in for an afternoon of Mahjong on Tuesday. Mama Jo rode herd over us, inspecting our clothes and our ears even though we would see the ladies only briefly when we came home from school.

We were expected to present ourselves, speak to each lady, then disappear.

Before we left for school, the girls to Saint Agnes on Vance and me to Saint Brigid's, I helped Moony set up the card tables in the parlor. Viola brought out the little Irish linen tablecloths.

Moony helped her straighten them. "This starch so stiff and slick a fly would slide off."

"Oh hush, Moony Franklin," snapped Viola. She was setting silver coasters on each table.

"I wish they wouldn't use these things," said Moony. "I'll be polishing into the night."

"I'll tell Miz Jo that you complaining again, you Moony." Viola threatened Moony like it was part of her job, but he didn't care. Mama Jo barked at him also, but neither one was ever all that mad.

"You didn't polish the card caddy," she reminded him.

Moony went into the wide entry hall and took the shiny silver caddy from the heavy walnut table. "It's fine, Viola," he said. "You don't knows nothin' about shining."

Viola glowered at him as he set the little silver piece down beside a china plate, with Mother's face hand-painted on it, that was held up by a brass stand like a portrait on an easel. The faint rose of her cheeks, the wide green eyes watching, the red-brown hair framing her oval face, were glazed in a fine sheen. The black metal clock near her face was guarded by griffins challenging time like monstrous dragons in the ancient mystic days of Irish heroes before the dawn of Christiandom. The clock sounded the half-hour, one deep gong that stayed in my ears reminding me that the school bell was ringing at that same moment.

I ran to Saint Brigid's and since I didn't have time to put my books in the classroom, went straight into the church for mass. George was in the pew with the rest of our eighth grade class. Sister Edith Ann sat in back like always and, like always, I had a hard time talking to George. We could both speak without moving our lips, but it was a hard way to make plans.

"Come over after school."

"I already am," he said. "My mother's going to be at the party."

I wondered if Rosie would stay sober. I knew that her drinking bothered Mother and Mama Jo. Dad would say, "Clare, why don't you just not invite Rosie if she won't stay straight?"

But Mother was loyal to Rosie and ignored the wobbling legs, misplaced syllables, and even the rudeness.

Mama Jo made excuses for Rosie, especially when George was around. "Rosie didn't have the hand of her mother," Mama Jo would say. Rosie's mother was Mama Jo's younger sister, Katherine, who had died giving birth to Rosie. Not much was ever said about Katherine. Mama Jo looked sad when the name was mentioned; the sorrow would come down over her face like a shade.

George never talked about his mother's problem, but when she drank, his blue eyes, usually bright buttons under his mop of curly black hair, would flatten out like the sick eyes of Moggy, our neighbor Mrs. Morganstern's old dog, who could barely lift his head off of the stoop.

"Moony's teaching us to shoot craps today," I told him. He was looking straight ahead at the altar, but the side of his bottom lip curved up like a sliver of quarter moon.

Then he looked at the crucifix hanging above the altar with its crown of thorns, its trickle of sacred blood, its nails, its wounds. He was thinking hard. I thought that I should do the same. I watched Jesus for a long time without blinking my eyes—it was possible that He might move a little or that a drop of the blood might run down onto the cheeks. I truly did want to see a miracle, but my patience was thin, my mind wandering where I didn't want to go—to the Phoenix, then off to Kansas, where I would attend boarding school in the fall. Weariness came over me when the dream of the past night again caught me. . . . I was standing in an old street in Memphis surrounded by ancient gray buildings. I was alone, but felt as though I were watched and in great danger. I looked for my father's face, but he was not there. I began to walk, although I didn't know which direction led away from the grayness, only that I had to get away. And inside myself I heard a man call. I knew that it was Leonard Jones and that I had to save him. My heart beat with each heavy footstep, the slow gait caused by the weight of the two dead men that I was carrying. I didn't know how they got on my back or why I carried them or who they were, but I had to do it. Something was chasing me and I began running hard, the weight pressing down until finally I couldn't hold them. The dead men slid off. But I still felt weighted down. I looked at them on the ground and saw that one had mean eyes. My heart was beating hard. The other one had a dark splatter on the lapel of his coat that began to spread, and as I stood there the oozing crept toward my feet and I ran and ran and ran until I woke in a tangle of sweaty covers staring into the darkness of the sleeping porch, saw the streetlamp glowing outside the window, and realized that my heart was beating in time with the thud of his cane . . .

I shook off the dream and saw that George was still watching Jesus. George would have seen the miracle, if there were one to be seen.

We struck our chests as the bells rang, three times for the consecration of the blood, three for the bread, and then filed silently toward the altar to receive the Communion. I saw Mama Jo watching us from a side pew. This was the second mass for her that day. I wondered how she kept her mind from wandering and how her old knees could kneel on the hard wood for so long a time. No matter the sacrifice, she was determined to keep Uncle Jim out of Hell.

After mass, we practiced for the Confirmation. The Major was to be my sponsor. My father would sponsor George. We traded fathers like we did books. The Major espoused duty and faithfulness to George in regard to the church, but I didn't think he was much interested in sacraments or ceremony. He did seem pleased when I asked him to be my sponsor. He said, "I'll stand up for you anytime." He shook my hand. "Remember Jim, Bishop Mahoney's harmless. Look him straight in the eye."

During practice, Red Shanley knelt in front of me, which was where I liked him if I had to be around him at all. That way I could keep an eye on him. He was much like my sisters when it came to sneaking up from the rear. Since the day I'd knocked him down, he had not looked me in the eye, but vengeance sat inside of him. I was sure of it. I didn't tell anyone, not even George, but I did not want to fight him again. It was May and the days were already muggy, but I kept my jacket on. The shoulder pads made me look stronger than I was. I hoped Shanley thought so, anyhow. Dad would have called wearing the coat "insurance." He sold insurance himself, and so referred to sure things with this term.

Dad said that Mama Jo had once begged Uncle Jim to hire Red Shanley's uncle, Jack Shanley. She had said that Jack Shanley needed a job worse than a devil needs a sinner, lamenting that no one would hire Jack because his father had been a member of the Mackerel gang, a band of hooligans who had no more sense than to rob other Irishmen. Jack had been tagged a hooligan along with his old man. Uncle Jim didn't want to hire him, but Mama Jo thought it was their job to take care of all the underprivileged and outcast Irishmen in the Pinch; she had nagged Uncle Jim until finally he was hired. I had heard this often enough that I could picture Uncle Jim talking to the big red man—his hands like mitts, his feet big in the brogans, his shoulders wide in his rough suit. They would have talked on the porch for hours at a time, Uncle Jim teaching Jack Shanley "his ways." Dad said that, after a time, Shanley had come up the steps wearing a new pin-striped suit. His new shoes were—as before—big boats, but were black and shiny; he stood straight and held his head high. Uncle Jim had glanced at him with a look of respect. But that was then. Now they were enemies. That was the reason I was an enemy of Red's. I was in the shadow of my great uncle Jim just as Red was in the shadow of Jack Shanley. I only hoped that any future fight with Red would be shadow-boxing instead of the real thing. My nose still hurt. But I wondered what had happened to Jack Shanley.

All day I grazed on the school work like the nanny goat on our scant grass. I worked a few arithmetic problems and wrote some sentences. It was a nibble here and a bite there, but never a whole meal. I was worrying about going to Saint Mary's in Kansas. I had heard that the Jesuits taught with their fists, and wondered if I would live through a whole term. One day Sister Edith Ann had pulled me aside. "Jim," she said, "if you don't cross them, you might be all right."

I didn't like the sound of the word "might." It was like a book without words or a house without people.

George walked home with me. I could hear his stomach growling. It went off like the gongs of the clock, every hour, every half-hour.

"Hope there's something to eat at your house," he wished.

"There'll probably be some cake left from Mother's party," I reminded him. He looked relieved, but his belly kept moaning.

We took the steps two at a time. Through the oval glass, I could see Mama Jo waiting for us on the stairs.

She held her finger in front of her lips. She spoke quietly like she was still in church. "Wash your faces before you speak to the ladies."

We looked at each other and decided not to argue.

Then she put her hand in her pocket and took out some letters. "Slide the mail under Uncle Jim's door."

I looked at the letters as we walked upstairs. They were mostly from local businesses. The Tennessee Brewery. Gingas Glass Company. Morton Furniture. Central Cigar & Tobacco Company. Two of the letters were from other states. A. E. Schmoldt of Beardstown, Illinois, and O. Hedermann from New Orleans, Louisiana. I decided that the one from Beardstown concerned the barge that he planned to buy for bringing in the booze. The one from New Orleans was more puzzling. It smelled the same as one of Mother's vials of perfume. I held this letter for several seconds, thinking how little I knew about Uncle Jim. That he might have a romance was a curiosity. But it was none of my business; I thumped each one under his door as though I were shooting marbles.

We went on in the bathroom and washed off the sweat. The stains from the inkwell took some time, but then we were not in any hurry.

In the parlor, Mother looked like a queen at her table. I was not given to notice such things ordinarily, but Mother was always an exception. Her dress was pale pink and she wore a deep red rose on her shoulder. Pearls circled her neck. Her hair was swept up to a wide knot on top of her head where it sat like a shiny cap.

The ladies had already taken their seats in front of a Wind: East, South, West, or North. The four tables each had four ladies. At Mother's table, the tiles were being shuffled by Mrs. Houston, who was East, and by Mrs. Espanshade, who was West. I could hear the clinking of the ivory pieces which they called the "Twittering of the Sparrows."

We watched from the door as the ladies began to build walls, which would then be pushed together to form the square walls of a city. Any space left at the corners was said to let in the devils of ill-luck. Dad had said that the space left at the corners also allowed the possibility of cheating. Mother did not think it likely that the ladies would cheat.

"Come meet the ladies, Jim," said Mother. "And this is Rosie's son, George, everyone."

The ladies all smiled and sipped tea. I could see that the Dead Wall had been formed. I had never played the game, but Mother had explained a little of it when she had gotten the ivory tiles out of the lacquered casket and polished them with a soft cloth. She had gently rubbed the Green Dragons, the Winds, and the Bamboos. She had shown me the Flowers and the Seasons, saying that while they were beautiful, they were not used much any more.

George gave his mother a polite hug.

"That's my man, Georgie." Her lips were stained deep red from the wine. She was a baby bird on a limb. Mother was there to catch her. I only hoped, for George's sake, that she wouldn't have more sherry. He would then have to listen to the Major's rules for reform all the way home. Rosie would ignore him, but George would memorize the entire message, such were his powers of concentration. I knew, however, that George would never need the Major's information; George was a peach.

When Rosie took a cigarette from her case, Mrs. Houston twitched a finger. "My nostrils are fragile."

Mother made a point of introducing us to Mrs. Houston, although I had met her before. She wore a dress with black lace cuffs and a collar that looked scratchy. She was fingering a tile with a rice bird carved on top.

"Your family hasn't been in America long, Clare. I can always tell," said Mrs. Houston.

"Oh, it's been quite a long time," smiled Mother.

"Your Jim looks like he just stepped off the boat like the rest of the immigrants in Memphis. He's got the Irish face."

"I'm proud for that," said Mother.

Mrs. Houston looked as though she couldn't understand why Mother would be proud. She had a monocle on one eye.

"It's true that the old ones came to Memphis before the Civil War," said Mother. "Ireland was home to our family for centuries. In ancient times, the family migrated from Spain to Ireland. Judging the length of *their* stay, I think we'll be here for a time." Mother's face was flushed.

"Clare has an interesting family history, doesn't she, Clotilde?" Mrs. Espanshade asked. "Where is your family from?" The question wore a scalloped edge, both sharp and soft at the same time.

"A village in England, as you well know, Ann Espanshade." Mrs. Houston had lost control and now tried to regain it. Her neck was wattled like a turkey's as she shook her head.

"And why did they come over here?" persisted Mrs. Espanshade.

"I think it was land they wanted," said Mrs. Houston.

"They might have wanted more food and less gin," said Mrs. Espanshade.

Then Mrs. Houston's turkey wattle really got going. The monocle fell from her eye, dangling from the black satin ribbon rooted in the pocket on the bodice of her dress along with

135

the black lace handkerchief. On its own, the round eye was red and smarting. She dabbed the eye with the handkerchief.

Mother sat up very straight. "Let's concentrate. We won't finish the game in time for dessert."

George and I went on to the kitchen for cake. I was still thinking about Ireland and the bright fierce look in my mother's eyes.

Mama Jo met us in the kitchen. "Give these lads extra big pieces, Viola."

Viola looked at my legs. She held the silver cake knife. "I'll give little Jim a big piece, but Mr. George's getting real stout."

"I'll worry about that some other day, Viola," said George.

"Miz Jo, why don't you go on and talk to the ladies," said Viola.

"Oh no, Viola. I'm joining the lads in the breakfast room." Mama Jo preferred our company to either the ladies or their games.

The girls came in from Saint Agnes and I could hear Mother introducing them according to age.

"Quong!" said one of the ladies in a voice louder than it should have been. I didn't blame her. She probably wanted it known before the jabbering of the girls got in the way.

"How is Saint Agnes, Kathleen?" asked Mrs. O'Leary.

"Perfectly wonderful, Mrs. O'Leary."

I looked through the doors and saw the disgusted look on Rose Kate's face. Her own answer was "Fine," which got a frown from Mama Jo, who was listening. I knew that Rose Kate would practice the proper response to such a question for at least an hour that night.

At Mother's request, Nellie sat at the piano and played the "Minuet in G," her latest musical conquest. Her piano teacher said that Nellie had a natural touch and a good ear. Kathleen and Rose Kate, neither of whom played well, were both happy with Nellie's success, since it took the pressure off of them to perform.

As soon as Nellie had curtsied, the girls came skipping into the kitchen.

"How about some cake for you little gals?" Viola asked.

"Great," said Rose Kate.

"I just want a small piece," said Kathleen. "I'm not going to be fat like some people." She was looking at George, who was not really so fat as he was stocky.

"I want a rose," said Nellie—an appropriate request; Nellie *was* a rose.

"I think I can fix you all up right," said Viola.

"Bring your cake to the breakfast room, little ladies. Viola has enough to do," said Mama Jo.

"That's the plain truth, Miz Jo," said Viola.

"Chow!" Mrs. Sullivan had picked up a discard. She was one of Mother's nicest friends. I was glad she had good luck.

"That old lady Houston's an old bag, isn't she, Mama Jo?" I asked after we sat down in the breakfast room.

"That may be, lad. But you don't talk about your elders that way. Besides, your mother is moving about in the kind of society that she's deserving of."

"Well, Mother's nothing like that old witch."

George agreed, but was busy stuffing himself, so didn't add much to the conversation.

I heard the back door shut and stopped eating. Uncle Jim bumped across the kitchen floor, letting his cane drag, then marked each step with it on the back stairway. When he got on the third step, Viola called to him. "Mr. Jim, don't you want some of this good cake?"

Motionless, Kathleen, Rose Kate, Nellie, George, and I stared at each other waiting for his roar.

"God protect me . . . for I have no friends here." He knocked the step hard with the cane, the kitchen windows rattling.

"Viola, you know what violence sugar perpetrates on my system. The only tolerable sugar lives in a bottle of bourbon. Have the kindness to keep your . . . confections to yourself."

"Oh, I'm sorry, Mr. Jim. I just hates to see everyone enjoy themselves and you not even havin' a crumb."

I thought him considerate in not cursing; most likely his restraint was not wanting to embarrass Mother or chafe the ears of my sisters. The ladies, absorbed in their game and conversation and being far away from the kitchen, hadn't gotten the thrust of his words. Mama Jo looked relieved as he continued on up the stairs, thumping each step.

He and I were the only ones in the house that used the back stairs. I went down them when I wanted to get away from my sisters. He used them because he didn't want the conversation that came from the parlor and the living room, although the back stairway was narrow and hard for him to maneuver. This didn't seem right, since both stairways belonged to him.

The girls ate greedily, except Kathleen, who just picked at her cake. "Mother looks beautiful," said Rose Kate. "She's prettier than any of the others."

"She always has been," said Mama Jo. "Your father knew it from the moment he laid eyes on her, even though she was covered with soot."

"I can't imagine her ever being dirty," said George, who had finished his cake. He had crumbs on his coat. He picked each one and ate it.

"Good heavens, George, have some more cake."

"That's okay." He was looking at Kathleen's.

"Mama Jo, tell us about Mother and Dad," said Rose Kate.

"Then it's a love story you want." Mama Jo looked pleased. She had a store of love stories. "The two of them, Mary Clare Slattery and John Ignatius Flanagan." She ate the last bit of pink icing. "Everyone was against it, that's for sure. Their courtship was a battle between the Pinch and Sodom. That's the truth." Mama Jo refrained from crossing herself like she usually did when it was the truth that was being told.

"What was Sodom, Mama Jo?" asked Rose Kate.

"An ugly term, to be sure, but one that was most appropriate." She folded the napkin and laid it on the table.

"The gangs in the south part of town started calling the north part of town—our part of town—Pinchgut." She held her stomach. "It was truly a jealousy on their part, you see. Ours was the eldest of the two neighborhoods and we were, of course, a bit more into things. We were the landing site for the great riverboats until the silt built up to where it was too shallow for the steamers. They became the new site and a better bunch of braggarts you've never seen. Not a modest one in the whole of Sodom. Except Nate, of course." She remembered not to count our father in with the rest of the Sodomites.

"That's Hand from Heaven," we heard Rosie say from the next room. She pronounced both "h's."

"How in the name . . ." said Mama Jo. "Your mother's having a good day of Mahjong, George. A lucky day."

He licked his fingers and smiled.

I only hoped that she didn't celebrate her luck with a double dose of sherry.

Mama Jo scooted her chair toward the table and rested her elbows on the white cloth, wrinkling it. We were quiet while waiting for her to begin.

"Earth's Grace," said Mother. Her hand was going Mahjong using East Wind's first discard.

"Sherry, Clotilde?" asked Mother.

Mama Jo's mouth turned up as she listened to Mother getting the best of Mrs. Houston; her eyes were crinkled at the outer corners.

"How did Mother and Father meet then, Mama Jo?" I wanted to know.

"By the barest, lad, by the barest." She put her hands in her lap. "You see, for all the high talk, there were not many jobs in the south part of town. Nate had to come to the north side to find a job. Mr. Robinson hired him at the icehouse when he was a young man. Your grandfather, Emmett, had a saloon down there on Calhoun, but he had so many other sons that he didn't have a place for Nate when it came time for him to work. Nate was youngest. When it comes to a line, that's the worst place to be."

She looked at Nellie, which was unnecessary. There was no reason to worry about her being youngest.

"When did he see Mother?" asked Nellie.

"I'm coming to it, dear." Mama Jo smoothed Nellie's hair. "I tried to make her a lady always, but it wasn't the easiest task, I can tell you!"

Mama Jo's gnarled hands were rough and red. They were the same hands I remembered in the tub each night when I was small. My skin stung just thinking about the scrubbing, but I have never been as clean since, nor felt so alive.

Mama Jo crossed her ankles. "Nate was never an iceman, mind you. He was too smart for that. He kept the books for Mr. Robinson. But one day when Mr. Robinson's icemen were both down with a fever, Nate helped him get the ice out. Just before he got to our place—we lived on Jackson then—other men were delivering the coal."

Mama Jo sputtered a laugh.

"My Clare was down in the basement stirring around like I had told her not to—as I told you, I wanted her to be a lady—when suddenly the coal went barreling down the shoot like rocks down the bluff. Black dust flew everywhere and she rushed the stairs like fire. She came out coughing and waving her arms."

"What happened?" George asked.

"Well, she was mad as a wasp. Her face turned deep red. She flew out the door and gave the coal men what for—like no lady should—just as Nate walked up with the ice. He laughed when he saw her. A heartier laugh I've never heard. Then she went from smoldering to blazing!"

"Did they fall in love right then?" asked Kathleen.

"Don't interrupt," said Rose Kate. "She'll get to it."

Rose Kate didn't like quick endings any more than I did. It would be like leaving a party while you were still having fun, wondering if you missed something even if the something turned out to be bad.

"Well, I think I can safely say that their love was formed by the Lord and that, yes, they were in love from the first moment their eyes met—hers green, his blue. You see the two of them blended together, the blue and the green, like the waters of the great oceans. Nothing could come between them, for they were deep water, undivided by islands."

"But you said that the people in Sodom were enemies to the Pinchguts." I reminded her so she wouldn't go on about the water.

"Yes, certain things had to happen. But Nate was a gentleman. That I can say for sure, even if most Sodom and Gomorrahs weren't! He came to the door the very next day. He knocked very quietly. Just a tap, tap. But I heard it and answered, thinking that it was O'Lanahan as he doesn't have the strength to knock loud. There he was, your father, dressed in his Sunday suit. He had a shyness, but still he looked me straight in the eye without blinking. He came right out with it. He said, 'May I call on your daughter, Clare, Mrs. Culligan?'

"I told him, 'Young man, you've asked very politely, but as you know, you're from the wrong part of town.'"

"What did he do?" asked Kathleen.

"He said, 'I'm for getting rid of the problems between the neighborhoods. After all, most of us are Irish. Our parents or grandparents came from the same land. There's no reason for all this fighting among ourselves.'

"'Tell that to your own father,' I told him. 'He's chased many a lad from the Pinch out of his saloon.'

"Then I reminded him that Emmett would point his old Betsy at the lads until they crossed Calhoun. He would spare no words in his denouncement of our lads, either.

"'Well,' says Nate, 'he's called me a few choice ones, I can tell you that. In between "scalawag" and "hooligan," he slides in some that can't be repeated to a lady.'

"'He'll borrow worse ones from the devil when he finds out that you want to call on my Clare,' I told him.

"'Oh no,' he says, 'he would never call a rose anything but a rose.'

"I knew then that he was determined and that there was no want for stopping him. Emmett or no Emmett.

"'You can come for supper on Friday,' I said to him, 'but you are on your own with her uncles and with the lads in this neighborhood. You need not fear my Captain Culligan.'

"'I'll take my chances,' he says.

"His smile was as pleasant as any I'd seen. He was a handsome prince. Even if he did come from South Main."

"Did he have to fight for Mother?" I asked.

"More like a war!" said Mama Jo. "Your uncle Jim howled like Moggy when I told him that Nate was coming to dinner. Uncle Jim had the bad limbs even then, but I can tell you that he nearly flew down to our brother Tom's store to discuss the business of Clare's future. And before she even knew that the lad was coming to visit!" Mama Jo folded her arms. She was a soldier poised for a battle that had already been won.

"It wasn't long before the two uncles stormed the door. The dearly departed John Culligan told me to just be calm. That it wouldn't do to deprive the uncles of their debate. 'Let them argue with each other, Jo,' he said. And he was a wise man. The two uncles came in letting off steam. They argued with each other even though they agreed with everything each other said.

"'We can't have the most beautiful girl in the First Ward courting with a Sodom,' said Tom. He couldn't forget politics for a minute. His Mary was killed by a runaway horse soon before this, but he was back pushing for votes before she was cold in the grave.

"'Clare is too good for the likes of one of them. I'll have Jack Shanley take the knot out of his tie.' Your uncle Jim would have loved to have done the unknotting himself, mind you, but he was already bent-bowed."

"Did Uncle Jim and Uncle Tom know Father then, Mama Jo?" asked Kathleen.

"No, dear. They wouldn't give him the time of day until they had to."

Mama Jo leaned back in the chair. The cane seat stretched. "It was quite a day in the Pinch. The people heard him coming."

"Who, Mama Jo?" asked Nellie.

"Emmett Flanagan, dear. Your grandfather. And with half of Sodom trailing after him. Friends of Uncle Jim and Uncle Tom had already gathered outside the house in case of trouble."

"Did they want trouble, Mama Jo?" George was almost as good as Moony when it came to figuring things out.

"If they had not found trouble, they would try starting some or been bitter for not."

"What did Mother say?" asked Kathleen.

"She walked in unawares as to what had been going on. She asked, 'Why are the men gathering outside the house. Has war been declared?'"

Mama Jo smoothed her forehead while she talked. "'Yes, dear,' I told her. 'It has.' Clare's brow creased with the worry of it. The uncles wasted no time jumping into the middle before I could explain.

"'Don't talk to him, ever,' advised Uncle Tom.

143

"'No, never,' Uncle Jim said.

"She looked at them like they were possessed by the devil himself. 'It's the young man, Nate Flanagan, they're talking about,' I told her. 'He's coming for dinner Friday night. He very politely asked to call on you.'

"Her eyes grew large like green balls when she heard this.

"'Did he not ask the wrong person, Mama? I have something to say about this.'

"'Right, lass,' says Uncle Tom. 'At least one of you has some sense. Your dear mother has forgotten hers for the moment. Inviting a Sodom to dinner. And feed him pig's feet? That's what they eat, don't you know.'

"'No, not pig's feet,' says Uncle Jim. 'Mule meat. They don't know any better.'

"'You may have eaten some yourself,' I told him. 'For you're as stubborn a mule as I've seen.'

"Just then a pounding sound like a wooden hammer started beating the door. I opened it and saw that anger himself had come to call. 'And you must be the father of Nate?' I says to him. 'Come to meet the Canaans?'

"His face was all wrinkled like an unmade bed. I wanted to laugh, but thought better of it. 'I've invited your son to dinner, not to a fight,' I told him.

"The rabble he'd brought with him was milling about outside, picking trouble with our neighbor lads.

"'There needn't be a dinner. Nate gets his fair share of nourishment at home,' says your grandfather.

"No matter what he said, he was born in Ireland and his words were beautiful in brogue. I was hard pressed to call him my enemy even though I was knowing he had come to disavow the intentions of his own son.

"But then a strange thing happened. Clare came into the room with the tray bearing glasses and whiskey.

"'And who might this be?' she said.

"'It's Emmett Flanagan come to call, Clare,' I says.

"Well, I expected a pack of words from the man, but instead he gazed at her and all his wrinkles fell away. He looked as though he were witnessing the vision of a saint, for he was speechless. His silence took me by surprise. Even the uncles were quiet.

"Emmett straightened his lapels, took a bit of a bow, then turned to me and said, 'It's kind of you to have my son into your home, Mrs. Culligan.' Then he went out the door. He gathered his rabble, quieted them down, and the whole brigade of them marched south."

"Did Father come to dinner?" asked Rose Kate.

"Yes, dear. And to many a dinner afterwards. And there has never been a prouder father-in-law than old Emmett on their wedding day, because there has never been a lovelier bride. Uncle Jim bought Clare the most beautiful white gown. She had white roses and gardenias in her hair and carried a rosary of pearls. Her face was the color of a faint pink flower. Nate was tall and handsome in his gray suit. His smile lit up the church like a row of candles.

"The people from the Sodom came to Saint Brigid's, many for the first time. They mixed together and talked, for it would have been a sin not to catch the happiness that floated in the very air that they breathed on that day. And when Nate kissed Clare I heard a lute playing far away, as sweet a sound as has ever been."

I doubted the part about the lute.

"Were the two sides of the family friends after that, Mama Jo?" Kathleen asked.

"Yes. And when little Jim was born, every last one of us celebrated the christening, for he was the first male child born on either side." She cleared her throat. "At least for a while Uncle Jim and Emmett were on speaking terms."

As she finished the story, we saw Dad coming in. He was

145

wearing his dark blue suit. He kissed my mother, then greeted each lady graciously, inquiring about the game and teasing the winners. They responded in sweet voices. He was a picture of the perfect head of the house. But the real one was upstairs, above all of us.

The ladies were gathering their belongings when the Major arrived. George and I were called in to assist with the wraps, a job both of us hated. The Major and Dad escorted each lady down the steep front steps to the waiting cars. As soon as the last lady had left, the Major began wagging his finger at Rosie and counseling her to remain seated while he and Dad talked.

"Nate. What did you decide about the race? Should you enter, we should discuss your strategic position."

Dad unbuttoned his coat. "I've not definitely decided," he said. "Haven't given it much thought." Then he saw Rose Kate's eyes, sunk in disappointment. "I'll let you know tomorrow. I might possibly sign up."

Rose Kate sat beside Nellie on the piano bench, turning pages, and began rapidly tapping her foot.

Mother was talking to Rosie, trying to keep her from falling asleep. The Major came over and helped Rosie to her feet. On the way out, he again raised his finger, which he shook as he lectured her on the problems of overindulgence, all aspects of which she ignored, and from all indications would continue to ignore. But the Major faithfully attended the cause of possibility. George followed them to the car.

I was still thinking about Mama Jo's story. I found her working in the kitchen and asked about the problems that had divided my great-uncle Jim and my grandfather Emmett, but she was not ready to tell me. She only said, "There was a disputation about a stolen ballot box." She wanted a smile on my face. No storm would cloud my days if she had any say in it. But she had no say in my dreams. And the dream came and went, and I always knew it would come again.

The Wake

1914, Jim Flanagan

O'Lanahan was an old family friend. Dad visited him regularly at Mama Jo's request. She said that O'Lanahan might need to talk to another man.

Dad would tease her. "Mama Jo, you just want me to get O'Lanahan in that tub of yours. Once a washerwoman, always a washerwoman."

As I have said, Mama Jo had a mean habit of scrubbing skin. I was sure that she had made every effort to get O'Lanahan in a tub, but the old man was immune to his own odor. Mama Jo had to content herself with helping him in other ways. She would leave a little money under the saucer. And I would always ask her, "Why don't you just give it to him?"

She would smile and say, "Oh no, Jim. You must leave him his bit of pride."

Dad also left him money, but instead of under a saucer he would leave it in O'Lanahan's hat, which sat like a bowl on a rickety table by his front door. The hat was fawn brown, turned dark with weather and age. Dad would leave O'Lanahan enough to pay for his whiskey and his weekly ride on the streetcar. The streetcar was fascinating to the old man. He would get on with his whiskey tucked in the pocket of his worn coat, deliberate over which window seat to claim, and spend the afternoon riding to the end of the line. He rode the route over and over again.

It was a sad day when Dad came up the steps and announced solemnly that "O'Lanahan has died with his hat on his head, ready to take his ride."

Mama Jo and Mother were both quite upset over this.

"I wish the Lord had seen fit to let him die on the streetcar," said Mama Jo. For O'Lanahan, it would seem the proper end, but death, I would learn, doesn't consider such things as time and place.

She started calling the old women of the church to make plans for the wake. The ones who didn't have telephones would hear it over the fences and in the aisles of Walsh's grocery store. For the wake, the ladies would cook cabbage gotten free from Mr. Walsh and corned beef bought secretly from Mr. Bluestein. Though their knowledge and interest in kosher meat was limited, his wasn't as stringy as Walsh's.

Dad and Mama Jo went to O'Lanahan's before the undertaker could get hold of him. I went with them, and since it was my job to stand guard until they actually got O'Lanahan clean, I knew that it would become my life's work. But Mama Jo insisted, saying that my participation was the "work of the Lord."

She said, "The undertaker might talk about O'Lanahan's bad habits. I won't let the man's reputation be ruined."

Dad swallowed a laugh. Letting his good nature slide, he could put on his solemn face when the occasion called for it, but fun still danced in his eyes. I copied his expression.

Mama Jo had brought one of Uncle Jim's suits, since the dead man did not have one without a frayed collar. She said that some people looked for such things, though I couldn't imagine closely examining a dead body or even focusing on one at all. Four years before, I had been expected to view my grandfather Emmett in his coffin. I had said a prayer for him, but never raised my eyes to see his face. Instead, I had stared at his second button, which had been left unfastened, then looked at his shoes and thought how strange for the dead to wear them.

Mr. Larkin, the undertaker, parked his shiny new green truck in front of O'Lanahan's little house. I guessed that business had been good, because when my grandfather had died Mr. Larkin was driving a horse-drawn wagon. "My father will be out in a few minutes to see you, sir," I told him. Mr. Larkin's hair was blond, his cheeks apple red. For a man spending most of his time with the dead, he seemed robust. He made himself at home, rocking back and forth on the swing, chattering as though death were a social call. The swing squeaked like a coffin closing.

Dad came out of the house. He was sweating like a laborer, even though he was a businessman dressed in a handsome dark gray suit. No matter what the request, he always obliged Mama Jo as though she were his own mother. Maude Flanagan had died giving birth to him. I thought that he felt guilty about this. He turned to me and said, "Your Mama Jo will have O'Lanahan back to life momentarily, Jim. He'll rise from the dead to protest her scrubbing."

"It's nice when the deceased have been well taken care of, Mr. Flanagan. We appreciate the affection," said Mr. Larkin, smiling broadly, then shaking Dad's hand. Mr. Larkin obviously enjoyed his work, anticipating a passing the same as I did Christmas. I did not want them to be friends.

"I'll take over now, if your sister will let us in," said Larkin. They talked over the arrangements. Dad said that Uncle Jim would pay for the funeral and for the headstone. He always paid expenses for Mama Jo's indigents, his knotty misshapen fingers grudgingly peeling off bills, his voice growing louder as the wad got smaller. When one of her poor friends died with no grave site, she would put the dead one in our family plot. Uncle Jim would curse and wave his cane. "When our time comes, Sister, there'll be not a shovelful of damn dirt left to cover either of us! They'll bury us in a pauper's wallow."

"Would you like a last picture of the deceased?" asked Mr. Larkin.

"No." Dad pressed his earlobe, a thing he always did when he was irritated. "My memory serves me very well, thank you."

"Then I'll have him back this evening in time for the wake." He cupped his hands, one inside the other, and looked as though the deadline was a challenge and he the man to meet it. His workers wrapped O'Lanahan's body in a sheet and carried him to the truck on a stretcher. Mama Jo handed Larkin the suit hanging on a hanger, and a white shirt, which was folded. It was a sure bet that O'Lanahan would look better dead than alive. I wondered then if Leonard Jones had been properly buried and where.

As I went into the house, the neighbor ladies were bringing rags for cleaning and vases for flowers. Moony and Viola came in with a broom and a mop. Their jobs were made difficult because they labored at cross purposes, the handles of the mop and broom clacking together as Moony mopped the same area where Viola was sweeping. "Moony, you gits over on the other side of this here room," admonished Viola. But he wouldn't move two feet away from her side.

Moony was suspicious. He did not like being in the house of a man who had just died. I didn't blame him. He and I were alike when it came to courage—we didn't have much of it. He whispered to me. "Little Jim. He's in here. I can feels him. You just looks at these here goose bumps on my arms."

"It is sort of chilly in here, Moony," I assured him. In truth, the room was hot as blazes. "But he really is gone."

"But not forgotten," said Viola. "Moon, you the scardiest cat in this whole world."

"Don't say cat, Viola. Cats has nine lives and knows a ghost when they sees one. If I got a cat and throwed him in this room, he'd shally out of here like . . . "

"A dose of salts." She finished his sentence. "You Moon. You always talking about salts. And the Lord God only knows a good dose would chase away that silliness in you. Plain silliness. That's what." She flapped her rag at his arm like silliness was dust that she could scatter.

Moony had the ability to seize the moment and squeeze the juice out of it, but his ambition didn't include spirits. I wanted to bet him that O'Lanahan would not rise from the dead so I could recover some of the money I had lost to him, but Moony would not scheme against what he could not see.

Mama Jo and the ladies bustled about the kitchen. Pans clanked, water swished, and the tea kettle whistled. Dad came inside. "Let's get out of here, Jim. If we keep standing still, we'll likely get cleaned and dusted."

We left O'Lanahan's and went on home. On the way, he told a story about O'Lanahan and my grandfather Thomas who had died in the yellow fever.

"O'Lanahan and your grandfather had a contest to see who could hammer the most horseshoes in an afternoon. They were both blacksmiths. It was hot and muggy and the two of them started slowly, one hitting, then the other. Before long they were grunting and sweating over the anvil, gouging the iron like two buzzards over a kill. Thomas hit; O'Lanahan hit, their strikes like echoes in rhythm."

"Like the chorus of a round?"

"Like that."

He was walking fast. I had to stretch my legs to keep up with him.

"They began talking between strikes. One started a story; the other one told a piece of it. Little by little the story unfolded. They struck in time and told in time. One. Then the other."

Dad dipped one shoulder, then the other. We passed Grobmeyer's Furniture Store that advertised coffins along with the sofas and chairs. Dad said that when the time came, I was to make sure that his was extra long, a comment I was to remember in later years.

"In the story, the two of them were the heroes. Thomas called himself Cuchulain; O'Lanahan was Brian the Bold. The story was about how they took up the gauntlet and slew a dragon.

"By and by, they sent your uncle Jim, who was a boy then, to fetch ale. They started drinking between the striking of the anvils and the telling of the tale. The anvils were red with heat, but not so colorful as the story. The drinking was done with the same attention to rhythm as the hammering and the talk. All three activities became faster, so that sound became part of the story itself. The gulps were symbols of swallowing fear, the belches—of which there were many—bursts of steam from the dragon, and the striking of the anvil was the hacking away at the flesh of the beast."

Dad imitated the noises they had made. I had not known that he could burp, but he was better at it than George and me when we drank soda pop. This was a surprise. His manners were the ones that Mama Jo had told me to imitate "all the days" of my life.

"It took three bottles of whiskey to kill the dragon," he said. "And a great heap of horseshoes supplied the Pinch for many months afterwards. Of course the death of the beast gave them an excuse for a well-earned rest. They curled up on a pile of straw on the floor of the blacksmith's shop. And sleep they did—from midnight until noon the next day."

At home we washed, dressed, and waited for the wake. Time dragged, then seemed to stop altogether when I heard the cane tapping its way toward the dining room. I was sitting in the living room. I wanted to ask Uncle Jim about the story of the dragon, but interrupted Dad instead.

"Dad, did you hear the dragon story from Uncle Jim or O'Lanahan?" I wanted it to be Uncle Jim.

"Both versions," said Dad. "From both men."

I wanted to hear Uncle Jim tell his version, but the dining room might well have been as far away as Ireland. As always, I said nothing.

In those days I knew very little about Uncle Jim's early years, but I did know that he was our benefactor. It wasn't just the fistful of coins that he doled out on Saturdays. Dad had a good job with the insurance company, but I knew that it was Uncle Jim who supplied the fine things. But now I wasn't sure that we were entitled to share his wealth, any more than I was sure that the church was.

Mama Jo came in the front door. Her dress quietly swept the stairs as she went up. I was sure that she was tired, but duty was life for her.

"What do the priests say about Uncle Jim, Dad?"

"Nothing. They can't afford to."

My question didn't even wrinkle the evening paper that he was reading. But he had always told me not to give up on something that was important and that curiosity was "a quality that will keep you moving forward," so I risked his irritation.

"What if he dies in mortal sin?" I persisted. "What will happen then?"

"He'll buy in, somehow." He continued reading, the presence of sin not a disturbance. His quiet confidence relaxed some of my fears; for a time, at least, they were moved aside.

Then Uncle Jim came in for his after-dinner whiskey. Dad got up and poured it for him and took one for himself. They clinked glasses in honor of O'Lanahan. Uncle Jim said, "Son of Erin, slip by the devil . . . go to rest!" They both took two short sips and downed the whiskey, Uncle Jim's face taking on a rose color. Mama Jo came in just as they made the "auh" sound.

She had changed from one black dress into another. Father

Pat had asked her to lead the rosary at the wake until he could get there. The first dress had been entirely black. This one had white cuffs, the hint of a nun's habit. She held her black rosary beads and her white handkerchief, both necessary items for the wake. She reached into her pocket, then handed Uncle Jim a small pouch. "O'Lanahan told me long ago that he wanted you to have the beads."

He looked inside the brown pouch and touched the old wooden rosary. It had belonged to his father, Thomas. Mama Jo had given the rosary to O'Lanahan in the old days as a remembrance of his friend. Then Uncle Jim handed the beads to me. "Keep these, boy. Might get you out of a jam."

I took the rosary and nodded my thanks, but he swept his hand up and left the room before I could say anything.

Then Viola brought out a large chocolate cake. "I'll carry it on over there, Miz Jo."

When I saw that she had put candles on it, I thought she must have stayed in the hot kitchen too long. Mama Jo didn't say anything about the candles. I thought that she probably hadn't noticed because she was upset about the death.

"Viola, nobody's having a birthday," I finally said.

"Oh yes they is." She was certain. "Mr. O'Lanahan's been born to Heaven on this very day."

"I'll take it, Viola. You go and check on the girls," Mama Jo said. She poured a sip of the whiskey and tossed it down. As soon as she heard Viola creak the stairs, she removed the candles and said that I could lick the icing off of them, but I told her to save them for George.

He soon came in with the Major. "From what the good Monsignor said of O'Lanahan after mass this morning, I thought he'd gotten the wrong man. I told Rosie, 'Let's go, we're at the wrong bereavement.'" The Major's hair waved in neat rows. "You can bet on the funeral going on for half a day. The Monsignor gauges the length of a homily according to the age of the deceased. Eat a good breakfast in the morning, Nate. We won't get out in time for lunch." The Major shook Dad's hand. He took everything in stride. The good had to move over for the bad, the bad for the good. In spite of his appearance, he wasn't really a perfectionist; he looked for balance.

George's hair was slicked down like his father's, but when it dried it would be curled all over his head. We rode together to the wake.

When we got there, Mama Jo and the old women started in on the Joyful Mysteries. Old men were quietly smoking and talking in the corners of the room. Without really looking at O'Lanahan, George and I knelt behind the row of women gathered around the casket and pulled out our rosaries. It was the first chance I'd had to look at the old wooden ones, the beads wearing the patina of many prayers. The rosary hadn't saved my grandfather Thomas from the yellow fever, but then again, O'Lanahan had lived a very long time.

"Hail Mary, full of grace, the Lord is with thee . . . " The lilt of Mama Jo's voice saved the prayers from the dismal flatness that otherwise belonged to them. Dad had Moony open the windows, the prayers and the smoke spilling out into the night.

Father Pat came in time to lead the Sorrowful Mysteries. The prayers droned on like the "Dies Irae" at a funeral as the smell of colcannon drifted from the kitchen. Irish whiskey was the only thing strong enough to mask it. The sipping began before the rosary was over.

Most of the old women left after prayers, but a few of them stayed, praying silently for O'Lanahan's old soul. The mourners who stayed ate heartily. George was one of them, until the odors of cabbage and bourbon began to sicken him.

"I'd better go outside."

"No, son. Stay and pay your respects to the dead. No doubt he needs the supplications of the innocent." The Major was

155

determined that George would have the self-discipline that his mother lacked. It was unlikely that Rosie had gotten many prayers said for O'Lanahan. She and Mother had taken the early shift, but had already gone home because Rosie had gotten tight, which had caused her to weep without letup.

Watching George, the Major drank his highball, its dark amber shining in the light from the oil lamp that hung from the ceiling by a thin twisted cord. Soon the Major was drawn into some talk about politics and forgot to oversee George's prayers, but he continued to say them without any prodding, having braced himself against the odors. I, however, was impatient and slacked off. My drifting was not meant as disrespect. I just had things on my mind. I had no reason to doubt the religion in those days, but it didn't seem right that Uncle Jim should give our family and the church so much and then end up on the wrong side for eternity.

Dad approached Mrs. McGillicuddy. "Go home and rest yourself. I'll sit with him. There's no reason for you to stay up all night. His soul's already up there."

"You think so, then." The idea of speeding to heaven had never before occurred to Mrs. McGillicuddy. Dad always knew the right thing to say, especially to the old ladies.

She got up slowly from the straight chair. Her knees popped like Mama Jo's.

Dad then tried to get Mama Jo to go home and rest, but it was no use. "He was almost like a father," she mused. "I'll sit with him to the end." She hummed a tune. Inside I hummed it with her.

The men gradually formed a large group. The latecomers had, for the most part, come in one by one, some of them miscalculating the end of the last mystery, others hitting it on the last "Amen." They forgot to whisper.

"It's a damn shame that he didn't get on the streetcar, the sweet man," said Mr. Lafferty.

"And see the trees laden with golden coins," said Mr. McCarthy. He laughed quietly.

"The sun was there to warm him." Old Finney said this. He was one of Uncle Jim's men. His little wrinkled face was fair and freckled, reminding me of Uncle Jim.

Dad was sitting in the chair vacated by Mrs. McGillicuddy. He stuck his long legs out into the room and pointed his toes. I guessed that he had cramps in his calves because of the calisthenics he'd done to get in shape for Doc Hollie's river race, although he had not yet committed himself. Mother had told Rose Kate to say no more about it, and while she obeyed in principle, her obvious reminders leaked out several times each day. She would simulate the crawl, her arms traveling in exaggerated arcs, then ask pointed questions such as "How is the best way for a tired swimmer to save himself? The backstroke?"

To which he replied, "If the swimmer is you, then it would be *herself*. And no, the breaststroke would be the better choice."

With fingers splayed, he stretched his arms out in front of him. His reach was such that I was sure that he would win if he entered, although I did not want him in the muddy water.

Although Mama Jo was not crying, she held the handkerchief in her lap, squeezing it with the upswing of the rocking chair, relaxing it on the downbeat. She yawned while Mrs. Hogan was cutting the chocolate cake, but seemed to gain spirit when she was presented a piece.

Finney spoke again. "Jerkins kept the trolley at the corner for twenty minutes waiting on O'Lanahan." He wiped his face hard with the back of his hand as though he could take the freckles off. "The riders got mad . . . excepting the regulars." He rubbed the other side. "The old regulars cursed the newcomers for their complaining ways."

"I wished I'd have seen that," said McCarthy, swallowing beer and wiping his mouth on his sleeve.

"Look at him there," said Finney. "He would have enjoyed it most of all."

"I'm sure he was there," said Mama Jo, finishing the cake.

"He'd just died, Mrs. Culligan." Mrs. Hogan had taken the remaining chair, the two women rocking slowly. "I don't think he could have gotten back down here in that short time. Not even an angel could fly that fast." Mrs. Hogan was looking at Dad as if to dispute his earlier remark to Mrs. McGillicuddy about fast-moving spirits.

He smiled at Mrs. Hogan's lack of faith in him and enjoyed his whiskey. He had brought his legs in close to the chair, since the protrusion had almost tripped her when she was taking her seat.

The men loosened their ties. They drank and told stories about O'Lanahan. Except for the Major, the men were slouched and comfortable. Next to them, the Major looked like the only straight picket on a worn-out fence. He stood erect each time he swallowed his whiskey, as if his glass were a bugle that he would blow from time to time.

Distance came in carrying a box of whiskey. Uncle Jim was behind him with a box of cigars. The men were attentive when he came in.

"Mr. Jim. What can I get for you?" asked Doolin.

"A little whiskey, Doolin."

Little John Finney's brothers, James and Joseph, flanked Uncle Jim. Gradually, the other men gathered round him. Father Pat looked over at Uncle Jim, but did not come near.

Bennie O'Levy lit Uncle Jim's Cremo. Mama Jo suspected that O'Levy was Jewish, although she did not hold him personally responsible for the killing of the Lord. Uncle Jim had said that O'Levy was one of his best men. Uncle Jim, I was sure, wasn't worried over anybody's religion or the lack of it. He took the whiskey from Doolin.

Devlin McBlue asked Uncle Jim what was to be done with

Crump. Uncle Jim coughed hard, his breath putting out McBlue's match just as he was lighting his Camel.

"Feed him," Uncle Jim said of Mr. Crump. He handed his hat to O'Levy. "Give him money and hope he ignores the Nuisance Act and never cottons to the damn prohibitionists."

O'Levy removed McBlue's hat from the hat rack and replaced it with Uncle Jim's. The hat was a plain black one, but somehow it had the status of a crown.

"If a man needs a drink or whatever, he takes it. Damn reformers. Soak 'um in lemonade. Drown 'um in swill. Give their rotten sugar bellies to the river. Catfish'll eat 'um."

Or gars, I thought. I wondered if Uncle Jim had ever been fool enough to swim in the Mississippi as I thought my father was planning to do. Moony had bet me that he would lose. I, of course, had to take his bet, but in spite of the possible loss of two bits—an amount I could not afford to risk—I hoped that Dad would keep hold of his senses and stay out of the race.

Father Pat accepted a small glass of whiskey along with the plate of colcannon. His Adam's apple poked out when he swallowed the whiskey.

Uncle Jim motioned to Distance, who offered cigars to the men, then took one for himself. Looking toward O'Lanahan, Uncle Jim walked over and tucked the Cremo into the dead man's pocket. "Looks nice in the suit," he said. He bowed to O'Lanahan—a serious bow for a man already bent over. All watched him, their eyes holding respect. I was one of them.

Dad was trying to prop up Mrs. Hogan's head. It had been hanging down like a tomato on a vine. The quiet snores of the two women went unnoticed with the attention focused on Uncle Jim.

Father Pat had forgotten to say the blessing before he had eaten the colcannon. Now he crossed himself. "Amen," he said aloud.

The afterthought got Uncle Jim's attention. He gave the priest a nod. "At least O'Lanahan won't have to put up with the lilies. He saw the best of the old days. He wouldn't want any part of a town gone lilified."

"Still, I wish he could have gotten on that streetcar," said Joseph Finney.

The Major toasted the thought. He drank the amber light, his feet placed evenly apart, hair symmetrically waved, then cocked his head slightly to the right as he watched my father.

"What is the decision, Nate? Are you in the race?"

"I'm leaning in that direction," said Dad. His voice had gathered strength with the whiskey.

McBlue said, "The Smiddy gang is betting on McGowen. Putting up some big money." McBlue and the others were watching Uncle Jim, waiting for his response. He drank his whiskey and refused to reply.

Dad coughed, and then paused. "My interest is purely sport," he said calmly.

"The deadline for commitment is Thursday," said the Major. "It should be an interesting race for you, Nate. Some fine competition." For some reason, he seemed anxious for Dad to swim.

Dad was rocking fast in the chair, the runners touching tips with the movement of his long legs. He stopped abruptly, stood up and ceremoniously raised his glass. "To the ride." He had a look on his face like a stopper in a bottle just ready to pop. "He'll have it!" he said loudly, then took a swig. "We'll take him."

Before anyone could say otherwise, Dad motioned to the three Finneys, who helped him hoist O'Lanahan out of the coffin and onto their shoulders. Father Pat crossed himself again. His mouth formed an "o" of surprise, his face white like the deep snow I'd read about.

"To him that was my father's friend and mine," said Uncle Jim. He took his hat from the hat rack and bade the men to stop while he put it on O'Lanahan's head. He knocked the floor with his cane three times.

"Hear hear," seconded the Major.

McBlue was singing "Kevin O'Donohoe" as we all began filing out of the house. Father Pat took out a small vial of holy water, poured a little into his hand, and flung it toward the men. Some of the men blessed themselves.

Moony had been hiding in the kitchen, the farthest point from the body. The singing had brought him out. His eyes were white plates when he saw the dead man being carried out the door.

"Moony, you stay with the women," said Dad.

"What if the ghost come lookin' for its body, Mr. Nate?" asked Moony.

"Tell him we'll be back by and by."

"It might be real mad about no body being in *that*." He pointed at the coffin, his finger trembling.

"Give it cabbage and tell it to sit tight," said Uncle Jim. He was leader and the meeting was adjourned to other quarters.

Outside, the singing continued as we stood waiting for the streetcar. Dad and the Finneys stood O'Lanahan upright, put the hat down over his eyes so the few passengers wouldn't notice the expressionless face, and dragged him up the steps of the streetcar when it stopped.

"Too much whiskey again, O'Lanahan?" said Jerkins, the driver.

"Just drunk enough to ride with you," said one of the Finney brothers as they hoisted the dead man onto one of the long seats and placed the hat on his chest.

Lying there, O'Lanahan looked just about the same as he had in the coffin, except that his face seemed more peaceful.

George and I sat as far away from the body as we could, but not so far that we couldn't see. The sign above the driver's head said:

DO NOT TALK TO THE DRIVER.
DO NOT SWEAR, SMOKE OR SPIT.

These rules seemed to have been written for the men, but they did all of those things. They also drank neat from Joseph Finney's pint of rum or from Dad's Irish whiskey or from Uncle Jim's bottle of bourbon. He said that bourbon made in Tennessee beat any booze that came from Dublin. McBlue was not prejudiced against any of the whiskey and sampled each one that was passed by him. Jerkins, the driver, declined the bottle, but joined in the singing even though he wasn't Irish. Following his lead, the sprinkling of regular passengers began to harmonize with the rest of the singers. Each one accepted a slug of booze. They sang, "Too-Ra-Loo-Ra-Loo-Ral."

James Finney put O'Lanahan's Cremo in the corpse's mouth, but O'Levy wouldn't let him light it. Jerkins passed by a group of people left waiting for the streetcar. He didn't think he could adequately explain holding a wake on public transportation to strangers. "They might lack my own sense of humor," he said. Then he laughed from deep in his belly until tears dribbled down his face.

We reached East End, which was the end of the line. The streetcar turned, then went past Overton Park and turned west toward the river.

"Looks to be enjoying himself," I said to George. He was also looking at O'Lanahan.

"Yeah," he said. "He probably didn't need any more prayers anyway. He was too old to do much sinning."

I wondered if O'Lanahan had looked at any bosoms when he was our age. "Dad would say that the prayers were 'insurance.' Maybe we should say a few more for him before we go to bed."

The streetcar finally stopped in front of the dead man's

house. The singing had died down, but a few soft notes still rippled the night air.

"Quiet down," said Uncle Jim. "My sister won't take kindly to the last ride."

But she never knew, because nobody told her. She was still gently snoring when they put O'Lanahan back in his box.

The Letter: Jo Whitaker

1890

Jo Whitaker tells O'Lanahan things that she would tell no other living soul. Not even Father Canfield. Information about the neighborhood is traded between them like sugar or flour. But he keeps to his little house or his blacksmith's shop and only leaves to ride the trolley car once a week. What with the constant striking of the anvil, he hears little of the gossip, so that the telling is weighted on her side. On this late afternoon in the shop, as he spreads the fire that it may die out, she visits with him and tells about her brother and the letter, and all the while worries that those things hiding in the corners of her mind, where the Lord cannot see them, will find her voice.

"When I heard the news yesterday morning, I went straight away to find him. Bedlam, it was. Men and mules everywhere and me among them wearing my apron. Such haste. Of all things, I'd worn it out into the streets. There, in the middle of the bustle, in a white apron with blue flowers sprouting all over it. Such a sight, I was." *She is out of breath and nervous.*

"The merchants are most polite to him, you know. And so they were with me. It was 'Good afternoon, Mrs. Whitaker. Yes, Jim Canaan's already delivered,' and 'How are you today, Mrs. Whitaker? He's been gone about thirty minutes, Mrs. Whitaker.'"

O'Lanahan stops her. "I'm bucking to ask the questions. What's got your kettle whistling?"

"*Well, as you know, life has been none too easy. But Mr.
O'Lanahan, as the Lord would have it, our luck is about to take
a turn for the better.*" *She pauses to allow him to take stock of
the matter.* "*Into Jim's hand, just yesterday, came a letter with
great black looping letters on the whitest of paper. The writing was neatly drawn, the letter meant for our own mother,
Kate, and our father, Thomas. The address was our own.*" *She
cannot read, but took her brother's word that it was so.*

*She sees skepticism walking across O'Lanahan's face as she
leans on his railing. He's right, of course, to have his doubts. A
letter from Ireland does not come over often and he, O'Lanahan,
is one of the few people she knows who ever receives one. She
thinks he might be a bit green over someone else getting word
from the old country as well, but he doesn't let on. He just sits
and listens. He's already told her about his ride of the past
week, and since the next one is several days away, has no fod-
der for the conversation. He scratches the stubble on his chin,
smearing the coal dust.*

"*Rosemary McGillicuddy was first to hear of it,*" *she says,
shaking her head with the wonder of it.* "*It was she who told
Annie Flaherty who said it to Mary Hogan who had the good
sense to rush over and inform me.*

"*The dispatcher told Mrs. McGillicuddy that when he had
handed Jim the letter that morning, that he stared at it in the
most peculiar way. As though it were a ghost. Well, Jim's a
strange one, sometimes. But a better brother hasn't been born.
Now don't be telling that to Tom.*" *She wants these things to be
true and constantly repeats them to herself. She is replacing
what she wants to forget.*

*She feels the secrets forming pictures in her mind. Her par-
ents have been dead such a long time now. Her hand covers her
eyes for a minute, but she knows full well that she will see the
pictures when they come.* "*After the death of Father, Mother never
sat still the whole day,*" *she remembers.* "*She took in more*

boarders than we could manage. The mountain of washing. And the mending and cooking for them. Never an end to it. And her . . . never a quibble."

"Oh, Kate was a scrapper," recalls O'Lanahan.

Jo tries to stop her feelings before they take over, but they swell inside her. The potatoes. Her mother, Kate Canaan's potatoes. She feels her stomach and hopes that she'll never have to eat another one.

Her mother had dug little wells all over her father's grave. Had seeded a potato in each one. She had made Jo help her fill in the holes and press the dirt close in. Jo could not understand her mother. What devilment had she been up to? In that low voice, she had told Jo, "Don't you be telling Father Quinn. You hear me now." Jo again sees the sin of sacrilege, covering her mother inch by inch in its blackness. She shudders in the sight of it.

O'Lanahan is waiting for her to go on with the story, but she is holding on to what she cannot say. She hardly believes that she allows herself to think these things and feels tired after the words run through her. But she gets hold of herself, then begins again.

"Well, as I was telling. I was looking everywhere for him and getting tired for all of it. I knew that he was most likely tired himself. Him having the lumbago and all. He suffers, you know. But Mr. O'Lanahan, for all of it, he delivers the mail fast as a fox. I kept missing him. It was 'he's already delivered, Mrs. Whitaker. He's just gone, Mrs. Whitaker.'" She remembers that she didn't like the sound of "Mrs. Whitaker," but tries to keep her mind on the telling. "I knew that if worse came to worse, I'd get hold of him at Tom's saloon later in the day. But I was not anxious to wait on the news."

O'Lanahan smiles at her, understanding her impatience.

"It seems that when he got near the boardinghouse where we all live—he decided to stop and tell of the letter. Of course, I was out roaming in the streets when I should have been home packing our things."

Now she hates to continue. Her marriage to Mr. Whitaker,
after the death of John Slattery, has met with the disapproval
of Mr. O'Lanahan. She and her new husband are moving to
another house and she does not want to speak of it. In truth, she
regrets the marriage, but cannot criticize what is sacramental.

The late John Slattery hadn't been much of a provider—he
was fired from his job at the icehouse because he told long tales
to his customers while their ice melted to wide puddles on the
floor; it would then have to be replaced free of charge, his wages
reduced to cover the expense. When reminded of this, Mr.
O'Lanahan said that at least he "was Irish." In truth, she still
misses John Slattery, although she nearly worked herself to
death tending to him.

She had thought that Jerry, being Mr. Whitaker's first name,
stood for Jerome. But after she had married him, she found
that it was short for Jeremiah. She then doubted that he had
really been baptized, since Jeremiah was surely not the name
of any saint she'd ever heard of. She did not want to know the
truth of it, and called him Mr. Whitaker to end any more thought
about the matter.

She would not let Mr. O'Lanahan in on her suspicion, and
continued with the telling. "Well, Clare heard him turning the
knob and the peculiar sound of his walk. She rushed up to him
and told how she hated moving." She thinks of Clare in the new
green dress. Jo takes great pride in the sewing, but feels some-
what guilty, since it is Jim who must come up with the money
for the extravagant material. She knows that Whitaker has no
notion of her dream. Would never understand.

"Well, I was rushing about looking for him when he was right
there puttering about, waiting for me, when I happened to stop
in to check on the girls and rest a bit. And he was surprised
that I was not busy with the packing, but to tell the truth, I am
not anxious to move—any more than Clare. I've always lived
with my family, you see. And I was worrying over leaving Jim
and Tom—we've always shared the same dwelling. Everything.

But the worst of it was that while I was packing that morning —before Mary Hogan told me of the letter—I found the brown dress that our sister Katherine had worn. I folded it and placed it on the green chair, for I cannot bear to give it away. It would be like turning my back on her. Anyhow, the old hurt was creeping through me once more, and so I was glad to leave the sight of it."

She pauses in memory. Katherine died giving life to Rosie, who, when she left the house, was sleeping soundly in the bedroom. Rosie's fifth birthday yesterday—and on the same day that the letter arrived—five years old, five years since Katherine died. Jo wonders if the letter is a bad omen.

"I still blame myself for her death. I promised our mother that I would see to Katherine and Tade." Tade's gone off to work on a barge, settling in St. Louis with his young wife. Jo thinks they'll be having babies before long. She would like very much to see them.

"There wasn't anything you could have done, Jo. Don't grieve yourself of Katherine," says O'Lanahan, which is what Jim always says, but he grieves himself.

"By then, he was in a hurry to finish the route. He didn't give me the letter, because he thought I'd not be able to make it out, fancy as the writing was." She does not admit to O'Lanahan or anyone else that she cannot make out plain print, either. "Can you imagine the man? Of course, he was thinking all the while that Tom, as eldest, should open it. He told me to meet them at Tom's saloon."

"Ladies don't enter saloons," O'Lanahan laughs. "But tell me, how is Jim really doing?"

"He's in pain, Mr. O'Lanahan," she tells him. "But I worry more about what's in his mind than the problems he has with the limbs." She sighs with the weariness of it all. "I watched him walk down the steps. He turned and looked back at me with a strange face.

"'Is there something you want, Jim?' I asked him.

"'It's Ola,' he said."

O'Lanahan shakes his head. He seems to know what's to come next.

"'Ola, is it?'" She remembers that her voice was soft, but her stony look had nowhere to hide, her eyes wandering from the sky to the ground, finally coming to rest on his. "'Ola's a lost sheep, my brother. I'm sorry to say it.'

"'She's had no chance. You know it,' he said to me.

"'It's not for me to say,' I told him. 'Better to pick a young lady who'd be but yours alone.'"

But she decides to change the subject. "How's it with you, Mr. O'Lanahan?"

"I'm spry, Jo. Real spry." He rocks back and forth. "Of course I'm a bit down in the back, but I hope the Lord's not listening . . . I've no cause to complain." He grins. His teeth are blackish. Jo wonders if his friend, the old priest in Ireland, is as far gone. She breathes shallow trying not to take in any O'Lanahan air. "Witch hazel is a fine thing for the skin, Mr. O'Lanahan. I'll bring a jug of it next time. And bicarbonate of soda, good for the teeth."

She hears the vesper bell tolling from Saint Brigid's. "But I'll go on about the rest of the day. . . . We don't have much time left for the telling.

"The letter, you see, was written by our mother's brother, the uncle we have never met." She had made Jim read it a dozen times so that she could commit it to memory.

She could hardly focus on the letter with the feelings about her mother pressing in on her. For her mother, the deaths of her husband and then her son, John, and later, the baby Meg, were lodgers that had blocked all faith. She had fought hard to stay with the Lord and to rid herself of doubts, but they had stayed around the same as bad boarders. Jo prays for her every day without fail.

Jo and Tom both receive daily Communion with reverence and hope for the everlasting as their father would have them, but she has seen Jim—as she saw her own mother—muse over his Host, doubting the Lord's power and majesty. How could they bear to think this way? The Saviour stands above them all. She is sure of it.

When their sin bears down on her until she can carry it no more, she draws water in the bucket, filling the tub on the back stoop many times. The pile of soiled clothes in the woven basket dwindles as she takes one piece at a time and scrubs each spot out of it, rubbing hard on the washboard, until her knuckles bleed. She then hangs each one on the line to dry and whiten. Now she shakes the thought of it out of her head.

"Well, when at last I met him at the saloon, he was sitting there with a stout glass of whiskey in his hand, listening to Tom tell of some important law, all of it high talk—blustery, I call it—but I didn't have to listen long. McNamara announced the beef and then Jim took out the letter and finally, after what seemed a year had passed, consented to read it. And it's our fortune that is coming, Mr. O'Lanahan. It may well be our fortune."

"A blessed thing, it is then," says O'Lanahan after hearing her recite the letter.

"There's something more, Mr. O'Lanahan. I said to them, 'If money comes, Jim could buy that saloon on Winchester and Front that he's had his eye on for so long a time. And get off of his aching legs.' And Tom allowed that it was a good measure."

O'Lanahan nods his approval. Jo helps him spread the ashes. She accepts his good wishes at the prospect of the great blessing that must surely be traveling their way that very moment, without really listening. She is remembering the expression that came over Jim's face on that day, thinking how he took out the letter, reading it again, and then how he put it back

170

*in his shirt pocket. His face had looked as if he'd been vis-
ited by the heaviest of grievances. But she doesn't say this to
O'Lanahan.*

*The ashes appear as downy feathers as she turns to leave.
O'Lanahan calls, "Take care, Jo. Keep the sun behind you."*

The Route: Jim Canaan

1890

He was delivering thick parcels of mail to the cotton factors on Front Street, who were steadily taking in and shipping out the harvest of white gold. Drays loaded with cotton that was wrapped in burlap filled the streets; the bales, piled five high, teetered above the draymen, who slowly made their way toward the waterfront. Waiting the cargo, steamboats crowded the waterway, their whistles singing out as they came to the mooring. A train chugged slowly toward the loading dock, its smoke like small round clouds, its steel wheels girding the track, straining with a hiss, nearly nudging a braying mule that balked in its path.

He crossed the street, alert to the drays. He wove a path in between wagons and avoided walking in front of mules, knowing the draymen would do nothing to stop progress even if it meant knocking a man down. Who could blame them? If one mule stopped, they all stopped. Cursing and fist-waving did little to stir a standstill.

"Good afternoon, Jim Canaan," said one of the cotton merchants.

Jim handed him his stack of mail and dodged a bale being unloaded for grading. "Better to stay inside, Mr. Saxon. It's taking your life in your hands out here."

"It's bedlam, Jim, I'll agree. But think of it. The muddy town's growing gold."

"For some, Mr. Saxon. For some." His cracked leather bag creaked as he hoisted it from one shoulder to the other. The brown satchel held neat stacks of mail addressed, fine hand, with curled looping letters. Except for the one buried in the bottom of the bag. Its writing was small and neat. The letter was meant for his own mother and father. The address:

> *Mr. and Mrs. Thomas Canaan*
> *19 Jackson Avenue*
> *Memphis, Tennessee USA*

And him who wrote it not knowing that Thomas had been dead over ten years and Kate almost as long. When the dispatcher handed him the letter that morning, Jim had stared at it like he sometimes stared at their tombstones.

After the death of his father, his mother's fiery nature was kindled and stoked by grief. She had taken in more boarders —washing, mending, and cooking for them. She had scrubbed and mopped. And always, she had harried her sons and bullied her daughters. At night, she would fall in a deep sleep only to wake at midnight and pace until dawn.

And the potatoes. She had tried to erase her sin with them. Increasing the size of her potato plot, she had hoed, weeded, and watered. When she had extras, she had made Jo and little Katherine take only a few of them to the poorest neighbors, but the kindness of her act had been made indigestible by her lingering stinginess.

In atonement for the neglect of her husband, Kate had planted the eyes on his grave. Jim had guessed at her hope—that they would somehow grow to nourish the old man. But she would not have wanted Father Quinn to notice the green vines that crept over the cob of earth that covered Thomas. To the priest, an admission that she doubted the afterlife and that her beliefs had been rooted in earth, not Heaven, would have been as much as a sacrilege, a ticket to Hell.

Her plait of reddish hair became a dry sandy nest, her cheeks hollow, her blue eyes a glaze of weariness. She died of exhaustion and grief.

And who would open the letter? He would finish the route, then take it to Tom's store on Market Square.

He walked past the firehouse topped with the American flag. Two firemen played checkers silently. They hunkered to low benches, ignoring the bustle of business, the clatter of wagons. The pump wagon waited for a fire call. Its brass fittings shone from the shade of the firehouse. The clang of the fire bell was the only sound important enough to interrupt the stir of workmen, the haggle of men bent on making money, or attention to checkers.

The big white mare swung her tail, stirring a breeze for Duffy, the fireman who brushed her coat. She was the pride of Firehouse No. 1. Duffy waved. "How's your brother, Jim?" He kept stroking the big horse.

"Oh, Tom's all right. He said to 'Tell the men to come down for one on the house.'"

"Or two." Joseph Finney looked up from the checkers.

Tom had a grocery-saloon on Main Street on Market Square. He had been a popular fireman, but quit in order to sell large quantities of whiskey and Irish stew. He gave away, free, great gusts of political opinions which were well received by the men who gathered around him. The stools at his bar were always filled, seats at the tables always taken.

Jim shifted his load. Only twenty-seven, but his shoulders ached like those of an old man. He straightened his arms, easing the throbs deep in his rheumatic elbow joints. He moved stiffly down Front Street, called Cotton Row, glad that he would not have many stairs to climb, since most of the merchants stepped outside to receive the commerce of a busy day.

In the distance, he saw the two parts of the bridge that when finished would lead westward out of Memphis. The gridworks

174

jutted toward the middle of the river, one from the Arkansas side, the other from Tennessee, gradually coming together like bride and groom. From his place on the bluff, he judged that the engagement would be a long one.

As the stacks in his bag dwindled, his fingers came closer to the letter on bottom. It lay flat and white under the other bundles. The letter was written by his mother's brother, the uncle he'd never met. The return address:

> *John Kearny*
> *Lishishkin Liscanvour*
> *County Clare, Ireland*

He came to the quiet end of Front Street. At least it was quiet during the day. At sundown, a blaze of lights, like beacons, showed the way to sin for some men and salvation for others. He approached the four-storied brick house that claimed almost the whole block. The Iron Clad it was called. Ola's window could be the one with remnants of blue, red, and black cotton, the colors of the skirt she had worn as a girl.

Ola met Jim each day expecting a letter. He wondered if she would have been better off in a fever grave, but when her turquoise eyes looked out of her delicate face he was washed with her beauty and stirred by his own feelings. It was the same on this day. He wanted to carry her.

"No, Ola. Maybe tomorrow." He watched her hope sink into her chest.

"He's promised to take me away from this house," she said. Her lids lowered, covering the turquoise. Her mouth, painted a thick red, pursed in a shell of small creases. He remembered her lips as they really were.

"A relative of yours, Ola?"

"No. He's a gambler. He comes up the river." She smoothed a wisp of hair from her face. "He promised he'd write. That he'd take me to New Orleans to live in a decent hotel."

175

"Jim, come to my room. I have a letter to send Joe. Please come take it now," said Ola.

Mr. Jolly was asleep in the corner, his big frame crimped in the small chair, his snores fluttering his lips. The maid moved one of his shoes, sculling the floor beneath him with her big hairy mop.

The desk clerk looked up from his counting to meet Ola's eyes. He licked the tip of his finger. "Remember, Ola. This is a business."

Jim wanted to hit him. But Ola seemed not to hear the clerk. She turned her back and led Jim down the hall, a cave of fractured plaster. She opened her door and he followed her inside. The scent of lavender softened the sparseness of the room. A lace curtain hanging at the window, its pattern a limp garden of roses, veiled the cobblestones outside that sloped to meet the passing river.

Jim glanced around her room, his eyes coddling her few possessions. A rag doll with no eyes sat on the dark heavy dresser. The doll's faded yellow yarn-hair had been neatly plaited. A broken hand mirror and a tortoise-shell comb lay aside. The lines of the mirror splintered from the main crack like the branches of a tree. The brush, an ancient Germanic salvage from an Ola Hedermann ancestor, rested on bristles that were held to rows by the enameled back picturing a lady carrying a blue bouquet.

When she touched his arm, he remembered to take the letter from her hand, and then he was staring at the lady in blue, her envelope hinting of the lavender, her writing gracefully slanted. Her hands were slender and soft when she touched his face, but the look of sadness made her seem far away.

"This Joe. He's the lucky man, Ola. If there's ever a problem . . . well, you'll tell me then." He backed out of the room, his steps faltering as he thought of the men who would come into her room late in the night. He knew that the man named Joe

would not take her from the city and that the line of men would grow.

Outside, he said good-bye to her and walked down the street, afraid to look back. The autumn sun blinded him until he found shade in the shadow of a sycamore that clung to the bluff. Leaves born by hot breezes retired slowly to the ground. Around his feet, scabs of fallen bark littered the scrub grass. He pressed his eyelids tight together. When he opened his eyes wide, the rash of blind spots cleared. The scene around him seemed tinted a faint brown that hid the colors that he knew were there.

He was near the boardinghouse where he lived. His sister, Jo, and his niece, Clare, would be packing their things. They were moving to another house with Jo's second husband, Whitaker, whom she had married after the death of Slattery, her first.

John Slattery had provided little besides his good nature, but at least he had put a twinkle in Jo's eyes. This Whitaker was not the man to understand the mind of an Irish woman, a task often impossible for an Irish man.

He walked up the steps and turned the knob. If he told Jo about the letter, she would needle him with questions. Tom was eldest and it was his place to open it. "Jo, I'm stopping for a minute."

Clare heard him and came skipping into the room. "Uncle Jim, I don't want to move." She ran her finger along the handle of the basket of tatting that sat on the table, its two small skeins of brown cotton appearing like eyes among the hanks of ecru. She carried a rag doll that wore a green dress that matched her own. A small lace collar lay beside the basket. A tiny one for the doll was unfinished inside. Jo had determined that Clare would be a lady and made dresses for her of velvet and fine cotton, fabrics they could ill afford, but he did not mind the indulgence since the dream also belonged to him.

Jim bent to pick her up, but he was stiff. At six, she was no longer a baby. He patted her hair instead. It was red brown and hung in plaits. Her face seemed small for green eyes so large. Her fair skin reminded him of Ola's, if only Ola had the same rose blush of good health. He trembled inside the hollow recesses where his longing for Ola lived, rubbing his arms, tightening the sinews. He felt the blackness.

Jo blurred into the room, working hurriedly, her puttering an attempt to disguise her jitters. "I've looked high and low for you, my brother."

He thought she was just worried over the moving—until he saw the brown dress folded on the dark green chair and knew that she was thinking of Katherine. In what now seemed the wink of an eye Katherine had grown to a bud anxious to bloom. Then she had died giving life to Rosie, who was sitting on the floor with her doll.

"There wasn't anything you could have done, Jo. Don't grieve yourself."

"Oh, I'm knowing it. The lads began following her and she let them. But I can't help stewing a bit." She wore a black dress that looked old next to Clare's new green one. She jiggled Clare's doll. "How's the route. Have you seen O'Lanahan today?"

Jim shook his head. "If he's finished with the smithing, he'll be at his gate like always. If it's still standing."

"He's all alone in this world. I feel obliged to ask after him. He was good to us when Mother and Father died." The ingredients in her stews included neighbors and friends as well as family, but in truth, O'Lanahan did go out. He rode the streetcar every Saturday.

Jim stood on one leg and then the other. It was a way of taking the pain. One leg would get all of it while the other got a few seconds of freedom. Now he stood on both legs. "Come down to Tom's store in about an hour, Jo. There'll be a bit of business that might concern you."

"You know the ladies don't enter saloons." She straightened

178

Clare's collar, folding it down and smoothing the edges flat to the dress, then smiled at her handiwork.

"You can stand in the grocery end, sister Jo." It was a game they played. She went to Tom's saloon whenever she pleased and thought little of it, but she would see to it that Clare would never go. She would not allow Rosie to go either, but Jim knew that this marked child would always hold superstition for her and that she would not be surprised by anything that happened.

Jo looked up. "Well. What's it about? Mary Hogan told me a letter came from Ireland."

"You're always talking about the virtues. You have use for one of them now," he said.

"You've got me stirring. For a letter carrier, you don't bring much news. Stingy is what I call it."

"Four o'clock, then."

She took up her broom, like she would give him a whack, and swept it toward him. He felt her watchful eyes as he walked down the steps. He looked back at her.

"Is there something else, Jim?" she asked.

"It's Ola. I want to marry her."

She swallowed and began to speak slowly, looking upward. "If she has goodness on the inside of her, and I'm thinking there is good in her—why, she wouldn't have you. She wouldn't be letting you marry second hand so to speak. Best to leave Ola to herself."

She had spoken her heart, but he did not wish to hear it. "Go back to your work, Jo," he said, his shoes thudding as he walked down the steps. She had never lied to him, but just then he hated her for it. He was the same as the fall, both the energy of love and the sadness of loss brought together by an October breeze, that damn fickle matchmaker.

He walked down the street and came to the Anshei Mischne Synagogue where the old Rabbi would receive the Jewish mail. The synagogue was balanced by two identical wings, each having its own door with a stone overhang peaked and pointing toward Heaven. In between the wings, the large middle section was arched at the top like a gate. The Rabbi came out from one of the doorways, his scholar's face brooding behind wiry brows. His black beard crinkled to his chest where it rested.

As mail carrier Jim Canaan got more than the usual nod from the Rabbi, who rarely spoke to other gentiles. Jim had become a familiar sight to all of the Jews in the Pinch. They had come to associate him with messages from their homelands which they anxiously awaited.

"Mr. Canaan, did you try the poultice I told you about?" The Rabbi had prescribed a remedy for the pain in his legs.

He nodded, but had no intention of trying the odd Jewish practice, though the Rabbi's concern for a gentile did seem genuine in spite of the flock of Jews that depended on him. Accepting the mail was one of the few times in the course of a day that he came out into the light.

"Not much mail for you this time." There was not much mail left on top of his own letter either.

The Rabbi spoke again. "Your brother has influence, Jim Canaan. It's the influence that I must have."

Jim waited for the reason.

"Can your brother get the water company to fix our leak in the basement of the synagogue? I cannot get them to do nothing." He was refined, but looked as though he wanted to curse.

"I'll ask him. But he'll be needing money for the election."

The Rabbi slid a drawstring bag of black velvet from his coat pocket. He took out several silver coins.

"The job will take more," Jim assured him.

The Rabbi's frown pushed his black eyebrows forward until they half covered his eyes, but water standing in the basement opened the bag once more. He handed Jim a stack of silver dollars.

"And remember the election," said Jim.

The Rabbi turned away. "Oh yes, the vote."

Coming down the street, a group of Jewish boys elbowed and shoved each other, until they noticed the Rabbi's frown, which starched their behavior. They filed behind him and into the darkness of the synagogue with quiet eyes. They would study until late afternoon, when they would come out squinting to hide pupils grown as large as black olives in the darkness.

Jim walked on down Overton. O'Lanahan was waiting by his rickety gate, both the man and the gate ready to fall. O'Lanahan drank steadily, forgetting any reason to keep clean, his beard a place for spittle to harden. Staying the same ground with him was an effort, since he bathed only on Saturdays, the ritual in preparation for the streetcar ride.

O'Lanahan sometimes got mail from an old priest in Ireland. They had been boyhood friends. O'Lanahan could not write, so Jim wrote to the priest for him. In the letters, O'Lanahan would tell about his streetcar rides, and what O'Lanahan saw on those rides was memorable: hickory trees with nuts the size of apples, houses like palaces, the river like silver. At least, thought Jim, he hadn't said that the streets were paved with gold.

"I was knowing it was not to be," said O'Lanahan when he saw that he'd not gotten a letter.

"My sister Jo asked about you, sir."

"Tell the dear lady that I'm fine. But tell me, Jim, why did she marry a bloke?" His disgust came out with a blast of breath. He scratched at his beard.

"He's good to her, Mr. O'Lanahan. That's about all I can say for him." He took another step back. "I'll come again tomorrow."

From O'Lanahan's gate, Jim could see the house down on Second Street that he had come to admire. He especially liked the porch; it was large and inviting, a place to sit, talk, and dream. It would be pleasant to live in such a place; some of the rooms would be dark and rich, others flooded with light.

181

"Young Jim."

"Yes, Mr. O'Lanahan."

"I don't mean to bring up the sadness where it might not be welcome."

"Go ahead, Mr. O'Lanahan. You're determined, I'd say."

"Well, Jim. Your sister Katherine. She was a lovely girl you know." He hesitated, waiting for Jim to give him the gate.

"Go ahead, Mr. O'Lanahan." He hunched up his shoulders, wanting the old man to get on with it.

"I think her path was a bit crooked, Jim. You see, the lads were following her."

"I couldn't lock her up, could I now?" asked Jim.

"I would've considered it, young Jim. I'd have kept my cap on it." The old man gave up and latched the gate. "Take care, Jim. Keep the sun behind you."

Old O'Lanahan had too much time on his hands, drank too much of the barleycorn, had too much imagination. Katherine had been a sweet, pretty young sister and he wanted to remember her so. Jim breathed in the hot fall air. He blew out the smells of old age.

He heard the cobbler's hammer keeping time to a silent song. When he entered the shop, Pagatini was humming it under the tapping sound. He was a short muscular Italian whose twin brother sold vegetables and sang Italian songs.

Rich smells of garlic, parsley, basil, and thyme drifted from the back room. The door leading to it framed only blackness. He surmised that the family lived in the dark.

The shoes and boots that had been mended were lined up on a bench; two customers sat at one end of it in their stocking feet. Pagatini looked up from his work, his eyes cutting straight to Jim's. "I've a got the promises for the votes. They know Mr. Tom can help them when the trouble comes." He looked toward the customers, who nodded.

Tom was a candidate for county committeeman of the First

Ward. He had gradually gained support from the Italians as well as the Jews.

"Some of them that would a voted cannot make citizen yet. Next time." The Italians knew the game.

"He'll know about your votes. I'll be seeing him in a few minutes."

He watched Pagatini's nimble fingers sort through the pile of tiny nails. "Here's your letter, Mr. Pago."

Dropping his good manners with the nails, Pagatini snatched the letter from his hand. He had immigrated to America a few years before and was one of a large group of Italians who kept the mail traveling from Memphis to Palermo. The letter was from his mother. He tore it open and read silently, rocking back and forth as his eyes devoured the pages. Jim left him.

Just then he missed his own mother. Her badgering had been steady and constant. The lack of it made his life uneven. Near the end, he had felt pity as he watched her try to swallow the Host just as she had tried to swallow stinginess. Neither went down easy, for Kate found, like it or not, that life was potatoes—it came from the earth and went back into the earth with the endless round of burials and births.

With each of the deaths, she had lost bits of her faith, struggling to swallow Jesus, getting Him down in a small wash of phlegm. He understood this.

Jim put letters into the burnished brass mail slip on the door of the rectory of Saint Peter's. His old man had visited the church not long before the fever felled him. He must have seen his own end, for on any other day he would have gone on to Saint Brigid's, a church built just for the Irish. "We were not civilized enough for Saint Pete's," he had said. "They had to build us a church of our own."

On any other day he would have talked Saint Brigid and some of the other saints into helping him out with the Lord as he had done every day of his life. "Saint Brigid, help your poor servant. Saint Patrick, chase the devil. Holy Mary, pray for us all. Amen."

It was supposed that God was in Saint Peter's, but Thomas Canaan had never been quite sure if the Lord—blessed be the humble—would take up residence in a church erected by the English.

The Germans also had their own church, Saint Mary's, a Gothic sanctuary where the carved pillars, spires, and statues cast medieval shadows. The Franciscans who ran it were a mean lot. Ola might have asked for their help were their faces not shrouded in hoods so dark, were their hands not clasped inside brown robes belted with ropes, were their feet not sandaled in bindings that creaked when they walked across the chill marble floor. For weeks she had hung about the pews carrying her sin, hoping for the courage to confess and, thereby, leave the black thing as one would leave a rotten egg; yet she, after a vigilance that had allowed the sin to grow as heavy as lead, shrank from the Franciscan frowns. They fed the poor and ministered to the sick, but fornicating sinners were ignored. She had stopped going.

Passing the apothecary, he was glad not to have mail to deliver there. Inside were shelves lined with toiletries—Odo-Ro-No for extreme perspiration, Mennen's Kora-Konia for chafing—but more importantly, the vials of patent medicines: Cocex for nerves and the essential S.S.S. for blood poison and sciatic rheumatism. One of them might cure him. Of what he wasn't sure. But with the letter waiting in his pouch, he did not want the distraction of his usual search for a new medicine.

A club of Chinese stood on the next corner. From the distance they appeared calm, their hands clasped in patience, but as he drew near he heard them chattering, all of them talking at once. Their agitation was part of a normal day, for when one of them received any kind of notice or letter, the whole group shared it. They gathered to sort things out, but the meetings became endless quandaries. Jim suspected that they enjoyed worrying, no matter how frightened they appeared. Mr. Wang was their leader although he was not really in control.

"What now, Mr. Wang?"

"A notice, Missa Jim."

"It's all right, Mr. Wang. It's for votes." He took the paper. It showed the name of Tom's opposition, Charlie Leary. Jim crumpled the bill. "No vote," he told them.

"No vote," they repeated, shaking their heads at the same time.

He knew that only a couple of them could vote, but he pointed to the poster of Tom's big smiling face on the side of the apothecary. "Vote," he said.

"Vote," they repeated.

He left them with their puzzle. He waved to Pat Ryan who was driving a load of cotton along Main Street. "Want a lift, Jim?" said Pat.

"It's time for the ale, Pat. Come join us."

"Train's waiting the cotton. Got to get on, Jim."

Pat Ryan had gotten yellow fever after reaching the Father Matthew camp, but unlike Jim's own father and brother and baby sister, Pat Ryan had lived to tell about the demons that had jeered at him when his fever was up and burning. He had been nursed back to health by the Dominican Sisters. Now he was a big strapping man diminished only by the pockmarks dotting his wide cheeks.

As Pat's wagon rolled by, Jim touched the edge of the letter, the last one in his bag. It was thin. Strange for an Irishman; he was thinking of the fat epistles that O'Lanahan received from the old priest.

Tom's store had the daily special posted on the wide window. Fish stew. Friday's fare. It was Tuesday; Tom had forgotten to change the sign again.

He saw Tom behind the bar sipping ale. He was holding a meeting with one of his supporters, police Captain John Culligan. They waved him over.

Two bartenders were serving drinks. A big Negro boy in his teens washed glasses between them, his arms covered in soap-suds up to his elbows. He bumped into one of the bartenders, causing him to drop a mug which shattered as it hit the floor, then looked up. "I'm sorry, Mr. Tom."

"Keep your distance, boy," said Tom. "That'll be your name from now on. It'll be Distance." The men all laughed.

Distance smiled and started picking up the pieces, the glass taking on his chocolate color.

Tom motioned to one of his bartenders to pour Jim his usual ale.

"I'll have a whiskey today, Tom," he said. He fingered the enve-lope, then glanced down at it. The writing had been formed by a disciplined hand. He placed it back in the bag. "Jo will be here in a minute." He took a sip of the whiskey. "The three of us have a letter to open."

"Addressed to all of us, is it?" Tom veered momentarily from political considerations to concentrate on the letter.

Jim didn't answer him. The unexpected tie to the past caused him an uneasiness that crept through him in what would seem a ghostly visitation. He had discovered the taste of mystery; he liked that the letter was still in his possession. He was savoring it while he studied Tom's face, knowing his brother's interest would quickly turn.

Tom went back to waving his arms in reaction to the Sher-man Antitrust Act. He said nothing favorable about its spon-sor, President Harrison, whom he opposed, but the passing of the act had made him happy. He was not himself affected by the law or the lack of it, but had often preached against monopolies and the abuses of industry (neither of which was a particular problem in Memphis) and so felt that the constancy of his lec-tures had been rewarded. He was nearly exhausted from the day's ruminations. Jim settled into the sound of his brother's voice, but didn't have to listen long.

Jo sprang into the saloon, the basket swinging on her arm as she walked about picking out her stores. Tom and Jim left their drinks on the end of the bar where the cigar box full of money had been set for the customers, who were allowed to make their own change. When asked about the possibility of theft, Tom had said, "If a man needs the money bad enough to short change me, then he must need it more than I."

They walked to the chopping block where Jo was watching McNamara prepare the raw beef. He held two cleavers and went at the meat with a vengeance, chopping it into fine particles, the sound in spirited three-quarter time. He then sprinkled it with cayenne and salt and piled it high like a hill. He offered the platter of Uneeda crackers to Jo. She took a cracker and put a pinch of beef on it. Approving its flavor, she took another sample. "You've not lost the touch, Mac," she said.

"She'll eat me out of house and home," said Tom as he reached for a cracker.

"Well? What about this letter?" She had swallowed the beef and wanted to know.

"Don't look at me, Jo." Tom stood near her. "It's your brother Jim who's keeping secrets." He looked impatient for once and drummed his fingers on the block. McNamara had to quit chopping.

Jim took out the letter. "I think you should read it, Tom." He knew that he did not sound quite sincere when he said this.

Tom examined the envelope, but handed it back. "No, you read it. You've carried it the whole long day." Jo agreed as she brushed the crumbs from her fingertips.

Jim reluctantly opened the letter, lifting the wax seal. He read the words slowly.

My Dearest Kate and Thomas,
I have no way of knowing if this letter will find its way to your new home. I pray to the Lord that it will. Two years

ago, I buried my sweet Maureen in the shadow of the tallest spruce that grows on these Cliffs of Moher. The Lord, in His wisdom, left us without the song of children.

In his way, there is always a message. It seems that he wanted me to serve Him. I am soon to enter the Benedictine monastery near Dublin.

Jo folded her hands. "It's a priest in the family. Bless him."
Tom smiled at her. The priesthood was almost as important as an election. Jim read on.

My small farm and worldly goods have been sold. It is my wish that you use these funds, in the Name of Christ, for a better life in America.

Sadly, I buried your Uncle Daniel last week. He was very old and died peacefully. He left no other heirs, so that proceeds from my worldly goods, along with the small sum of his estate, will be sent to you if you receive this letter and reply to it as soon as you are able.

Of great importance is for you to know that the Canaans have died out in this village. It is your duty to insure that the ancient name does not die out. May God bless you and may He always keep the rain from your sweet faces.

Yours in Christ,
John Kearny

They said nothing. Tom took up one of McNamara's cleavers and chopped softly at the meat. Jim folded the letter and put it in the pocket of his jacket.

"It's up to you, my brothers," said Jo. "I can't give the name. You'd better be proposing to Mary McPartland, Tom. That is if you can give up the politics long enough to ask her." She didn't look at Jim.

Tom's face was crimson. He smiled and made a show of his big white teeth. "Well now, I guess the old name must stay alive. The letter's a command."

"There's something else, brothers," she said. "If money comes, Jim could buy that saloon on Winchester and Front that he's had his eye on for so long. And get off of his aching legs."

"It would be a great day." Tom approved of great days.

Jim took out the letter and put it in his shirt pocket. Inside him was the emptiness of autumn. He could have given the Canaan name, if he'd saved Ola.

The Mississippi

1914, *Jim Flanagan*

I have always been afraid of the Mississippi with its alligator gars that fishermen and rivermen told about. The gars speared hogs, drug them to the bottom, and ate them. They were as large as any demon I'd ever dreamt about and the reason to stay away from the river. But not everyone felt that the Mississippi was bad. Dad was not afraid of the river. He was afraid of fire and of lightning, he said, but river fears never got hold of him. He said that death by water would be soothing, but that dying in fire would be punishment. So I wondered why it took him a long time to enter the river race, what with Rose Kate pushing him on one side and the Major tugging on the other.

I never wanted my father to get into either the river or the race. The year before my fears were waylaid—thank the Lord, as Mama Jo would have said—because according to Mother, he had taken a cold. But this particular year, 1914 to be exact, he was in good health, although I was sure that he would not be after swimming in the river.

When Doc Hollie rang the doorbell, I shook with the jangle, because I'd seen him mounting the steps and knew why he'd come. Dad had been exercising for weeks and was ready for the invitation.

He greeted Doc warmly. "I've been expecting you."

"Well, Nate, you know if an insurance man will swim in my race, it'll give the fence straddlers a push. And the race is more fun when a bunch of people swim in it."

"And more profitable, I'll wager," said Dad.

"You've got a bet," laughed Doc.

I also had a bet. Moony, who could talk his way into my bank with the ease of a snake charmer, had managed to increase our wager to a buck, my life's savings. He said, "Mr. Nate's not going to win, but I am." I was sore about it. Not just about the possibility that I would lose the money or that Dad would lose the race, but that I was in some way a participant in a sport that was opposite my strongest belief; I counted the Mississippi a troublemaker.

Doc Hollie then looked at me. "How about you, Jim?" he asked. "The river's real tame for this time of year."

"No *sir*, sir." I said.

"Well, you have made up your mind at least. Some of the young ones want to go, but can't quite say 'yes' nor can they come out with a 'no.'"

"No," I emphasized. His idea of tame was that no floating trees had been sighted in a couple of weeks. It was true that the river had behaved better than normal in the early spring —the reason that the race was moved up from the usual midsummer—but trusting something with a proven record of wildness was unreasonable. They both laughed and continued the press.

"He'll change his mind some day, Doc," said Dad. "Don't you give up on him."

"I won't, Dad."

Doc straightened his hatband. "We'll start at Island 40 and go to the Frisco Bridge. That's ten miles. It'll be Doc Hollie's Fourth Annual Mississippi River Marathon."

Dad stretched his long arms. "Jim, you and George and Distance can follow me in a skiff."

"Miz Clare and the girls can ride on the excursion steamer," said Doc. "We'll have music and refreshments."

"Distance is afraid of water," I told them. "He hasn't even been baptized because of it." In this situation, I would have lied, but Distance had common sense and counted the river as I did, a body of water fit only for the sizable fish that were in it.

I was not happy about riding in the skiff, but did not want Dad to know that I was in no way as brave as he was. Gars were bigger than skiffs.

"What time will the race start, Doc?" Dad asked.

"I'll wave my hat on Island 40 at precisely 8:00 A.M."

"No starting pistol, Doc?"

"No, Nate. There's always so much ruckus the swimmers couldn't hear the gun anyhow. I'll put a red band on this old straw hat. You'll be able to see it a long way off."

Dad beamed.

I quaked. "Our Confirmation's Saturday, Dad," I reminded him. "And Mama Jo thinks that Ted and Pearl are coming from St. Louis." I was sure that the impending visit from cousins whom the whole family was preparing for would counter his need for this risky venture.

"Oh, I haven't forgotten. Your Mama Jo won't let me. We'll be finished with the race early enough. Plenty of time between."

I tried to think of another reason to keep him out of the race. "I think George gets seasick," I said.

"Maybe he's not the only one," Dad said. "Don't worry Jim. The day will be a fine one, from start to finish."

Doc began to shuffle and pat his coat pocket. "I know Miz Jo and Miz Clare don't want cigars in the house. Mine's waiting to be smoked, so I'll be off."

"You can light up if you want to. You know Uncle Jim's not going to be held back by the women. The house wouldn't be the same without the aroma of a good cigar."

"Thanks, Nate. But I like to keep the ladies happy. So I'll just see you on Saturday morning." He covered his bald pate with the round straw hat. "Too bad about what happened at the Phoenix. Sorry it was the lad's first fight."

Dad's smile quickly wore out. "Yes, well . . . such things happen. Unluckily."

I wondered if Dad had dreamed about the fight. Leonard Jones was heavy on my mind, but this was not a subject that I could speak of to anyone. Until the night at the Phoenix, I had given little thought to death, as though it were a stranger walking the streets knocking on doors that were safely beyond my reach.

"Like Jim said, Ted Canaan might be coming down from St. Louis, Doc. He's a strapping young man, just the right age to give the old river a tryout. I'll try and persuade him to enter."

"From what I hear, Jim Canaan's waiting for Ted with plans already blueprinted. He's counting on Ted to go into the business, Nate. That's the rumor."

Dad's face showed no expression, so I knew that he was already expecting Ted to join Uncle Jim's enterprises. I wondered how Dad felt about this. How he would feel if Ted were his own son.

Doc tipped his hat and walked across the porch and down the steps. Dad left just after him. He was headed for the stockyard where he had business with one of the mule traders who bought insurance from him. Dad had said that Memphis was the "Mule Trading Capital of the World." He hadn't said anything about it being the "Murder Capital." I knew that Uncle Jim and his kind of business had contributed to the distinction. I thought that Mr. Larkin, the undertaker, was probably glad for the business, but wondered if he felt a difference in embalming a man who had been murdered compared to one who died of a natural cause, say influenza. If Ted linked up with Uncle Jim, what kind of jobs would he be asked to do? I went out to practice mumblety-peg, postponing my home-work for as long as I could get away with it. My mind was running.

As I pitched my pocket knife, Mama Jo was leaning out of the window talking to Mrs. Morganstern about green beans.

"Mrs. Morganstern, have you seen Mr. Sites?"

"That worthless jesbah, no," said Mrs. Morganstern from her porch. "He promised to bring fresh eggs this morning. But Mrs. Culligan let me tell you . . . if the galoot shows up in this afternoon heat, the eggs they'll be hard boiled."

Mrs. Morganstern placed her hands on the sides of her head as if to straighten it. "The man's heart does the promising, his head the forgetting."

Mr. Bluestein came out of his small store. It was next to Mrs. Morganstern's house. He took the flag from its holder by the front window. Its reflection in the glass striped the chick-ens hanging in the window red, white, and blue. When she saw the flag, Mrs. Morganstern got to her feet, stood straight as an elm with her black-laced shoes tight together, and saluted. Moggy managed to get up from his resting place. He propped himself on his hairless haunches and watched his mistress as though she were a fresh bone. As she lowered her hand, he fell back to his space on the porch floor, worn smooth from his naps, and went back to sleep. The ritual hadn't required much of his energy, but clearly he was exhausted. If dogs dreamed, his would be epic.

I sat on the ground in the dirt, the grass all but gone from the short stay of the nanny. Escaping the appetite of our guest, the wild blue hyacinths that Mother loved were just up by the house. Near them, I scratched out a map that had rivers and roads, none of which led anywhere in particular. I knew from the long hours of history that Memphis was once the hunting ground of the Chickasaws. Herds of buffalo had probably passed by this place. Rumor held that black bears still hid in the deep green thickets not far upstream. And wild hogs. The Chickasaws most likely camped where I was crouched, traveling alongside the Mississippi, fearing to cross it.

I began smoothing the dirt with the blade of my knife. I heard the dull tap of Uncle Jim's cane, the yawn of the chair. The Major's voice trailed after the sounds. "Nate signed up today. He held out until the last hour."

"For Clare's sake, he ought to stay out of the damn river," said Uncle Jim. His smoke slipped away from the porch. "I'll have to bet on him. Probably lose a stack."

I coughed, so that they would know I was there, but they did not hear me.

"Of course the possibility exists that he may not go through with it," said the Major. "McGowen is a fair specimen. He appears to be the favorite."

"God forbid Smiddy's man should win," said Uncle Jim. "Nate's got to go out and show what he's made of. I know it's in him somewhere. Clare wouldn't have married him otherwise."

"My instinct declares him loser. He's not a combatant."

In a loud voice that curled my ears Uncle Jim said, "He's an Irishman of good stock, by God. Much as I hate to say of that damn grappler, Emmett Flanagan. I'm putting my money on Nate. It's high time he took his place as head of this house. I can't live forever."

"Speaking of forever, you need to appoint someone to administer your estate. I do not believe that Nate could properly manage things in your absence."

"I'm not going today, Merlin Mahon. And if I were, I've made my will and that's the way it stands. Place your bet."

"Well, I had not actually planned to wager against Nate."

"It's the only way you stand a chance of getting money out of me anytime soon. Except for your damn legal fees."

"One hundred dollars, then."

"You really want him to lose, Major. Well, we'll see. The bet's on."

The Major said, "Of course, in the interest of family harmony, my bet must be kept secret."

"Jo would likely kill you, Major."

"Exactly . . . submerged in a tub of scalding water."

"Be on," said Uncle Jim. "I've got a long night. Got to have rest."

I was silent, staying on the ground, imagining myself growing out of it. Betting against George was something that I could never do. I felt that the Major had slapped Dad hard across the face.

He walked down to his car as Uncle Jim went inside. Even after they were gone, I stayed put without moving for what seemed an hour while the anger built inside me like a fire. I stood up, my legs unable to support me, and lunged at the house, stabbing at the clapboards, making thin gashes in the white paint and blunt pain in the palm of my hand. My chest and arms collapsed against the house. I held on.

"Jim," called Mother from our porch. "What a lot of noise. Look up and tell Mama that Ted and Pearl will be here on Friday. They've sent a telegram. They'll be here for the Confirmation and the party."

The feeling in my legs returned with the smooth sound of her voice and I folded my knife and with it, the anger.

Pearl and Ted were my cousins. They were older, young adults actually, and unlike most relatives, kind of exciting. "Mama Jo, they're coming, did you hear?"

"Yes. Happy days." Mama Jo leaned so far out of the window that I held my breath. Ted and Pearl were Mama Jo's niece and nephew, and were faithfully accounted for in her daily prayers. She worried about them when she wasn't worrying about Uncle Jim or the rest of us. I was especially glad that Ted was coming, since being surrounded by sisters wasn't the best thing. George, of course, kept me from going loony, but he and I were shadows of one another and having Ted, I thought, would be the same as having an older, wiser brother for both of us.

"I knew it first," said Nellie from the playhouse.

"No you didn't," said Kathleen. "I heard it first."

"I saw it being delivered," said Rose Kate.

Mama Jo was inside of the window now, her large bosoms resting on the wide ledge like dark melons. "You three sound like hens in a henhouse. Next you'll come to pecking."

Three heads peeked out of the playhouse door. "Can we go meet them at the train station, Mama Jo?"

"We'll see. But not if you don't stop that squawking. Mr. Bluestein will think we've made off with his chickens."

Mr. Bluestein wore the hat that he'd had on at the Phoenix, but he didn't look the same as he had at the fight. His apron, as always, was bloodstained; his face relaxed and calm. I wondered if the death of Leonard Jones had made him sad and if he would ever attend a boxing match again.

I cut a trail in the dirt with my knife, connecting the pockmarks left in the middle of the yard from mumblety-peg. The rut formed a meandering stream, a reminder of the river that I would meet on Saturday.

Ted and Pearl's train would chug across the bridge. They would see egrets flying away from creosote hitching posts; then they would watch tugboats push barges upstream. Whirlpools would tumble and swirl and seem innocent. They would look down into the water, but never see the gars.

The Visitors

1914, Jim Flanagan

A wandering German painter came through the Pinch. My sisters, vain as they were, begged Mother and Dad to let them have their portraits painted. They sat individually for the artist, one Mr. Hoffendorfer, who made them pose like statues for hours on end—a sort of purgatory, although Nellie was the only one to complain. They wore white lace dresses for the sittings and, I thought, looked about right for the ordeal. But when Hoffendorfer unveiled the likenesses—if they could be called such—Kathleen and Rose Kate, even Nellie, wore the faces of adult women. This was bad enough, but worse was that only Nellie's face was beautiful. After the awakening, both Rose Kate and Kathleen were sullen, since beautiful was the thing that they had expected to be. The expectation wasn't altogether their fault. Mama Jo had told them often enough that they were "beautiful little ladies" and that they should also "act beautiful." They paid little attention to the "act beautiful."

Mama Jo allowed only Kathleen and Rose Kate to accompany her to the train station when Ted and Pearl came to visit. She told me that she needed to spoil them a bit so they would quit worrying about the future.

I waited on the porch with Nellie, who was already beautiful and in no danger of becoming otherwise. Nellie was charming even as a little girl. She liked following me around and although I didn't admit it at the time, I enjoyed her company. She danced, sang, and was cheerful even on rainy days. I, of course, called her a pest, which was expected of me.

"Pearl and Ted might bring me a present," she said.

"Your birthday's a week away," I told her. "And don't ask. Mama Jo will be mad." I knew that the money for whatever present they might bring would actually come from Uncle Jim's pocket; he had been their sole support since they were small children. Their father, Uncle Tade, whose picture looked exactly like Ted, had died a young man, leaving his wife, Fannie, to raise their two babies alone—the upshot being Uncle Jim's money, which he sent regularly. I wondered if Ted and Pearl knew that the money was more black than green. I hoped Nellie would never get caught in the quandary about the source of Uncle Jim's money, that guilt over it would not infect her, that she would spend it happily on such things as the nickelodeon where the flickering pictures would always get her laughing, the high-spirited sound of it making me and everybody else around her certain that the show was the greatest on earth.

I was reading the book that George had brought on Saturday. I read it out loud to entertain her, but she became bored and went up to Uncle Jim's room, which was forbidden. I think she just wanted to look around while he was gone. Getting the money on Saturdays didn't take long so her curiosity about his room hadn't been satisfied. While there, she climbed up one of the pilasters that supported the mantel. There wasn't much space between the fireplace facing and the column; she got her knee stuck between the two. Uncle Jim was soon to come home, so she began calling me to come and help her.

"Jim . . ." I heard her from the porch, her small voice floating in the air. "Jim . . . Jim . . ."

She didn't holler, because she didn't want Viola to know

that she was in Uncle Jim's sacred place. Viola would tell him.

Since I had never had the courage to snoop in his room, it didn't occur to me that she was in there. Besides, I had always thought that his door was kept locked. It was the sound of the andirons clanging against the marble hearth that led me to her.

The knob turned with a twist of my wrist, the door opening, the hinges groaning with its weight. Her brow was wrinkled in frustration above her green eyes that were the color of Mother's. Her leg was wedged between the walnut column and the green tile facing.

"Hurry up." She was wriggling in desperation, the knee red and swollen. I wasn't mechanically inclined and just aggravated her leg by pushing and pulling it. When George came upstairs and found us, he looked over the situation like a surveyor, his mind working hard under the cap of black curls, his black eyes piercing through the problem to find a solution. He was able to beg a piece of bread and butter from Viola in the kitchen without suspicion. In fact, she was expecting him. He came back upstairs and sacrificed the butter for Nellie's freedom.

While he worked, I glanced at the many books that rested in bookcases flanking Uncle Jim's fireplace. Between some of the books that Mother had borrowed for me—*Oliver Twist*, *Hiawatha*, *Luck of Roaring Camp*—were some that I had not seen before. *Eugenics*, *The Art of Fencing*, and *Leonardo Fibonacci*.

George rotated Nellie's leg, a greased pink pig, ignoring her squeals, knowing the job had to be done and quick. We had heard the car pull up outside. He freed her and I wiped the butter from the pillar with a towel. We ran down to the porch, which was where Mama Jo said we should be waiting.

Ted and Pearl had grown up in St. Louis. We had only seen

them twice before in our lives, Nellie only once. Their father, Uncle Tade, had been shot in a train robbery. I had always assumed that he was the victim of the robbers, but with my new understanding of Uncle Jim's "business," I reconsidered the innocence of his younger brother. I did have enough sense not to ask which side of the law Uncle Tade had stood on.

It took both cars to haul the visitors, their bags, and the family from the train station. Distance got out and opened all of the car doors for the ladies who were riding in Uncle Jim's car. Ted stepped out of Dad's car and swept his arm aside with a flourish as the ladies got out. For a moment I thought he would bow.

He wore a gray pin-striped suit with a pink boutonniere in his lapel. He helped Pearl out of the car. She was dressed in a navy blue traveling suit, her tatted jabot held to her blouse by a cameo.

They had gone to fine schools in St. Louis, Uncle Jim providing the money. Dad said that the finishing school finished off Pearl. She smiled at his joke. She was very fair with the skin that Mother wanted for the girls. She looked like an Easter lily.

They both hugged Nellie, who had "become a person" since they had last seen her. Then they hugged and squeezed George and me when a handshake would have gotten the job done.

Mama Jo was all swelled up with their arrival. She was popping. Under her direction, George and I lugged their bags upstairs. Mama Jo had decided that Pearl would stay in her room, where we lined up the five suitcases she had brought. The amount of clothes that Pearl required most likely kept Uncle Jim fingering his roll.

Mama Jo would sleep in my bed in the hall. Ted's clothes were put in Mama Jo's room also, but he was to sleep on the sun porch with me. That was the plan, although it didn't work out.

With their things successfully stowed, we all sat on the front porch listening to the two of them talk about life in St. Louis. Pearl had become impressed with the German musicales that were held there. Uncle Jim said that the Germans had left Memphis during the fever of 1878. That most of them hadn't had the courage to return. Ted laughed and said that courage was a commodity owned by dead men. He crossed his leg and swung it like Kathleen did. Uncle Jim was watching him.

Mother had planned a party for them. She began telling about the guests who would be coming. Then she asked Ted if he would like to ride down to the Tennessee Brewery with George and me. He seemed glad for an excuse to be done with the ladies although he talked much like they did, his hands keeping time with his voice, his fingers motioning as though he were playing the piano.

Uncle Jim gave Distance the money for the brew. Most of the party guests would drink highballs, but he liked having a variety of booze on hand for such events.

We drove down on Butler Street to the brewery—it was a fortress, foreboding and grave. The low massive arches gave me the feeling that nothing could get in there, and that nothing inside could get out. The building made the beer seem important.

The brewers wore uniforms like the Texas Rangers, the kerchiefs around their necks knotted under metal tie holders. They had on western hats and boots. The owners had big bellies and puffy faces. They were dressed in suits. Every one of them, brewers and owners alike, was neatly groomed—hair, mustache, and beard trimmed and combed.

The brewery was immaculate, the copper boiler shining, the floors spick-and-span, the windows clear glass encased in wooden frames that captured the bright green trees and robin egg sky outside.

Mr. Schorrman and Mr. Blochman were pleasant men who accepted our order for a barrel of beer, saying that Uncle Jim was their best customer. Then they insisted that we view the Mississippi from the brewery's tower on the sixth floor. Ted went up with George and me while Distance paid for the beer. We climbed up the stairs with the aid of bannisters made of wood and decorative wrought iron which matched the columns that supported the interior. We reached the first balcony and looked down on the atrium bathed in sun pouring in from the skylight.

"A great place to play Juliet," said Ted. He clasped his hands, swinging them up to one side of his chest.

> *"Ay, those attires are best, but, gentle nurse,*
> *I pray thee leave me to myself to-night,*
> *For I have need of many orisons*
> *To move the heavens to smile upon my state,*
> *Which, well thou knowest, is cross and full of sin."*

He flapped his eyelashes slowly and swept his hand across his forehead. "From *Romeo and Juliet*, men," he said. "Act four, scene three."

We clapped, which he greatly enjoyed. Mr. Schorrman and Mr. Blochman, plus many of the workers, clapped from below.

There were identical balconies on the third and fourth floors. Ted performed on each one. George and I, as well as the workers on those levels, were his audience as he played Roxanne, then Ophelia. George's face said what I was thinking, that Ted's choices of leading roles were odd, though he seemed natural in each of them, even while wearing a suit. But why not Romeo or Cyrano? When he finished with Ophelia, we all climbed to the tower.

I was not anxious to look at the river, although I will admit that the view was the best in Memphis. And far enough away to forget about the treachery that lay underneath the deceptively innocent body of water, eddying, whirlpooling, rolling, tumbling down to New Orleans.

When we came back down, I rubbed my arms, as the brewery was cold. Mr. Schorrman told us that the walls were eighteen inches thick, which kept the building cool no matter how high the temperature got outside. The temperature control was an important element in brewing. He also said that he was afraid that the prohibition law would close the brewery unless the brew masters could figure out some way to manufacture another product such as "Near Beer." He shook his head when he said this as if "Near Beer" would hardly be worth drinking. "I've experimented with it at home," he said. He straightened his tie. "I lost respect for the N.B. when *it* froze before the *milk* did."

Dad had said that he couldn't imagine Memphis without "Goldcrest," which was the name of Mr. Schorrman's real beer. He had told me that the city dads had asked Mr. Schorrman to quit giving free samples because the frequency of trains stopping in front of the brewery for the refreshment of both passengers and conductors had held up the rail traffic in Memphis like a line of sluggish mules.

Outside, the windows were arches grouped in series which got smaller as they went higher. As we left, the building seemed less like a jail and more like a home, or in Ted's case, a theater. We went on to the Central Cigar and Tobacco Company and bought boxes of Cremo cigars. Ted lit one. He blew smoke as though it were bubbles. Then he said, "No offense to Uncle Jim, men, but I can assure you that these cigars are absolutely horrible." He coughed and stomped his stogy out on the cobblestones before getting in the car.

We dropped George off at his house before arriving home, where everyone was involved in getting ready for the party. My sisters picked four-o'clocks in the side yard. Although they were unreliable as cut flowers, Mother said nothing. She most likely wanted the girls out of the way. She and Pearl were arranging roses in vases in the breakfast room while Mama Jo showed Viola what dishes were for certain foods. Dad was mixing a batch of "Pink Ladies" for the women. When we came in, Ted began arranging the sprigs of mint into bouquets that he set in miniature silver goblets, an unusual job for a man, I thought. I helped Moony with the coasters and ashtrays that he hated polishing.

The beer was delivered in a wagon and placed, with great effort, in a huge washtub in the large closet under the stairs. Moony loaded the tub with block ice, chipping away at it with an ice pick.

Dad let the beer settle awhile, then sampled it to make sure that "it wasn't poisoned." Ted also poured a glass, but didn't drink it. He handed it to me saying, "I never touch anything less than eighty proof."

Dad watched disapprovingly as I took the glass.

"He may as well have a taste," said Ted, who had probably just remembered that I was only thirteen. "After all, it's not poison. You said so yourself, Uncle Nate."

"Just one glass, Jim," said Dad. "The hosts are supposed to stay sober. You have to help with the guests." He smiled his handsome smile. "I'm expecting you to dance with Mrs. Houston."

I gulped half a glass to rid myself of the thought. He knew what I was thinking and clinked his glass against mine. "May nothing so hazardous happen in your lifetime."

Then Ted relented and had a glass himself. "I'll have to taste Mr. Schorrman's pride." He took little sips and mulled over each one.

Mr. Sites finally showed up with the green beans. We heard his wagon pull up in front of the house. Dad motioned Ted and me outside. "It's the best show in town," he said.

We watched from the porch as Mama Jo and Mrs. Morganstern picked over the beans that were, according to Mrs. Morganstern, "barely mature," but Mama Jo said that they were "green enough" for Sunday dinner. Next Mrs. Morganstern inspected the eggs that he had brought, announcing that she found the specks of offal disagreeable, but she bought a dozen anyway. He also had a bushel of early corn, which Mrs. Morganstern referred to as "pig corn." Mama Jo agreed with her description.

Sites seemed anxious to move away from Second and Overton even though his wagon sales kept him alive. The women didn't notice his restlessness and continued clucking like hens.

Sites' helper was named Mose. He held old Lucy's reins tautly, although the ancient ragged horse wasn't about to go anywhere. Mose nodded his head toward the wagon bed and mumbled something unintelligible to Mr. Sites, who understood perfectly.

Sites opened two crates of strawberries, causing the women to swoon. The berries were red and bursting. Mose stared at one of the crates as though his eyes were tied to it.

"I'll take the whole crate," said Mama Jo.

"Which one, Mrs. Culligan?" Mrs. Morganstern wanted to know.

"This one," said Mama Jo, pointing to the one that held rapture for Mose.

"Well, Mrs. Culligan," said Mrs. Morganstern, "it seems that we agree on most everything. I want that one, too."

Mr. Sites wasn't sure how to handle the popularity of the berries. "Well now. This crate belongs to Mose. He grew them in his row."

Sites realized that he was putting a terrible burden on the black man, whose brow had become furrowed. But Mose, who was intent on the sale of his berries, said, "Hafs."

The solution found, Sites removed half of the strawberries from his crate and put them into a bucket, replaced them with half of Mose's, then gently poured the ones in the bucket into Mose's crate. The two women were drooling.

"You do have a way with the berries, Mose," said Mama Jo.

"M'nure," mumbled Mose as Sites handed him his share of the profits.

By this time, Lucy had become accustomed to her parking place and was much like Moggy in his attachment to his special spot on the Morganstern's porch. Lucy refused to move on. Sites yelled and flapped the reins. Still the old horse swished her tail, dreaming in the sunlight, ears shut down against the flies flittering around her head.

Mose picked up a stout piece of cane from the floor of the wagon. I thought he was going to give her a whack, but he merely held it alongside one of the big eyes which wizened with the sight of it, the revelation causing the horse to nicker and pull away from the curb with a start that pitched Sites backwards into a bushel of beans.

Then the band members began trickling in and started setting up in one end of the parlor. They wore uniforms with brass buttons, but not all of them wore the hats that were part of the ensemble. The bass drummer wore a red cap much like my brown one. The alto saxophonist wore a pith helmet. The snare drummer, one of the trombone players, and a trumpet man all wore dark suits and derbies. The man with the violin had on a beret. As we dressed for the party, they started tuning up, tooting and rapping in a cacophony that was rhythmical in spite of the dissonance.

Distance served as chief bartender that night, although he had Moony do most of the work. I also helped them by pouring beer from the tap. Ted hovered over all of us. For a man who hardly drank beer, Ted was meticulous in his instruction of pouring it.

"Jam the handle down quick, Jim." He jerked his hand down hard, making his veins pop out like blue vines. He talked like a teacher. "You must angle the glass to disallow the foam."

I didn't get this. The foam had always seemed the fun part, the whole reason for swigging the stuff.

"Of course, you may get someone in the crowd who likes to blow foam. Someone crude."

But Mother and Dad's friends were not crude. Not even Uncle Jim's men were crude, although they did tell off-color jokes on the porch, but always in low tones out of respect for my sisters and, of course, for my mother. I didn't think Mama Jo would have been all that offended by a dirty joke as long as the Lord's name was not involved.

That night Mama Jo wore a diamond bar pin at the throat of her black dress, the one without cuffs. Mother was beautiful in a red dress. Pearl was late coming downstairs because my sisters were captivated by her and chirped like crickets while she was trying to get ready. When she finally floated down the stairs, she wore an ice-blue dress that shimmered as she walked.

Uncle Jim did not socialize with Mother and Dad's friends. He sat on the porch with several of his men and smoked like a furnace. I asked if I could bring them something. McBlue said that he was hung over from O'Lanahan's wake and that yes, he would like a beer. He wasn't the only one. The requests for brew were constant; Uncle Jim's men never came into the house, which meant that I was kept busy serving them.

Then George arrived. He had on his coat and knickers like me. This would be one of the last times that we would dress this way. Rosie wore a dark red dress that was dull beside Mother's bright one. Her face was bluish.

The Major looked crisp. "Reason enough for a party. Reason enough." He was always ready for one. Accepting a highball, he sipped it, then proposed a toast. "To the race!" He clicked Dad's glass, Dad countering, "To the race!"

That the Major was a traitor took more understanding than

I could find. As I looked at him, my teeth were sliding, the bottoms against the tops. In telling Dad that the Major had bet against him, I would have been forced to admit that I had eavesdropped, the same as Rose Kate. There was no question that she would be forgiven. We didn't always operate under the same set of rules.

"Careful what you eat and drink tonight, Nate," said the Major. "Early call tomorrow."

It was then that I wanted to punch him in the stomach. To shout out loud what I knew. Dad was looking at me hard. "Don't neglect the porch, Jim," he said. "See to Uncle Jim."

Uncle Jim requested "The St. Louis Blues," his voice suggesting that it was his favorite tune.

> *I hate tuh see de evenin' sun go down*
> *I hate tuh see de evenin' sun go down,*
> *Hate tuh see de evenin' sun go down,*
> *Cause my baby he done left dis town.*

The song got the party going. Dancers crowded the living room and parlor while the three Finneys kept us hopping. George and I steadily carried out beer to them and the other men on the porch who had increased in number. We edged through the crowd, threatened by the red-tipped cigarettes, like hot fingers, held by some of the dancers.

> *Feelin' tomorrow like I feel today,*
> *Feelin' tomorrow like I feel today,*
> *I will pack my trunk, make my get-away.*

Rose Kate and Nellie were sitting at the top of the stairs looking down at the party like two eagles on a perch, their toes hooked over the edge of the step, elbows braced on their knees, hands holding up their faces. We looked up at them every time we got the beer.

"Bring us a glass, Jim," said Rose Kate.

"Mama Jo'd be switching you for sure," said George. He'd already had a glass himself.

In fact we both had. At first it was because we had a tendency to overpour and had to sip it down so we could carry it. After awhile, we learned to like it on its own merit.

Ted checked on us more than was necessary. He had consumed a number of his "eighty proofs" and, as a result, had become excitable and bossy.

"George," he said. "Ask the lady in the corner, the one ugly as sin, if she wants a toddy. Jim, pass that tray of chicken livers around." He shuddered when he gave the order. I felt a special kinship with him over the hatred for liver.

Kathleen's time of greeting the guests was over, but she wore ambition along with her pink satin dress. Ted noticed it and invited her to dance. This, I felt, was a kindness that she would not receive often in life.

George and I got casual in attitude and began feeling sorry for Rose Kate and Nellie in their nightgowns, watching from their bird's view, tapping time with their toes. Viola had said that "Chiwrens love beer," so we poured them both a glass of it. I left a lot of foam on Nellie's because I thought she'd like it. They both stuck their noses in the fluff, drank some of it, then licked their lips. Nellie sipped hers, but Rose Kate began to guzzle. Both girls soon wanted more. Their wanting more didn't surprise me.

Ted escorted Kathleen back to the stairs. "I bid you goodnight, my dear lady." He bowed deeply. He was performing again, our house the stage.

Then he walked up the stairs and invited both Nellie and Rose Kate to dance with him at the same time on the landing. I guessed that he didn't want to play favorites by picking one to go first. The violinist was playing a solo. A waltz. Ted twirled the girls in and out as though he were doing a rope trick using their arms as the ropes, their nightgowns swirling, them giggling. When the song ended, he saw them back to their places on the top step. As he bowed, he made them curtsy, counseling that they needed more practice in the art.

"Ted," said Rose Kate. "Sit next to us at the race tomorrow."

"I accept, my dear little lady. With great pleasure."

Then he bounced down the stairs, melding into the crowd, looking for a larger audience. Nellie had held off a burp until he got out of earshot. Then she belched loudly, which disgusted Kathleen—that is, until she found out that they had drunk something that she had not been offered. Not to be outdone, she stuck out her curved hand for a glass of it. We had to give her one to keep her quiet.

George watched his mother; she was tippling the "Pink Ladies," but on this night he wasn't worried about her. He was weaving and said that he sure could stand another beer, using the accent of the Finney brothers. We both started laughing which suddenly became uncontrollable. My ribs were hurting from the vibration. Then I remembered the men on the porch who were probably dry. The day I'd fought Shanley I became a member of their squadron, and now needed to supply the ammunition. George and I carried two trays of glasses out the door, spilling only a little of the warm foam. The music kept us moving. We walked in time to the beat.

People in the neighborhood were sitting on their porches listening to the music, except for the Jewish people, who were observing the Sabbath. I wondered if the noise disturbed the Morgansterns. Moggy was out there alone on the porch. Now and then, he would howl like a trombone.

> St. Louis woman with her diamond rings
> Pulls dat man roun' by her apron strings.
> 'Twon't for powder and for store-bought hair
> De man I love would not gone nowhere.

Uncle Jim and the men seemed oblivious of the music in spite of their requests for it. They were, as always, entrenched in discussions about Mr. Crump, the worth of a good cigar, and the fight game. They didn't mention Leonard Jones or his brother, Joe, but I was certain that Joe would never box again.

The girls were finally sent to bed when Mother noticed Nellie soundly sleeping on the top step. Dad carried her. At the same time, he shooed Kathleen and Rose Kate, hurrying them along, singing "Buffalo Gal" in his melodic voice.

While Pearl was flirting with one of the young men, Ted was busy being the life of the party. The more he drank, the more lively his arms, the more exaggerated his walk. Pearl cautioned him to slow down on his "eighty proofs."

Mrs. Houston, I am sorry to say, came to the party. She wore a dress that was black taffeta which made an annoying sound when she walked. I avoided speaking to her. I think Mother was sorry that she had invited Mrs. Houston.

"Why, Clare," she said. "Is that a new ring?" Mrs. Houston was referring to Mother's big diamond.

"My engagement ring," said Mother.

"It certainly has *grown*," said Mrs. Houston.

Mother flicked her finger. The diamond caught the rainbow of colors worn by the guests dancing around them. She motioned Mrs. Houston toward the dining room crowded with guests who were eating shells stuffed with cream cheese, tiny cream puffs, little cookies with icing, cashew nuts, and rare roast beef piled on Viola's small rolls.

Dad came up behind Mother, caught her waist and danced her around the room to the tune of "St. Louis Blues." Dad was one of the few men at the party who could dance the tango, the newest rage. Following his lead, Mother smiled at his skill and held her head high. Holding her in his arms, smiling widely, he was clearly having a ball.

My beer hauls became less frequent as Uncle Jim's men gradually filed away from the porch and went on. Uncle Jim and Distance left in the car. Uncle Jim stayed out late almost every night. He had not even sampled the food.

The guests, stuffed and happy for the most part, began leaving on unsure legs. The Major was on the porch steps calling for George. He had already put Rosie in the car. She passed out on the horn, a blaring siren that ruined the band's last tune. Dad patted the Major on the back and tried to ease the situation. "I've heard enough music for one night, Major, but Rosie is one mean trumpet player."

The Major threw up his hands and gave a half-smile, his expression that of a stalwart. "Let's get your mother home, George."

George made his way across the porch, his face white as a ghost. He had upchucked in the bathroom, but the Major was not wise to him. After the heaving, George had warned me to stay out of the beer or get sick like him. But I kept on sipping.

When most of the guests had gone, Dad noticed that Ted was missing. Pearl was leaving with some of the young people. They were dropping in on another party. She told Dad not to worry. "He sometimes disappears. But he always comes back."

I slept on the sleeping porch that night. The house was quiet, the only sound the deep restful breathing of people who had enjoyed themselves. I wasn't one of them. My sleep was fitful, the beer inside me rolling like the river.

Finally I slid into sleep. This must have lasted awhile, because when Nellie shook me, I was startled, or I should admit, scared. I had been in the dream of gray streets again, the apprehension of meeting the dead holding me as before.

"Snakes," she said.

"What are you talking about?" I yawned when I saw who it was. "Go back to bed . . . snakes. You're just dreaming like me."

"You're dreaming about snakes?"

"No," I said. "Snakes would be better."

"Mine's not a dream. They are in my room. Dad won't wake up and kill them."

"There's no such thing as snakes in our house, Nellie," I said. "You're just imagining things. Like when you play with your dolls."

I got up and walked her to the bedroom. Mama Jo was sleeping on her back in my bed in the hall, her lips sputtering peacefully.

The girls—dead lumps in the feather bed—were, in truth, passed out. Nellie had tried to wake them, but she said they wouldn't budge. Kathleen's arm dangled down the side of the bed like a broken tree limb. Rose Kate lay on her back with her mouth open as if she would sing.

Nellie pointed to the bookshelf. It was low and wide; among the books and figurines were many dolls—one of them, wearing a little straw hat and a plaid dress, looked like Nellie going to a party. She kept her finger aimed toward the shelf without saying anything. Even in the dim light from the hall, I could see her eyes big with fear. I turned on the lamp to show her that nothing was there, except her cherished things. Her face relaxed for a moment, but then she remembered and covered her eyes.

She was crying. "There *are* snakes on the ceiling," she said. "They're just invisible now."

In spite of my concern, the light, faint as it was, hurt my eyes. "There's nothing bad in here, Nellie," I told her. "You just had a bad dream." I was feeling none too good and was anxious for her to quit seeing the snakes. "Go on to sleep."

From the foot of the bed, she crawled through the space between Rose Kate and Kathleen, got under the sheet, raised the covers over her head, then pulled them back down just below her eyes so that she could see me. "If they come back, will you kill them?"

"Sure," I promised in a slur. I was just sober enough to know I was still drunk.

Her eyes were shut tight as I turned off the light. I stumbled back to the sun porch, fell in bed, my body light and floating, my ears ringing. I couldn't go back to sleep. My stomach was turning flips, my head whirling. I could see colors flashing in the dark—streaks of red, bursts of yellow, glares of white.

In between the fireworks, I could hear Nellie's feet again padding the floor. My head was twirling like a top when she tugged at my sleeve. There were two of her standing beside my bed.

I walked her back to her room, carefully placing one foot in front of the other. Getting up with her the time before seemed to have increased my intoxication. The hall was waving. "Were the snakes big?"

Nellie's fingers trembled as they came together, her small arms forming a circle out in front of her, indicating the thickness of the serpents. She did not say a word. She stared at the shelf, then looked up at the molding around the high ceiling, turning slowly, showing me that the snakes surrounded the room. Her cat green eyes watched the fearful night things. They were lying up there in control of her. She looked down at the bed and whispered that the small ones were crawling on Kathleen's feet. I reached to touch a foot and bring her dream to an end. She called out, her voice a quick strike in the darkness.

"Auh. You killed them." She shuddered, but her voice was gaining confidence.

Then I understood the mission and set about killing the rest of the serpents. I took her pillow and threw it up at the molding.

"You got him!" Then she pointed to the window ledge. "Get that one!" She was emphatic about this particular viper. It must have been the most menacing. I took the umbrella, which was propped in the corner and stabbed at the ledge like a fencer. Then I sat on the bed bouncing on each place where she saw a snake. Caught up in the execution, I waited for her to point to the next victim. I became swelled up with my ability. When she ran out of snakes on the bed, I made her look under it. She was losing fear and became bossy.

"Kill the one inside." She was pointing toward the armoire, holding her arm straight as an arrow, her fingernail the little sharp tip of it.

I hurriedly took care of the mammoth things that only Nellie could see, thrusting the umbrella at pythons, pounding my fist into anacondas, stomping my foot on the heads of moccasins. Everywhere she pointed, I disengaged the serpentine enemies, then charged to the bathroom where my own demons were heaved into the john.

The purging left my stomach flattened to the backbone. I stood up slowly, head swimming, urgently needing to leave the bathroom, since my presence in it would interrupt Uncle Jim's routine. He would soon be home. But two of me looked out from the mirror. I was spinning. I sat back down there on the floor, hugging the commode for a long time before I tried walking again.

When that happened, I looked in on Nellie before going downstairs to find some ice. Nellie smiled and yawned, a princess put to rest. The stairs squeaked in the darkness as I made my way to the parlor, guided by a small lamp left burning near the clock in the entry hall. It gonged three times as I reached the bar and stuck my hand down in the ice bucket for the cold prize. I put it in my mouth, letting it roll over my tongue, the melting cold trickling down my dry throat. I drank the icy water from the bucket.

My teeth were crushing a cube, the little hail-like pieces falling into the lower crevices of my mouth, when I heard Pearl and a young man coming up the porch steps laughing. Then I was the eavesdropper. A spy.

"I hope you're not in too much trouble with your old uncle," the young man said.

"He didn't like our running out of gas in the first place," she said. "But going into his old saloon burned him up. I didn't know he could move so fast. He flew to the door when he saw us coming."

"No place for a lady, Pearl. I shouldn't have let you go in with me."

I saw their shadows move close together in the oval glass. Their arms were around each other. He held the back of her head, stroking her long hair, which affected me like the snake song at the peep show. Then I knocked over a glass—the sound of the crash a ringing that interrupted Pearl's love life. She came inside quietly and quickly crept up the stairs. Not wanting her to know I had been watching, I stayed still in the darkness of the bar for a long time and waited for her to get to bed. I stood there missing my pillow in the quiet.

Just as I was going toward the stairs, I heard a car stop. I was forced back into the parlor and to the safety of the bar, where I could see my own silvery black silhouette in the mirror. The thump of Uncle Jim's cane stopped when he got to the porch. I listened for the click of the brass doorknob; the only sound came from the runners of the rocking chair.

His presence on the porch, I thought, was for the benefit of Pearl. It turned out that I was wrong, as I was often wrong about many things. He was there for Ted.

Soon another car stopped and I moved to the window. With the glare from the arc lamp through the pattern of lace curtains, the night seemed frosted. In the darkness, the street was a different place with a time all its own. The black taxi eased up to the curb, Ted getting out, attempting to pay the driver, the driver refusing the money.

Uncle Jim had moved to the south part of the porch where I could see him. He held up his hand to the taxi driver, who got out.

"Wait there," he said to the driver.

"Still up, Uncle Jim?" Ted tried to focus. His tie was askew, his shirttail rumpled.

"Pack up, Ted," said Uncle Jim. "Bill will drive you to the station." He flipped his stogy into the street where it humped over the cobblestones, the fire glowing and shooting sparks as it rolled.

"Don't wake up Jo."

"But I'm to leave next week, Uncle Jim." Ted was in a stupor. He hadn't yet figured things out.

"You're leaving when I say you're leaving." Uncle Jim jabbed at the night air with his cane. "Now."

The taxi driver was unhappy with his passenger. "Do I have to take him, Mr. Jim?"

"I want him gone, Bill."

"Okay, Mr. Jim," he said. "Whatever you say."

"Uncle Jim, what's wrong?" The whiskey made Ted ask the question, but I thought that he knew the score—that he was being culled from the barrel, like a bad apple.

I wanted to hear the reason, but it never came. Uncle Jim said to him, "You're no son of your father. No nephew of mine."

Fire and Water

1914, *Jim Flanagan*

The day started like a strange tune with no words. Nothing was said about Ted. George never asked me about what had happened, although he must have wondered where Ted was. Most likely his lack of curiosity was due to his condition, which was the same as my own. He refused all offers of food, his face the color of clabber, his eyes begging to shut. After getting a load of him, I avoided the mirror altogether.

Mama Jo was like a clock that had stopped. She and Pearl sat holding hands on the porch for a long time. Mother stayed busy doing things that she hated. She sewed up the holes in Dad's bathing suit while he was touching his toes, stretching, limbering up.

Rose Kate pulled me aside and begged to know about Ted. From whispers in the kitchen, she had learned that Uncle Jim had told him to leave. I lied, not only because the darkness of what I suspected was unmentionable, but also because I would have been forced to admit that what I knew was learned from an invasion of Uncle Jim's privacy, though I had not listened intentionally.

She accepted my claim of ignorance with skepticism. She felt that Uncle Jim's dismissal of Ted was a cruelty. Building on this, she decided that Dad should bring him back, inform-

219

ing Uncle Jim that guests, especially cousins, should be treated with consideration and respect.

The veins in my head were pounding. She had somehow escaped punishment, and was focused on Ted and on the race that she knew our father would win.

As it turned out, the Major, George, and myself were marked for the skiff. Distance had excused himself. "Mr. Jim can't spare me."

Moony laughed at this. "The race'd be over before Mr. Jim even get up. Seems he had to works late running a queen out of town."

"That mouth of yours ought to be put in the jailhouse. Lock up yo' tongue." Distance's forehead spoke a language of frowns. Moony saw the ridges and quit pushing, but Distance wanted to make sure his words stuck. He reached inside Moony's white coat and popped his red galusses, making the sound of a slingshot. "See that yo lid *stays* shut, boy." Distance only called him "boy" when things got out of hand.

But Moony wasn't disturbed. Uncle Jim had given him some of his old suits. Moony had auctioned them off on Beale Street, claiming that they had belonged to a "czar" and held special protection from evil. The curved backs of the suits undoubtedly sagged on men with normal posture, but his sales were brisk. With the revenue, Moony had paid a tailor to make his white sharkskin suit with the ivory buttons. I wondered if his Carrie had noticed the ensemble.

With half of us assembled on the front porch and ready to leave, Uncle Jim, wearing his brown fleece bathrobe, came out and tapped the concrete, nodding toward the Major. "Make it two hundred," he said.

"A bit steep, isn't it?" replied the Major.

"The stakes are higher now. Take it or leave it."

They, of course, were unaware that I knew that the Major had wagered against Dad. But when I saw Dad's expression, I knew that they had underestimated his insight.

He stared at the Major. "I understand that reprisals from the Smiddy boys are often more swift than the current of the river. They don't like it when their man loses."

The Major leaned on one leg, uncomfortable, not willing to question the turn in conversation.

Uncle Jim examined their faces. "The Smiddys be damned. No match for the Finneys."

"I seem to remember someone near and dear to you that isn't around to enjoy spring, or any other season," said Dad.

"You can't live in a Goddamned box."

"No. And neither can my Jim." He was standing very tall, speaking as clearly as I'd ever heard him. Mama Jo and Pearl had stopped talking and were looking at him.

Uncle Jim looked at me, then turned and went back inside, his bedroom slippers shuffling for traction on the waxed floor.

When Mother and the girls joined us, we filled up two cars and drove toward the Beale Street landing. Distance drove Pearl and the girls. They had been instructed not to ask her about Ted. The request, I felt, was beyond them.

The Major, having brushed off the possibility that Dad was aware of his faithlessness, did most of the talking in our car. He gave Dad advice about the race as though he were a past champion. He spoke of the velocity of the waves, the pull of the undercurrent, its speed.

"Major, you should have a go at it next year—when we swim upstream." Mother smiled at Dad when he said this. She held his hand.

The Major grew quiet and concentrated on his driving.

We parked and boarded the excursion steamer. It was dressed up with pennants and American flags that flapped loudly.

The band wore red uniforms with gold braid. All members had matching hats. They were polished and spit-shined like soldiers. With their leader, Herr Gruber, standing straight as the teeth of a comb, I knew that would be no solos as there had been with the black musicians at our party. He had led every parade that I'd ever seen down Main Street, the eyes of his musicians keen on watching his directions. Since there wasn't any music appropriate for swimming, the band played marches. Ordinarily, the music would have inspired me, but today I could not wait for it to stop. George covered his ears.

The skiffs had already been loaded onto the big boat. There were three stacks of them on the deck. Each of the seventeen swimmers had to be followed by at least two men in a skiff. Doc's rule.

I had learned to swim at the Linden Natatorium. Swimming was fine as long as I could see the bottom and what was on it. My mind was much like Nellie's when I could not. It was easy to imagine large coiled river creatures napping on the soft mud bottom of the Mississippi River.

The steamer moved upstream, the river brown and running. George and I sat on a bench and held our heads as the boat, with its whistle shouting, plowed against the water's strength, turning it up, kicking it out. Once they got accustomed to the churning waters, Mother, Pearl, and the girls got caught up in the excitement. Before this happened, Kathleen skipped up to mother with the news.

"Mother!" She was tensed up with the telling. "Rose Kate said 'My G . . . !'"

"Well, dear. That's all right."

"But Mother! She said, 'My *G*!'"

Mother was trying to watch for Island 10, but she was patient as always. "Kathleen, a lot of the young people say gee whiz and all. It is slang, but it won't hurt to say it occasionally."

"No, Mother. I mean she said the *real* 'My G!'"

"Dear, whether it was the real G or the wrong G, it really doesn't matter." Mother was peering across the water and never did catch on that Rose Kate had taken the Lord's name in vain. Kathleen, unwilling to commit a mortal sin by repeating it, retreated in frustration.

Dad was looking down into the water. "I feel like diving very deep to see how long I could stay under," he said. The words were chilling. They came inside of me, filling up the empty pit of my stomach with a cold knot.

The Major ordered George and me to find paddles. He had already inspected the skiffs, picking out one that had recently been caulked. We hung our jackets on knobs, then rolled up our sleeves. The Major had already taken off his coat, but his white straw hat hugged his head, his hair curling around its border. The hat had a green band that matched his bow tie. His sleeves were rolled evenly as though he had measured them.

The steamer pulled up to Island 10, the gangplank eased to the ground. The boats were carried down it, shoved into the water, and lined up for the race.

The swimmers were stretching on the sandy beach, touching their toes, bending over side to side from the waist, reaching out in front with their hands cupped in the swimming position. The bathing trunks were mostly made of knitted material colored in striped bands; one of the competitors wore red, white, and blue. Dad wore solid black.

Doc Hollie stood on a chair so the swimmers could see the crimson band of his hat. He teetered back and forth as the chair legs weaseled into the sand, finally settling under his weight. He wore a stiff white shirt with a polka dot tie that matched the purple suspenders holding his pants to his wiry frame. Doc called the roll of his entrants, checking off the names as the men said, "Here," pausing after each one, which gave the crowd a chance to clap.

The Major led George and me to our skiff. Had I not been hung over, fear would have eaten me alive. As it was, I kept my mind on simple things like walking and talking.

"I'll do the steering," said Major Mahon stoutly. "You two will supply the power. Two steam engines. That's you."

George's face blanched. In the transparency of flesh, I could see blue lines traveling across his cheeks. When the Major gave us the word, George croaked a cough that sounded like an engine giving up for dead.

The Major took the stern position, putting George in the bow. He motioned me to push off. George watched me. He looked grateful for the precious few minutes left to him before he had to join the navy. He cradled the paddle as though it were a baby, rocking it gently.

I was able to stand up on shore, but the push was something that sent me close to my own end. My legs waffled in the sand. I was shoving the boat at the same time that my shoes sank into the gumbo. I held onto the splintered gunwale while my body stretched outward from the point of my anchored feet. The river wanted the boat; I was the rope holding it to the shoreline, the current a medieval rack pulling me from fingertips to toes. The Major finally grabbed my hands, jerking hard, but my shoes stayed bogged in the gumbo. With great effort on his part, George leaned over, caught my pants, and pulled one leg free. Then I was able to get the other one out and clambered over the side. My shoes were great boots of mud. I dangled them in the water one at a time trying to dissolve the brown casts that were hardening like plaster of paris. Finally, I took them off, a struggle in itself.

The Major tried to straighten the course of the boat. Doc was calling for the start.

"Why the hell does your dad have to swim in this damn race?" George whispered. These were the first words he had uttered in over an hour. Since he never cussed at all, I figured that the devil was knocking at his door, which had been damaged in the flood of beer.

Trying to rest up after the launching, I could barely answer him. "The Lord only knows," I finally said. The temptation to uncover the Major's deceit rose in me, but telling George would serve no good purpose.

"Carry on, boys." The Major had his hands full of the river. "Man your stations."

The cold water had at least made me feel alive again. I slapped my paddle in the river, splashing water on George to help him get over his misery, but he only managed a weak smile.

Doc waved his hat, a crimson blur, and we both had to set aside all personal problems. Dad was in the water with the others; the race was on.

At first, we paddled only enough to keep the course while the swimmers got out ahead. The river gave their natural abilities a push, carrying them quickly past us. Then the brigade of boats maneuvered to follow and possibly to rescue the swimmers.

Steering us into a position within ten feet of Dad, the Major kept his eyes on his charge at all times while barking orders to George and myself. He had a way of inflecting his speech which made us speed up or slow down. His voice was a throttle. "Hey up!"

I looked over my shoulder and saw the excursion boat easing away from the shore, but I couldn't take time to look for Mother and the girls because of the Major's orders.

"Pace it up on the starboard," he yelled. That was me letting down on the job. I began counting "two and a" after each of George's strokes which were "one and a." He was working the bow. I was in the middle.

The back of George's neck had come to life. It was bright red. I could feel the pulse in my own neck, an unwanted reminder of the constant work that would make up the day's naval exercise. The current helped us, but I wanted to invent another word for paddling. The word sounded fun; it wasn't. Grinding was the word I would have picked.

The Major steered well, but he was also dead weight. He was a true leader. He did as little as possible.

Once George and I got in rhythm, my stomach and head quickly learned when to expect relief. I cruised on the first beat, surged on the second. I watched Dad's arms come up, out, down, and back. His was four-four time, so I started counting this way.

"Two and a," I said.

"One and a," stroked George.

"Three and a," I pulled.

"Four and a," he joined. He caught on without my having to waste words.

"Pull port," called the Major.

With this command, George had to take "four and a" as well as "one and a."

Dad was swimming strongly, breathing easily, his kick barely rippling the water. There were three swimmers ahead of him as the steamer tooted twice, the signal for two miles. Following closely, each boat was in the same stage of the race as the swimmer it guarded. We caught the spirit of the race, which had to do with heart; it was definitely not stomach or head. We wanted Dad to win.

"Port and starboard together." Dad was pulling away from us. "Hey up! Pull one. Pull two. Pull three. Pull four." The Major kept a different tempo. His was *allegro*, a term I remembered from Nellie's music book when I sat on the piano bench watching her play. George and I pulled together to the beat, our arms aching, bodies straining. We were horses running without oats or water. The emptiness was settling in on me. But Dad was depending on us. I pulled. George pulled.

Five toots. Five miles. We could see the Frisco Bridge and in the distance, it looked small. Dad was still ahead of us. He was no longer gaining, but he held his own, his stroke strong and steady. We were allowed to go back to our regular pace. *Moderato.* "One and a," groaned George.

226

One powerful stroke at a time, Dad was pulling into second place. I looked back at the steamer, wondering if Mother could see him. I knew she would be proud.

"Heads up, Jim!" called the Major. My curiosity had made us list to starboard. I pulled one. Pulled two. George breathed hard on my pulls as well as his own—as though he were helping me. I thought as how he shouldn't waste his strength.

Eight miles. Dad was swimming past Mud Island when he gained the lead. *Accelerando.* He had gone past McGowen who was the odds-on favorite, George and I cheering from the pits of our ravaged stomachs. "Uncle Nate, go it!" George yelled.

Dad's kick became stronger, his feet sending steady brown beats that foamed and bubbled as he crawled like an Australian through the old man river rushing past the city.

George looked back at us. "Pull together. He's leaving us behind!"

"I'm giving the orders," said the Major. "Pull together, men. Keep it steady!" It was then that he joined the hands on the lower deck. "Pull one. Pull two." I had no time to sort things out. I only knew that his was a spirit with grit and that he was keeping ours going, money or no money.

He was pulling on one side, then the other. *Allegro con brio.* George and I called on muscles we didn't have to keep up with him. We were following Dad closely when McGowen started gaining on him. "Get him, gar!" I hollered. I hoped no gar was near, but if there was one, McGowen seemed the best meal. He was young. Not tough meat like Dad.

Dad was breathing on the starboard side and saw McGowen slide by. Dad kept his pace for a few minutes, then sprinted several knots, but McGowen spurted out for a lead of three body lengths. *Presto.*

The Major railed at him, "Push forth, Nate!" He himself was oaring so hard that I was afraid we would soon clip Dad's toes. But then Dad slowed down—*poco a poco*—and seemed to just die in the water.

The Major muttered "Harumph" and slacked off the pace. "What's up, Nate?" he called.

Dad waved, then disappeared under the water. *Misterioso.* My eyes dug into the brown hole where he went. I stared, not wanting to lose the place. "He's there!" I yelled.

The Major turned the skiff to the starboard and we all pulled hard. "Pull it! Pull it! Pull it!" We were on top of the hole when the Major dove into the water. I jumped in after him.

"Jim, hold onto the boat," yelled George. The Major had forgotten to take off his shoes. He was struggling in the water. I reached toward his hand, afraid that he would be carried off, but he pulled off his shoes and dove under. I was swimming toward him when he came up gasping. "No, Jim," he hollered. "Stay with the boat." He went under again.

As I got back to the boat and held on to it, I felt something clamp my foot, my heart beating out of time as I jerked my legs like a jumping jack. Hand over hand, I ran the gunwale, my feet running under the water. It caught me again, clawing my ankle, my head going down in the darkest brown, my arms fighting to rise above the graveyard of gars.

I came to the surface like a water spout. He was there beside me.

He laughed in the face of my drowning. It was a joke. "Where's the Major?" he asked.

George was shouting. I was jabbing my finger. "Under," I said. "Looking for you."

Just then the Major came to the surface red faced and panting. His hair hung in neat wet rows. "Nate." He was barely able to speak, his voice a gargle of water. "What happened?"

"I saw that I couldn't win. I had to dive." His face showed that he was sorry for shoving us into panic. "I had to do it. I don't know why."

Even the slowest of the swimmers was now well past us and kicking hard toward the bridge, throwing small wakes.

The two men held on to opposite sides of the skiff as George helped me in. Then we held the balance as they rolled over the sides.

"I could eat bear," said Dad. I didn't think much of his choice of food nor of his cheerfulness, and neither did George or the Major. But at least the worst had not happened. We paddled in silence toward the bridge where we would surrender the skiff. Dad had given up, a thing that he had counseled me never to do.

We drove the short distance home without talking much. Mother tried to smooth things over, but time was Dad's only ally. The Major said that river races were for fish. He had scuttled his shoes in the Mississippi and was barefoot, a disparate picture both funny and sad.

At home, Rose Kate refused to speak and ran straight to her room, in spite of Mother's counsel that sometimes people we love disappoint us, but we don't love them less because of it. Viola said, "I do believe you boys are peaked." Moony was in the corner of the kitchen grinning at the results of the previous night's inebriation. He was talking with his eyes, the same as fingers pointing. When I offered to square the bet, he said he'd rather I'd keep it for him to "draws" on.

Distance came in for his coffee, looked at us, then shook his head. "Viola, looks as if these boys could stand a dose of Mr. Jim's medicine." Distance had told me never to take up "coke," but he hadn't said anything about the effects of beer. I wished he'd been more thorough with his advice.

When Uncle Jim came down and handed the Major an envelope, he refused it, requesting that he give it instead to Mama Jo. "A true penance on my part," he said, and went to the parlor for a rest. Dad sat alone in the living room.

Viola didn't give us medicine, but she did fry some potatoes. She salted them heavily. We both felt better after eating and went up to get ourselves ready for the Confirmation.

In a way, I had already become a soldier for the Lord on Palm Sunday of this same year even though the Confirmation wasn't official. Father Pat had called me out of a sound sleep early that morning as he always did when one of the altar boys feigned illness. Living close to Saint Brigid's, I was an easy touch. This time it had been Mingo Campdonico pretending mumps. I'd gotten on down there and was bundling the palms in the vestibule—Mingo always layed out when there was work to be done—when Monkey Angelo, the Pinch idiot, snuck up from behind and coldcocked me over the head with his bat. The rumor about Irishmen being hardheaded must have been true, because I sustained the blow and still had strength enough to wrestle him for the palms. I didn't really win the wrestling match—he was scared off by the sound of Monsignor's footsteps—but I did prevent him from stealing all of them. He only made off with one armful. But his desire for the palms was so intense, his smile over his small pilferage so wide as he limped away, that I wished I had just given them to him.

George and I had gotten sunburned on the river, which made us look healthy, but this was like women putting rouge over sickly white complexions. Tiredness was our shroud that no one could see. We did feel somewhat better after the food; the energy from it would get us through the Confirmation, after which we would die in bed, buried under cool sheets. That's what we thought, although things turned out somewhat different. For my own part, the strangeness of my father's behavior had as much to do with my exhaustion as Friday night's dissipation.

We looked handsome—or so everybody told us—in the new white suits. The long pants went a long way toward making me feel up to receiving the sacrament of Confirmation. As we marched down the aisle, I wondered if Uncle Jim would come to the church. Of course, he would not.

Bishop Mahoney was an elegant shepherd though somewhat squat. The wearing of the hat, I thought, must have been tricky; it was so tall that a tilt of it would have toppled him over. His tall staff was walnut rubbed to a fine finish, although it was not as beautiful as Uncle Jim's old shillelagh that was kept propped against the hall tree. He didn't use it anymore, opting instead for the more modern cane, but Mama Jo kept it there, saying that it was a sign of his honor and strength, that it had seen war and that it deserved its special place.

The choir sang "Panis Angelicus" and I became lost in the wonder of the Latin words. The hymn bore me up from the fraudulent body, moving its buried spirit to the surface of my skin where I could feel it. I was ready for the Lord's army and stood straight in my place in line while the Bishop solemnly, slowly pronounced the words over us while chucking our shoulders with his staff. At the same time, our sponsors clasped our shoulders to show the solidarity of the religion. In my case, the Major had turned out to be a fine choice. He had acted as a hero.

When the ceremony was over, we marched out of Saint Brigid's as the choir sang "Ave Maria." Mother was sitting in our pew with her hands crossed in her lap. The veil over her face stopped just below her chin. Rosie and Pearl were on either side of her. I wondered what Mother thought about Dad's performance. I loved them both, but his behavior on this day was a clot that blocked my admiration for him then, although I never uttered the word coward to a living soul.

Viola had punch made when we got home. We ate cookies and cakes and small sandwiches. Mr. Wang, one of Uncle Jim's tenants, brought sacks of fireworks which gave us another jolt of strength just as we started to fade. Uncle Jim said that George and I would be in charge of the fire show.

The girls had on their white lace dresses with white shoes and stockings. Each sister had a different color ribbon in her hair—Kathleen's was pink, Rose Kate's blue, Nellie's green. They had all complained about one thing or another all day long. Nellie's stomach. Rose Kate's and Kathleen's heads. Although their cheeks had changed from rose to lily white, not even Viola suspected them of quaffing the brew, but all three of them suddenly felt better when the sparklers were revealed. They were set for the dazzle.

The noise of the fireworks made me jump even when I was the one lighting the fuse. George's neck would jerk when he lit one. "I feel like a gunner in a firing squad," he said. But we both became somewhat proud and slightly cocky when some of the kids in the neighborhood gathered on porches and all along the sidewalks to watch. Having an audience shot some spirit into us.

We had set off about half of the firecrackers when two Jewish boys across the street started fighting. This didn't strike me as unusual, but Mama Jo said that they shouldn't be boxing on their holy day. Uncle Jim, who paid little attention to holy days, took notice of the two when he saw that one of them had a stick, the other one only a wad of paper. He was standing on the porch with Mama Jo and leaned over to speak to her. She then stepped quickly into the house and out again carrying his shillelagh, which she gave to him. Motioning me over, he handed me his weapon, and pointed toward the warring Jews. "Even it up," he ordered.

I walked over and gave the Irish club to little Marty Bluestein, who, needless to say, had a field day battering Justin Schwartz, who had been whopping him with the stick.

We were all watching the match when Rose Kate started hollering. Her sparkler, which she had lit without permission, was blazing in the grayness of evening. It showered down, burning her hand that she was waving frantically. The sparks leaped toward her dress, catching fire to her wide lace collar. I heard the crash of dishes and a rush of footsteps pounding the porch. Everyone was yelling as Viola threw the table-cloth over the railing. But Uncle Jim was beside Rose Kate. He had smothered the fire with his coat. Mother wrapped her in the cloth and held her as Dad ran inside to call Dr. Brennan.

Rose Kate was badly burned on the neck, her lace collar shreds of black. Nellie and Kathleen were both crying. I forced my own welling down into my chest because although Rose Kate's eyes were hurting, she never shed one tear. She held enough courage for all of us.

My eyes then fixed on Uncle Jim's gun in his shoulder hol-ster as he retrieved his coat. Viola was behind me. It was she who had yanked the cloth from the breakfast room table, send-ing the American flags crashing to the floor. She had sprinted outside to smother the fire that Uncle Jim had somehow got-ten to first. She looked at me intently with her big black eyes, but said in her everyday voice, "Don't you worry none about that gun."

The Czar

1914, *Jim Flanagan*

Sunday morning, I overheard my father. "Uncle Jim's name is on the editorial page again. This time they're calling him a 'Czar of the Underworld.'"

"I'm thankful that you never went in with him, Nate. There wouldn't be time enough left for the prayers needed to save more than one. I'm just praying that I can live long enough to fill the Lord's requirement for my brother," said Mama Jo. "He'll ride out the storm."

"I hope so, Mama," said my mother. "But Uncle Jim's problems are growing. Nate and I feel that Jim should board with the Jesuits. The girls will be all right here. They're young enough that we can protect them. But Jim needs to grow up away from this publicity."

"Don't worry, Mama Jo," Dad said, "the Jesuits will make him a 'Soldier of the Lord' as you would say."

I could imagine Mama Jo crossing herself even though I couldn't see her from my place in the hall.

"He'll be in the Lord's hands, then," she said. "Is the school very far?"

"In Kansas . . . Saint Mary's, Kansas. He'll ride the train."

That night Uncle Jim was arrested. Officers O'Leary and Nash came to the door looking timid. "Sorry, Mr. Jim," said Nash. "Orders from City Hall. They've raided one of your places on Fourth."

"Sons of bitches."

I could see Uncle Jim take his hat from the hall tree. Distance helped him with his coat.

"Go with him, Distance," said Dad. "I'll be right behind you. I'll get the Major. We'll straighten this thing out."

Go *now*, Dad, I wanted to yell. Don't let him go *alone*. The door shut as I heard him phoning the Major. It seemed then that when Dad should have been driver, he chose to park the car or let someone else take the wheel. The ticks on the old clock pricked my ears as I crouched behind the curve in the bannister. Mother and Mama Jo stayed upstairs. I could hear them whispering while the backs of my thighs grew to the backs of my calves. My arms held my legs together like partners, but somehow I wasn't sure the parts belonged together. I was an owl guarding an old tree. Late in the night, my eyes wide open and staring, I heard Uncle Jim's cane strike each step. At the count of nine, I straightened my legs numb with sleep and moved through the dark to the bed in the hall. I slept under it.

For the next few days, Uncle Jim held strategy sessions on the porch with his lieutenants. In a cloud of cigar smoke, they traded words for hours. Mother and Dad went about their normal duties. They avoided the porch. Mama Jo went to Saint Brigid's.

During these days, I considered the many things I had learned that I hadn't wanted to know. And I thought about the Confirmation and about the Jesuits. I would soon be packing the trunk for Saint Mary's in Kansas. I was supposed to carry the family faith like Mama Jo, but wondered if I would be able. I held less resentment for my sisters and their spying and eavesdropping. I understood that it was just their way of looking up to me. But even more, I knew that I was the only one of them to understand that although the house looked the same, it was not.

PART III

PART III

The Garden

1921, *Clare Flanagan*

I remember the year that Jim left for Kansas. It was in the fall of 1914. Mama was wearing her white dress. I do not know whether Jim sensed that the dress was an omen or if he just didn't like seeing her in white. He told her how pretty she looked, then asked that when he came home again, would she please wear the black one.

Mama was dying even then. Jim said his good-byes without knowing of her illness. After rubbing his head and wrapping her big arms around his shoulders, she let go of him and stood on the porch, watching as he walked toward the car where Nate and the girls and I were waiting. His forehead was moist under the heavy blanket of afternoon air, the last dog day of his summer in the South that year, but it was neither heat nor humidity that caused Nate and I to send him away. We considered Jim the standard-bearer for the family and for the Catholic faith that was still less than acceptable in the South and we wanted him prepared to defend it. He got into the car and waved to Mama. Her lips stayed closed, but curved into a faint smile. The little dent above the bridge of her nose seemed to connect the dark circles of her deeply set eyes as if she were wearing glasses, although Mama had perfect vision. She did not want to ride to the train station. She knew there would be tears. And she did not want sadness to send him away. Seeing her standing there, a plump angel in white, I suddenly missed her. It was as if I were going. "Jim," I said. "Go and hug your Mama Jo one more time. It will be a long while before you see her again." He ran up the steps, threw his arms around her, and nuzzled her round face.

She had been saving the white dress for the time when she would be reunited with Captain Culligan. Nate would ask her what she planned to do with my father, John Slattery, and with Mr. Whitaker, when she got to heaven. She would look bewildered at the thought of meeting the three of them at once. "The Lord takes care of such things," she would whisper. "You can be sure of it."

Now and then, she would fuss over the dress, threatening to put it on whenever we teased her about wearing black, but she never did until the day that Jim was leaving.

Uncle Jim watched from upstairs, his breath a patch of fog on the window. Jim saw him as he climbed back into the car. He hesitated, then waved awkwardly and muttered, "Goodbye." Uncle Jim nodded and closed the curtains. Jim looked much the way that Uncle Jim had looked as a young man. And I hoped, in spite of the reputation, that Jim had inherited Uncle Jim's integrity and stamina, though some would disdain such aspirations. Mama had said that Uncle Jim's business was religion to him and that he followed the rules faithfully even if they "were of his own making." He would gain no eternal reward for such a "religion," but inside I knew that he had sacrificed himself for the safety and comfort of Mama and me and that he had wanted the best for Rosie and for all of the children, especially Jim. He had done it the only way he knew how.

Mama struggled to live, even though Heaven was her aim. She felt that as long as she was on earth, she could save Uncle Jim from the devil. At the same time, she was distressed over the prospect of the demise of Uncle Jim's tenure as chieftain in North Memphis. His position was just as important to her as life itself. If I had to comment, I would say that Mama ate from both cakes. She wanted the legacy to go on, probably because she remembered the bad times in her own youth and didn't want any of us to have them. She understood little of her own illness, only that it grew inside her. But she was not bitter for any of it.

The newspaper had seemed heavy in my hand during the days that Jim remained at home, the words in it firebrands that raised blood to my face, the flush of anger and fear worn like a red veil. I wanted him spared from the disgraceful publicity. I was not ungrateful for the many opportunities that Uncle Jim had given me and my family. He was responsible for the happy days. And it was Uncle Jim who paid for my son to be instructed by the Jesuits, a dream long held by Mama and me. But we were climbing to a place in the sun, growing like flowers in the garden. I wanted for us to be roses on deep blue-green stems, long lasting and beautiful. It seems, though, that we were four-o'clocks. We grew hardily, spread, and bloomed a bright red in late afternoon, only to fade in the morning light.

Mama gave me life, but very much more. I mean it is more than just the great mammaries that grant sustenance. She taught me to be a lady. It seems strange that she was able to teach the modes and manners of the day, since she herself had no such exposure. I suppose she was just a keen observer and remembered the essential things until such time that she passed them along to me. She and I then taught these things— posture, grooming, and the like—to the girls. They learned these things and more, for I ran with people of society who had benefited from the most careful teaching of etiquette.

I was able to careen about in this society because of my appearance. Lest it be thought that I am vain, let me remark that I received beauty, not from my bloodline, since neither my father nor my mother had been blessed with it, but rather from the greatest giver of all. So you would call it, if you will, a gift. The society ladies considered me the wild Irish rose who was not only pretty, but also charming. For my own part, I played the role well and it was in this manner that I gained, as I have said, some brief place in the sun. That I was admired was Mama's greatest pleasure. But this was all to come back on me, for I suppose that the use of my gifts was not, after all, pleasing to the one who granted them.

As Viola sometimes said, Mama "was stout," her roundness a pleasant, comfortable kind of warmth. She pulled the children to her and they held on as though she were a great pillow. She herself would have had many children, if "the Lord had seen fit" to give them to her, but He gave them to me instead. She took care of them for me. She was fond of them all, but it was Jim whom she loved best, for he was a "fine lad" as she called him, the son she never had.

Even though Mama had no education, she had more business sense than either Nate or I. After Mama knew that she would not live to see the children to adulthood and not be around to help protect them, she would often tell me, "Clare, don't sign anything," a phrase that would come back to haunt me. She had seen to it that I would inherit all of Uncle Jim's property and most of his money. This may not seem fair, since Rosie, Pearl, and Ted were equally kin to him, but Mama said that she knew I would take care of Rosie. And yes, I told her, I would "always take care of Rosie"—all of the days of my life. Mama said nothing about my responsibility for Pearl or Ted, so I made no prediction in their behalf.

Rosie carried a stigma known to neither Merlin nor George, nor to my own children. Rosie's mother, Katherine Canaan, had held a romance in the shadows. She never said the name of her lover and not even Uncle Jim, with all of his contacts, lieutenants, and watchdogs, had ever been able to find him out. Rosie was born from the unholy union. Mama always felt that Rosie's trouble with alcohol was the sign of the devil's presence and that he could come and go in Rosie as he pleased. I was the only one who knew the reason that Rosie drank, a secret I never divulged and will not now.

What Mama never knew, and I am grateful for it, was that the devil repeated his angry work in our fairest flower. If the malignant thing had not killed Mama, the words that told us of Nellie's sin would have. That Mama died well in advance of Nellie's disgrace was my greatest blessing.

As I have said, the newspapers were full of political warring that came from three directions: Mr. Crump, Chief of Police Mayo, and Uncle Jim, who seemed for the reporters a symbol of all that was wrong in Memphis.

The stories centered around Chief Mayo, who had once been Uncle Jim's ally. Nate said that Chief Mayo had a kiss-and-tell sort of life as witnessed by the stories. He did not want me to read any of it, afraid that such things would fade my beauty. His intuition was well perceived. I certainly began to feel less than lovely as time went on, though I think the fading was due to the constant pounding of my heart.

Some of the stories were about the raids on Uncle Jim's establishments, which took place just before elections in order to satisfy the reformers and church people. Great crowds gathered to watch these raiding squads vainly trying to hammer their way through the brick walls of the Monarch. Once the election was over the "lid was lifted," to use Uncle Jim's words, and people went back to doing whatever they did in the Blue Goose and in the other places that he owned. Nate would read the paper and remark that things were "hot for the underworld" and that the progressives and the reformers were gaining momentum. He talked of it as though it were something that affected the rest of the people and not us. Even though he had predicted the raids, he seemed surprised when they occurred. I don't think that Nate saw things as they really were, until it was too late for him.

Mayo constantly gave orders to the police to strike out for the enforcement of the law. But the reporters said that the public should watch him closely, because old political enemies might attempt to trouble him. I wasn't sure if they meant Mr. Crump or Uncle Jim or both. Then Chief Mayo charged that before the 1909 election Mr. Crump, posing as a reformer, ordered the gamblers to shut down, but after he won and the wheels of his machine began to turn smoothly, the gamblers were soon in full swing again.

Words of Uncle Jim's business dealings had been written in the paper before, but always in the form of innuendos or hints. Now he was subjected to a galling fire because the chief of police, I believe, was filled with all sorts of venom for him. I myself felt the hot flames.

While the news centered on Crump, Mayo, and Uncle Jim, I felt that my family and I were also watched and whispered about. My posture improved at this time, the rigid upright position a model of carriage and poise. I attended all events as usual and spoke not a word of the trouble that was knocking on my door.

According to the papers, the canvassing of Uncle Jim's Front Street property resulted in closed saloons, the quash of gambling, and an end to ballot stuffing, but Nate said that the campaign only encouraged the bootleggers. Uncle Jim plodded along as always and said nothing about his success or lack of it. But each time his name appeared in the paper, Mama grew a little worse.

Mayo was claiming that Crump had wanted to get rid of him after the first election because he knew too much. He also charged that the gang—meaning Uncle Jim and his men —had started a propaganda of lies against him which had finally resulted in his quitting as police chief. When he rejoined the department this year, Mayo said that the gang chancery court to have him ousted. He charged that Uncle Jim was financing the trial in order to get rid of him.

It appeared that Mayo was wedged between right and wrong, but it seemed to me that any sinning that had taken place had been done by all three men, but to what degree I would not conjure a guess. I only knew that my family and I would pay the price.

At least Jim was spared the humiliation that would have come to him had he remained in Memphis. The Jesuit mold would right any stigmas attached to him. I always looked forward to his letters, but the frequency of them left me thinking that he was homesick.

I saved his letters.

We do have a good time when Mr. James O'Sullivan comes to visit—he's "an old St. Mary's boy." That only happens every two to three months, but I will tell you what it is like when he comes.

He brings prizes for the students and sets up games in order to win them. The prizes are things like box hockey sticks, baseball gloves, and kites, which are great on the Kansas plains, since there are no trees to catch them. Sometimes the prize is money. The best of the games is the Jackrabbit Hunt. There are hundreds of them on the plains with few places to hide. The trick is getting the greatest number, since all hunters are equally hungry for the prize.

On Friday, Mr. O'Sullivan drove up in his chauffeured limousine loaded with fresh fruit for the priests. Needless to say, his presence sent a wave of excitement over the school as soon as the word got out. The recess bell brought all of us to our feet as though we had heard the cry of fire. We ran to the dining hall where Mr. O'Sullivan announced the plans for the hunt. It was to begin after the hours of study were over.

My friend James Gutherie and I formed a partnership for this event and, I thought, would win, since he runs as fast as any rabbit and I am not far behind him. (By the way, his legs are wiry and slightly bowed like some of the famous track men and I think he might one day be an Olympian.)

Outside the main walls of the campus, the land rolls and the trees shade much of the grass, except for the athletic fields. Farther still lie the plains where the aforementioned Jackrabbit Hunt takes place.

James Gutherie, as I have said, was my partner and we raced on out to the plains sure that we would be champions and win the prize which on this occasion was ten dollars, an extravagant sum you will agree. We already had the money divided and spent.

We both had burlap knapsacks with drawstrings that Mr. O'Sullivan had provided. There were about fifty of us boys out there, each group hurrying along so as to beat the vesper bell that would signal the end of the hunt.

Each boy had a big stick. In case you think us cruel, I guess we were so. However, the plan was just to stun them as usual. Once they recover from the whack, they just sit quiet while we add more rabbits to the sack. You will be glad to know that after the hunt's over, we set them free. This part is almost as much fun as winning a prize. When the sacks are opened, each rabbit leaps out like a jack-in-the-box, hops over his fellow rabbits kangaroo-style and the derby is on. Father O'Connor, the track coach, wants them for the hurdles. But what happened on Friday made every boy in the school hot. Except the one who did it, of course. But let me explain.

We were all out there on the plains beating the wire grass around the holes with our sticks. It was a rabbit day, warm and sunny. But after we had been out there for forty-five minutes and time was running out, not one rabbit was sighted. It was strange, you see, because rabbit holes dot the plains like air holes in bread and are as common here as the rats in the Gayoso Bayou. It was as though a piper had called them all away. When it became obvious no game was to be gotten, we began to discuss this in groups. Not even the smartest guy, Stuart Holbrook, could figure the lack of long ears, fuzzy tails, and thumping feet.

Finally the gong of the big bell called us back to the church steps where the prizes would be awarded. We walked to the grove of trees, crossed the creek where we skate in winter, shuffled down the path toward Sleepy Hollow where we kicked up the dust that chased out backs, then swarmed under the arch toward the church. (Seeing how many can get through at once is one of our pastimes.) After the rush, we began walking slowly since it had finally dawned on us that we had nothing to show for our efforts and no reason to tax ourselves.

Then the unexpected happened. There on the steps of the church, beside Mr. O'Sullivan, Father Morgan, Father Donahy, and Father Charles O'Brien, was Fuzzy Coony, his six croaker sacks jumping off the ground like Mexican jumping beans.

Seeing that there was no competition, Mr. O'Sullivan looked puzzled as did the priests and all of us boys. Mr. O'Sullivan had always enjoyed the count and seemed disappointed at the lack of ingenuity by those of us who were empty-handed. Fuzzy Coony, on the other hand, had a smirk on his face a mile wide. When Mr. O'Sullivan handed him the ten spot, the smirk broke open to a smile that showed his big buck teeth. The worst of it was when our patron handed him the second prize, which was five dollars, then the third, which was two-fifty. We were every one of us rocking with unrest, while trying to maintain the look of sportsmanship—hardly possible with Coony as winner. He'd brag about it forever.

Not one person asked him how he'd gotten the rabbits, because no one wanted to listen to the long-winded way he would tell it. Two days passed before the truth jumped out. James Gutherie was running on the plains when he discovered the pen that Coony had built to house the rabbits. He'd been feeding them carrots and lettuce that he'd stolen from the dining hall. He had taken a lucky guess as to when Mr. O'Sullivan would show up. Coony had cornered the market on rabbits and was living the high life to prove it. His greed was somewhat understandable, but the fact that he'd piled on the second as well as the third prize grated on the nerves of us who had come up short. Coony knew that we would never rat on him—code of honor—but fear of a solid thrashing kept him doling out the money to us for as long as it lasted.

Well, I will close for now and try to concentrate on Alexander the Great who, I'm afraid, bores me stiff.

Your son,
Jim

Mama's pain became great; she did try for so very long to keep it under the covers and away from the girls. But finally, the suffering broke down her resistance and the screams were part of every night on Second Street. Monsignor Canfield came to pray with her every day now.

There was much concern in the neighborhood. Mrs. Hogan and Mrs. McGillicuddy brought pie and cake that Mama could not eat. Mr. Bluestein sent chicken soup. And from Mama's window, I often saw Mrs. Morganstern standing on her porch, her hands clasped and resting on her stomach, old Moggy sagging behind her, their eyes looking up toward me. She would see me, then fold her hands and nod.

Uncle Jim would sit outside her door then. He would offer not one word. Uncle Jim wasn't nearly as old as he looked, although people, especially Jim and the girls, thought him ancient even when he was still fairly young, because of his carriage or, I should say, the lack of it. But now he was more stooped than usual as though he were bearing the burden of her pain. But it was Nate who was most affected by her illness. Her cries were almost unbearable to him. He would pace the floor in the dining room, going round and round the long table. Then, without saying anything, he would walk out the door and stay away for hours. I think now that it would have been better for him to have taken his leave until Mama passed away. He stayed, but his presence was not a comfort. I knew that his was a nightmare that did not end at dawn.

His behavior hinted what was to come, but I was tied to Mama's bed and had little time to worry over him and no understanding.

Something dormant awakened and slowly grew to fill him. During these days he began drinking at hours that he would never have approved of in the past. The drinking was not for the sociability, but for the effect. He was never without the smell of whiskey on his breath, although I rarely saw him swallow it. What had been a festivity, a party, became the thing that governed him, his habit well established when Nellie's sin came into our lives, whiskey the friend sitting beside him, brooding with him, when he could bear no other. When he did talk aloud, whiskey led the conversation. It had become so much a part of him that I believe he was trying to get into the bottle itself.

But he was always loving to me and I knew that I would have to keep the strength of him in the eyes of the girls. If I said something often enough, then it might become true. At first the words were hard to come by, for I had learned that he was not strong or brave. But later, with the repeated use of "Lionhearted" . . . "Stout fellow" . . . "Firm" . . . the words became comfortable in my mind and voiced with ease, a conscionable habit that grew in its very impetuosity and appeal so that I myself believed him brave.

When the girls worried over him, especially Rose Kate, I would remind them of those days when life was a crackling fire—like Christmas Eve when their father would shut himself away in the parlor to decorate the spruce tree, carefully hanging each glass ball, each piece of glistening gold tinsel, the cascades of red and green garlands, while they impatiently threaded popcorn on a long green string in the breakfast room with Mama and me, and lastly Jim carrying it in to him while we waited . . . so that when he opened the doors inviting us all to "behold the miracle of the tree" with their own white offerings spiraling from the full-skirted bottom, around the girth, then upward, a trail that ended at the foot of the angel with the golden wings and hair, how their eyes, like shining stars, would light up the night. And as we watched the magnificence of the tree, the candle flames steadily burning on the mantle, the gas lights a smoky glow, we sang out "Silent Night" and "Adeste Fidelis" as directed by his long graceful arms while Nellie played the piano.

I kept these memories alive while Mama shrank in size and spirit until she prayed for the Lord to take her. I shared her wish. I did not want her to suffer anymore, although I knew that I would be quite alone in the world without her. I would have my children to love, but no one to share in the responsibility. I clung to the sadness of it as though it were a thing alive, the thing inside me that I loved most. To let go of it would be to let go of her.

In the months of her suffering, I did not let Jim know. I sometimes wondered if sparing him was a shield against honesty. But that, I knew, was not my virtue. Besides, Mama did not want him to know—I kept faith with her wishes and satisfied my own as well.

Nate called Saint Mary's when Mama was on her deathbed, his voice wavering so that I wondered how the message was delivered. Father Morgan arranged for the train to wait in Topeka for Jim, who was then out on the field for spring football practice. Father Morgan called Jim out of the game and told him about Mama's illness. Jim raced to the showers, washed quickly, threw some clothes in his bag, and drove the twenty-six miles to Topeka with Father Morgan, who broke the speed limit while reciting his prayers aloud.

While Jim was making the long journey home, Ted came back to Memphis for a brief stay. He had written to me that Mama meant as much to him as his own mother and he wanted to see her in her bad times. He was handsome in the uniform.

His visit brought a touch of happiness into the house. Kathleen quizzed Ted about Pearl and her social life in St. Louis. He assured Kathleen that Pearl had danced the soles off of dozens of shoes, but that she still hadn't found the right arms to spend her life in. This did not surprise me for I knew that Uncle Jim had constantly sent her money for dresses and I understood her desire to appear in each one for all to see.

Kathleen was charmed by the stories about Pearl and her suitors, but not so much with the thought of it all ending in marriage. She herself was then thirteen and waiting for her own social life to begin.

Rose Kate, always the militant, followed Ted around. She admired the army uniform and wondered aloud if he would fight with Teddy Roosevelt, who had asked President Woodrow Wilson for permission to equip and train men for the fight with the Germans. Ted said, "No, Wilson won't allow Roosevelt the right to lead the lambs to slaughter. He'll pick a less colorful shepherd."

Rose Kate ignored the prediction and continued to support the spirit of fighting for the honor and glory of America, which amused Ted. "Rose Kate, you can take my place."

Uncle Jim had said that Ted was not a man. But Ted never flinched or showed weakness in the face of Mama's illness. He was holding her hand when she died. He folded the covers neatly below her chin and smoothed the hair away from her face. Knowing that he was not welcome in Uncle Jim's house, he left thereafter and began his search for adventure, and for life.

But while Ted was with us, Nellie, who was still only a child, listened to the fabulous accounts of his social whirl while dreaming of her own dance. Her dreams and her girlhood would both come to an abrupt end when the woman in her emerged sooner than expected. But it was I who would allow Nellie the freedom to sin. A few years later, when she had grown quite lovely, she would tag after Jim, Kathleen, and Rose Kate, who attended the many dances, because it was I who wished for her to be displayed for all to see—for her beauty was so great, greater than my own. It was my wish that Nellie live out my life—for I knew, even then, that I held the same malignancy as Mama.

I made Uncle Jim recite the Confiteor on his deathbed, but it was I who needed to confess.

Mr. Jim

1921, *Viola Jones*

They needn't have worried over Mr. Jim's gun. I told them, "Mr. Jim couldn't hit nothin' if'n he tried." He were old now, you see. It weren't like that when the man were young, I can tell you. But these days, the man were just wore out. He done everything for the family, you see. And him always hurting so.

Then after Miz Jo passed, it were like he were set free. He got on that train and headed for Miss Ola. Bound for glory, he were. He weren't planning no trip back, I can tell you. I know about it because he bought me a little house just before he left. It were Mr. O'Lanahan's little house. I weren't to say nothin' about it or the train ride. I'm good at sayin' nothin', but Moony ain't got this here kind of zip on the lip, so he's the one spread all about Mr. Jim going on the train with all his money in a bag. I wouldn't have told nobody nothin' about no train ride excepting for Moony having told it anyhow. Distance, he knowed about it, but he's got the ways known to me. Distance and me, we the only two what knowed about Mr. Jim giving most of his money to Miss Ola. Mr. Jim did save a good bit of it for Miz Clare and some for Miz Rosie. If he'd of known about how things came to be with Miz Clare, he would have saved more. But he did not know.

Distance got Mr. Jim's car of which he were mighty proud, it being black and shiny and all. Moony were sent by Mr. Jim's instruction to work over at the Monarch as the manager of the whole place. Moony seem some taller since being the manager.

But I can now say about all this dying. Once it got started, it weren't no time until all of the main folks done passed. Miz Jo, of course, she were first to go. Then Mr. Jim got real sick in New Orleans. Miss Ola sent word on back to Memphis—I sure she the one who sent the words telling about him coming on back this way. A telegram with no name. Not even an X. Miz Clare didn't know nothin' about Miss Ola, but Mr. Merlin, he knew. Miz Clare, she thought it were the conductor man what sent the telegram and then done started Mr. Jim coming on back home. But it were Miss Ola what got Mr. Jim put back on the train. Mr. Jim, you see, wanted Dr. Brennan to look him over. Didn't want no strange doctor seein' to him. Can't say as I blame him for that. Them Witch Doctors down in Louisiana is liable to do mischief to a body. But weren't nothin' Dr. Brennan could do to save Mr. Jim. Wore out is what he were.

I wanted so to sing at Mr. Jim's day. I'm not big and stout as some singers in my church—although the Lord God knows I've tried to get that a way—but even without the stoutness I can get higher than most. Lena Goody claims she weighs in at 207 pounds. Done weighed herself on the scale at Mr. Slocum's feed store. She can get high as a tree and low as its roots, but I can equal out to her highs. I just can't get down so far as she can. She sounds like she down in the cellar. But Mr. Jim didn't have no regular day like Miz Jo did. The singing in that church on Miz Jo's day was frightening, I'm here to tell you. I had no understandin' of them words. Not the slightest. Not wanting none, either. It were like they was arousing up the devil so creepy it were, and so sad. But Mr. Jim's day, it were just a bit of praying in the house. Miz Clare were most sorrowful about this. But this here Monsignor wouldn't let Miz Clare bring Mr. Jim into the church for no funeral. She being the one to make Mr. Jim say he were sorry just before he died, she were mighty outdone about his not going into church for his day. I don't think he really were sorry, mind you. But then again, I don't think he had all that much to be sorrowful about. He just liked "colored ways" as he sometimes would say. But the way folks acted, it's a wonder they let Mr. Jim lie in the dirt at that burial ground called Calvary. But they done it, thank Jesus. The jest of it were that they didn't put no headstone on Mr. Jim. But I marked it with this heah cobblestone from the driveway that were a-loose. Distance, he drove me out to the burial ground, and I placed it right over Mr. Jim. I scratched his name on it as best as I could:

MISTER JIM

The big men in town, they went in and out of the house that day. I can tell you that they liked drinking Mr. Jim's bourbon. They were all them politicians and such. The colored folks came all around the house also. Distance, he made sure that they all got cigars just the way Mr. Jim would have wanted.

Then Mr. Jack Shanley come into the house—nobody thought to stop him. He done come into the parlor and everybody got real quiet. Mr. Shanley looked at Mr. Jim real close. Put his face right down into Mr. Jim's. He seemed sad and glad about Mr. Jim all at the same time. Whilst Mr. Shanley was busy staring at Mr. Jim, Miz Rosie nearly burned a hole in him with her eyes. He must of felt the heat, 'cause he turned around and looked back at her with his old tired-looking eyes. The eyes must have sent some kind of spell, because Miz Rosie did not drink even one drop that night.

Mr. Nate and Miz Clare and also Miz Rosie and Mr. Merlin tried to open Mr. Jim's safe after he done passed and had been set into the ground. They had quite a time trying to open it.

Had to call a locksmith. I can tell you they were mighty disappointed when that safe were opened. It didn't have quite the money they was expecting. There was a few gold bars and deeds and such. And I knowed where a mess of it were and couldn't say nothin' cause it weren't my place to tell about Miss Ola.

Little Jim he got the farm of Mr. Sites. Now little Jim he's a city boy. And me I can't see him on no farm. Mr. Jim most likely figured little Jim would take up country ways, but generally that don't work out with folks what's been reared up in the city. Miz Rosie's share of the money were attached up somehow with Mr. Merlin. He done stood by Miz Rosie and I guess Mr. Jim done want that he should see a reward for it. Mr. Merlin had stood her from harm for the most part.

Miz Clare she got all his places, but she didn't seem all that happy about it. She didn't say nothin' against them places, but she wasn't dancin' over 'um either.

I guess Mr. Jim thought he'd sent enough to Miss Pearl and Mr. Ted, because he left them nothin'. He didn't cotton much to Mr. Ted and he knew that Miss Pearl were soon to marry a rich man anyhow. Of course, I said nothin' about my little house that Mr. Jim had give me, but Distance he had to show them the paper where Mr. Jim had give him the shiny Ford, 'cause they naturally suspected that it were theirs.

They soon found out that Mr. Jim had drawn all the rest of his money out of the North Memphis Savings and Loan. They were mad with him then. They faces wore fire they did. I myself kept my money under the mattress, but Mr. Jim said it wasn't the best thing. Anyhow, I liked looking at my dollars, but I guess Mr. Jim had so many that he been tired of seeing 'um. They said he done had $150,000. More than a body could count. That's what.

Moony hung around listening, but found out nothing more than he already knowed from Mr. Jim's people. It tickled me to see him so curious. The hair stood up on that boy's arms just like the cats he was so scary of. And all the while, I knowed that Miss Ola got most of Mr. Jim's money and how he would be proud for her to enjoy herself.

Mr. Merlin knowed about Miss Ola, but he had in mind that Mr. Crump had got Mr. Jim's money so's Mr. Jim wouldn't have to go to no jail. I guess he couldn't figure that Mr. Jim would give such a chunk of it to no woman what wasn't his kin people.

Mr. Nate then were just a worrying hisself to death. He wasn't no ordinary worrier. He were just a worrying down in the bones. He would talk so cheery and all, but his face showed what were going on inside of him. That man's eyes weren't hardly even blue no more. The worry ate at him like a little finicky chiwren picking at their food. Then again, he made tracks around the dining room table and just wore out the floor in the parlor. "Mr. Nate," I'd tell him. You must rest easy, now." Then I would try to get him to take a glass of my nerve tonic, but it weren't no use. He were stubborn against it, though he were all too ready to take the devil's drink. All too ready, I can say.

Then it were that Mr. Merlin, the Major they calls him, went on down to New Orleans to see what happened to Mr. Jim's money. He could not find no sign of Miss Ola. He went to the hotel where Mr. Jim were staying, and found out that Mr. Jim done put down a whole year's rent money, so a few of his things was still there. Some of his black suits, a few hats, and a wad of socks. Also, there were this bottle of absinthe. He brought all of these things home.

When Mr. Merlin brought the absinthe in the house, it came to be a bad thing. Mr. Nate—I know because Moony done told me—started to drinkin' that bottle and then got hisself more of it. It were green and smelled of things uncommon. Mr. Nate he were a man happy in happy times. He jest could not take no black clouds.

All this time, little Jim and George was makin' suds in the

kitchen, then keeping the bottles in the basement. All of these things were beginning to get on my nerves and I began thinkin' of the time I would spend all my days in my little house away from all that I were bumping into around me. Working for white folks is often times intolerable at best. They act up in strange ways, I can say.

Then, some later, Miz Clare got to lettin' that little Nellie go round with the older chiwrens. That little gal should of stayed close to her mama's skirts, but Miz Clare had the intention of letting her "go on and be happy." Me, I think Miz Clare knew she herself were not long for this world and were jest dressing Miss Nellie up so she herself could show out.

The Trunk

1921, *Jim Flanagan*

I can still hear the vesper bell telling its story—of a man traveling the cypress swamps, its trees rising from the black water in skirts, him winding in and out of them, losing the map of time to the beggar knees, then finding the compass of the sycamore white against the growing darkness of a winter's sky. I watched Coach Metheny's lips, but heard only the song of ages. Then Father Morgan came out to the football field and told me that Mama Jo was mortally sick. He whispered as though she might live longer if he didn't enunciate.

I raced to the showers, washed quickly, threw some clothes in a bag, and rode toward Topeka in his old black car, holding on to the door that rattled, hoping that the grinding motor with the reputation for contrariness would not give in to its age on this day. Father Morgan was speeding and praying at the same time, his face lined with intensity and smeared with gloom. It was the first time I'd seen him with any expression at all. Mama Jo was dying and it was death that got him creased up around the mouth and crinkled about the eyes. The air blew in the window, his thin brown hair standing away from his head like angel wings.

I shut my eyes for a few minutes, the tiredness not so much from spring football practice as from my turn at watch the night before. John Cleary, who had little if any brains, had

259

drunk a whole bottle of Virginia Dare Hair Tonic, the challenge taken from the product's name. From Cleary's reaction, the alcohol content must have been 80 percent. At first he acted dumb like a clown. He threw cold water on Jim Gutherie in the shower, a stunt that always raised retaliation to high art. He also put water balloons in Fuzzy Coony's bed, which found no objection from any of us on the third floor of the dorm. But later, after he'd fallen asleep for awhile, he woke up with delirium tremens and saw us all as vampires and devils. We had to take turns keeping him quiet so that the prefect of the hall, Mr. Eagle, would not get wise to him.

At the station, I thanked Father Morgan, patted the car, then ran up to the conductor, who was standing outside the engine studying his watch. He looked at me with steel gray eyes that seemed powerful enough to interrupt the magnetic field. I was glad it was not judgment day and happier still that he was not the judge. "I've held up the train for the likes of bean?" His voice was disgust and I was the reason. He took the cap from his pointy head, punching the inside of it until the roundness of the crown was restored. He saw Father Morgan in the distance and tipped it toward him like a cup. To me he snapped, "Go on, take a seat."

In the rush to catch the train, I had not had time to relieve myself, the inside of me now like one of Cleary's water balloons—stretched like skin on a fat man and ready for bursting. I went from car to car searching for the men's lavatory. I located it and gratefully rushed inside. I passed the sinks and tried to turn the knob of the door that led to the stalls, only to find it locked, which is the way it is when the train is in the station and the demand for the bowl a high calling. My need, however, was so great that I unzipped my trousers and let it fly, so to speak, when the station master came in with a rattle of keys in his hand and saw *me*—the one prayed for by Jesuits *who had the power to stop trains*—desecrating the sink. The keys clanged together in his fat fist that waved back and forth like a speeding metronome as the smoke blustered out of his ears.

My haste to get home was needless. Mama Jo died about the time I was passing through Little Rock, Arkansas.

The house was still and lifeless then, the quiet a stuffiness that filled space like spring always does when the sun heats an already warm room before the windows are let up. The clock had not been rewound, but as I reached under it for the brass key, it was Uncle Jim who motioned for me to stop. He gave no explanation, saying only that he wished that I had been born sooner. I understood then that he was quite alone, a fact that had passed by me until that moment when it played like a brass band. I wanted to hear the ticks and gongs of the clock, but the silence went undisturbed. In this way, the pulse of my own life was strong, a thing I did not want to think of or feel, but the perception was one that I would come to know well.

The march of death was on now. It was relentless and swift.

George sat with me in the parlor. Mother's white pearl rosary beads were intertwined in Mama Jo's bony fingers that were folded in a tight pale knot. Her white dress was hideous, the face a thing unknown to me. I had learned duty and patience at Saint Mary's and George still had hold of his. We stayed in the parlor making sure that the strange body was not left alone. An understanding surfaced in both of us at the same time—if we didn't look at each other or speak of it, we wouldn't have to acknowledge the poor thing in the casket.

Later, I went searching for her upstairs as though I were not entirely sure that she was really dead, a feeling gotten from the slightness of the strange form stiff in the box. In her room, the midday sun was alive and lighting the shower of dust that rode the air. I walked through thousands of sparkling dots. It was here that I gave her spirit a good-bye as I touched her

MARGARET SKINNER

missal, her shawl, and the miniatures of her parents, Thomas and Kate, grim in portraiture. The serious faces of the two hardy souls who had dressed in their best black to record the misery of their life together were somehow comical. I laughed then; it was as if she had seen to it that I would find the funny side of things in time to ease the wrenching loneliness that came from knowing that she was gone.

Uncle Jim came up the back stairs, a habit formed in avoidance of Mother's friends, in this case Mrs. Lafferty and Mrs. Dugan visiting with her in the living room. Framed in my door, he was an ancient picture even though he wasn't all that old. He saw my cap on the spread and said, "No hats on the bed," a peculiar law that was his. Mama Jo's straw garden hat was perched on one of the four posters of her bed; I wondered if this counted. His displeasure with stray hats was some sort of superstition that had come over from Ireland with his parents, although it was Mama Jo who had catered to such things.

These were the last words that he spoke to me. He left for New Orleans soon after Mama Jo was buried, but his trip was a long joy ride that began and ended on Second Street. He had heart trouble in New Orleans and came back to Memphis for treatment.

When I picked up my cap, he turned away and left me. Then it was that I saw the picture of Ted smiling from her dresser. It was beside the one of me in the football uniform. We were shoulder to shoulder in our frames, the large *M* on my jersey looking silly beside the army uniform that he wore. I wanted to change my shirt in the picture. His blond handsomeness was large in the frame, his jaw firm, his eyes intelligent. He had found redemption behind the glass.

He would travel to Washington by train, then to France on a troop carrier, fight his way to Château-Thierry and live to tell about it. Upon return, his swagger would be tempered by inward pride, the refinement a maturing of the elegant actor.

262

That Uncle Jim booted Ted out of Memphis and allowed him only a brief stay when Mama Jo was dying was a sore that never would quite heal, although my attention never focused on it for long. There were so many other things festering in the years that followed.

When she found that Uncle Jim was next in line for a visit from the reaper, Mother had placed a single rose in a silver bud vase on his bedside table. She was setting the stage for his confession, a mission that woke her each morning and stayed with her until she slept at night. So far he had stubbornly refused.

He then asked for me. When I entered his room, he knocked over the vase as he reached for his wire reading glasses. I stood at the foot of his walnut bed, the green blanket dark beneath the crocheted spread that Mama Jo had made for him. His pink lips quivered when he opened his black wooden box, his hand feeling around in it, the fingers walking through his papers. The freckles dotting his hand that held the box reminded me that he was once a boy. The creases on his forehead relaxed when he found what he was looking for. He motioned that I was to come forward, then handed me the key, cold in his cold hand. He pointed toward the trunk that sat under the two tall windows, anchoring the bottom of the closed draperies that were billowed out with hot wind, some of its heat escaping from the sides, warming the room. The hand that had drawn me forward told me to leave, then rested on his chest. His eyes were closed, his lips silent and peaceful.

After his death, the sound of Uncle Jim's voice still rang in my head, while his essence, recondite and slippery as moss, stood in the distance. The days of the street wars when he had fought his way up to become a political chieftain, and the rise of Boss Crump who pushed him back down again, were whisperings. When I opened the trunk and read about his life and times in the papers that he left to me, these shadows became images. I pieced these things together in a way that he would have called "motley," but I was named James Canaan Flanagan—the James Canaan in honor of him—and called Jim just as he was; his life was part of mine and so I have tried to understand how he could have been, at the same time, a "Czar of the Underworld," "a black sheep," and "the best of us." While tracing his life and the events in the life of my family—events that led to the destruction of all that I had known—I tried to imagine the younger face of him, that of a ragged boy silently searching for his father in the streets of a city dying of pestilence brought by the *Aedes aegypti*. And I think of him now as I have often thought of him since the day I began searching for my own father.

The Yellow Jack: Jim Canaan

1878

Jim Canaan crawled backwards out of his narrow place in the bed between two older brothers, his hands and knees flattening the straw that poked through holes in the ticking. His rough shirt stuck to his wet chest. His face was warm and tilting toward the hitch in his neck. He got up, and pulling the oilcloth aside, peered out of the window into the grayness. The dark silhouettes of grave diggers carrying shovels over their shoulders filed along Front Street. It was 1878. The Yellow Jack was paring people from Memphis like skins from potatoes.

Tom's arm flopped on the empty space. At seventeen, he was oldest and took up most of the bed. John was sixteen, Jim fifteen. Jim had been awakened from his dream by Tom's snoring, the sleepsong a tune of honks and whistles. The wheezing in John's chest had kept him awake, his sound steady like the complaining axles of the burial wagons that signaled dawn and the seventh day of Jim's search for his old man.

He stepped over his thirteen-year-old brother, Tade, then over his sister Jo, ten, then over Katherine, six—all asleep on the horsehair pallet. He moved quietly toward the door carrying his shoes, not wanting to wake his mother and the baby, Meg. Outside he stretched his neck, pulled on the tight brogans and took to the streets.

.   .   .

In the dream, he rode in a wagon, listing and swaying, Mr. Fowles pulling the reins one way, then the other, weaving the mare between the black ruts and potholes revealed by the full moon following them. Jim remembered the words. "I don't know why you want to move him. He's under that big cottonwood tree. It's as good a place as any when you've passed." Fowles' face was white in the dream light. His teeth were gapped, the sign of a liar.

The sun was a pink glow on the horizon as Jim walked to the house on Jackson Avenue where his search had ended the day before. He walked up the steps to the rotten porch planks and for a moment stood watching a wagon roll past, its wheels bobbling on the cobbles. The horse, a dapple-gray, his mane a tangle of knots, clip-clopped along like the tick of a clock, the driver's head nodding, the lumps under the black muslin cloth in back rising and falling. A straggle of four-o'clocks grew beside the front steps.

Jim had learned not to breathe much in the boarding houses that he searched. He held his breath as he entered the hallway. He walked slowly, knocking softly on each door as he passed, his footsteps loud in the silence. As he listened for an answer, he straightened the crucifix hanging slanted on the yellowed wall; the air hung heavy with the heat of July, but the figure of Jesus was cool. No one came. He knocked on the next door and waited. He felt the quiet surround him.

An old woman creaked a door, her head bending out with suspicion. He could see the whites of her eyes in a squint. Her face was dry with deep wrinkles.

"Would you know Thomas Canaan, ma'am?" Jim asked.

"No, lad. Stay away." Her voice quavered. "You should not be abroad with the sickness . . . we've an old man die in this very house in the night. Before that, it was a young girl . . . a bit younger than yourself. They've all died and gone."

The door opened halfway. She wore an apron soiled and tat-

266

tered. It covered most of her black dress that had a faint purple sheen. A small table and one chair sat in the middle of the room; on it were a stub of candle in a pool of tallow and a black iron pot. The putrefaction of the old boiled cabbage made his head light.

"The Lord is taking those he wants." She shook her head from side to side. "It does seem cruel with the young ones. All the weeping mothers . . . you'd not tarry. You'd be staying home with your own mother, if you still have one."

A rush of hot air brushed his face as the door shut. He steadied his legs and walked down the hall toward the porch. Black dots floated in his eyes as he stepped outside and felt the slap of sun. He tripped, fell, and landed on the boards, his hands catching splinters that stuck up in his skin like a dead forest. He pulled out the biggest ones, ignoring the rest. He smoothed his palms on his shirttail, then stuffed it down into his sweaty brown pants.

Smoke from the torch drifted above him. In the dream voices singing hymns came from distant bonfires that licked the night, the low voices sounding of loss, the emptiness riding with him in the wagon. An owl swept down from the cottonwood. It chased a jackrabbit, caught it, and carried it off.

Jim heard the metronomic booms of the "Little Democrat," a cannon that was fired regularly by Mike Moran, a saloon keeper who thought he could shoot germs. Moran also thought that the smoke might cleanse the poisoned air, but mostly he just hoped to be passed over like the biblical Hebrews, a feeling shared by the group of men who gathered every day to witness the cannonade as if it were a religious rite. In truth, the saloon keeper was like Cuchulain of Merthemne, the legendary warrior who fought the sea—for the emanations of the fever swelled like waves, so thickened and stimulated were they by the cannon's smoke and its noise.

Jim walked along Market Square, stepping over broken glass, the sign of the Mackerels, a gang of marauding thieves who stripped the stores at night. A few were still open, the owners sitting inside with loaded guns. Jim had already searched most of the buildings along Market Street; he nodded to the guns as he passed. He saw himself in the cracked glass of Schuyler's Beer Hall, his blue eyes bright against the forest green reflection of the elms growing in the square. Sprigs of his sandy hair showed between the letters of the sign painted on the glass:

WIENER SCHNITZEL ON THURSDAYS

His father had said that he "wished old man Schuyler were Irish" so he could eat the veal every week, but good as it was, he couldn't stand the German music. "The timing's off, Jim. And worse, the words have the hard edge." Jim thought of Ola. Ola was German.

His old man had looked sick and weak before leaving home, but insisted on helping Father Quinn. The priest had asked the men of Saint Brigid's Church to visit the houses in the parish, to get people who were still healthy to move to the Father Matthew Camp outside the city until the fever left town. The men would repeat Father Quinn's words. "You're crowded up in here," he had said. "You're just keeping the fever in a huddle. Get yourselves out to the camp. Save the children."

People thought the world of Father Quinn, but not so much of their neighbors. They worried over leaving their scant belongings. Most of them had come to America to escape famine in Ireland, but found the Civil War and hard luck instead of food.

Jim's mother and father, Kate and Thomas, had told him how they had trailed behind the Union Army doing odd jobs, getting small portions of food for their labors. At the siege of Memphis, they had quit the army and settled in Happy Hollow under the bluffs where the Wolf River joined the Missis-

sippi. Jim was born in one of the huts held above the muddle of waters by rickety stilts. Chickens, cats, goats, dogs, and rats shared the teeming shanties. When Thomas began to make good wages as a blacksmith, the family had moved up the bluff to a boarding house in Pinch where life was some better, until the town felt the sting of the Yellow Jack.

Jim saw a man sitting on the corner holding his head. His skin was yellow. Tom had said, "Fowles has the ambition to bury one hundred men." Then he had whispered, "It's been said that he sometimes sinks a live one."

No food was coming into the city. Quarantine. The big stone row house, hiding the sun, stood on the corner of North Second Street and Market Square like a giant tombstone. The old man could be lost in there and no one would find him. Jim wished his old man would come out on one of the enclosed porches high above where the ragged wash, in faded reds, blues, and dingy whites, hung stiff and hard like forgotten flags. He wished the old man would wave and say, "I'm fine, Jim. Just stopped over for a snort with O'Lanahan." It would mean he would have been drinking for a long time, so long, in fact, that he would fall. Not even his old man could stay drunk that long without falling.

Ola Hedermann stood in the street. He was surprised to see her there. Most of the Germans had already left. The Irish never knew when to give up. The Germans were smarter. And most of them had more money.

Ola's hair, like thick golden wheat, was tied with a black kerchief. Blue and red figures dancing on the border of her skirt touched the tops of her thick black shoes. She was thin as a willow and graceful. She smiled at him, then looked down at her shoes. He watched her with half-closed eyes as if the seeing might last longer.

She looked up at him; her eyes, like turquoise glass, held him in their blue gaze.

Jim didn't have to ask why she was in the street. He pulled the crust of bread from the pocket of his trousers. He reached for her small hand, placed the bread on her palm, and closed her fingers around it. Her arms came round him, her head against his chest, her hair soft on his mouth. He closed his eyes and reached to touch the hair, but she left him—like his dream at dawn.

He felt the rising in his groin, a welling that made him ease up beside Dromeyer's Grocery. He pressed his backbone against the bricks, feeling the leanness of his body. He was hungry in a way that he had not known before.

He heard the scrape of wheels, shook his head, brushed away his thoughts, and stood up straight. His friend, Pat Ryan, was coming down Market carrying a bundle, trailing behind his mother and father, who struggled with a cart piled high with pots and pans, bed clothes, and chairs. Straw fell out of spaces between the slats. Pat's father was bandylegged and walked with a jig.

"Jim, we're going out to the Father Matthew Camp," hollered Pat Ryan. "Have you found your old man?"

"It'll be Mr. Canaan to you," Mr. Ryan poked in.

"Well, have you?" Pat asked again, setting down the bundle.

"No," said Jim, not wanting to say it. He gathered an armful of straw, stuffing it into the corners of the Ryans' cart. Pieces of straw stuck to his pants.

"I'll help you look for him," said Pat.

"You'll do no such thing," said Mrs. Ryan. Then she looked at Jim with the look that mothers give. "But we'll be praying that you find him, young Jim." She made the sign of the cross with the tip of her walking stick and kept hold of the wagon handle with her other hand.

"And how's your mother?" She remembered to ask.

"She's fine. Just fine, I think."

Mr. Ryan's coat was flecked with the straw; bits of it stuck up on the top of his brown hat as if it were growing there. He swatted a mosquito. "Damn gallinippers," he said. "The lot of you had better be going on out to camp, Jim."

"I have to find my father. And my mother wouldn't leave the potatoes anyway."

"Better to eat gruel than potatoes if it's the Yellow Jack who's coming to supper," said Mrs. Ryan.

She leaned forward, prodding Pat with her walking stick. Jim watched them move down Market. As they turned the corner the pots spilled out, clanging on the warped cypress blocks, a rotted pavement stinking of mule and horse waste and spilled garbage. The Ryans scrambled to pick up their belongings.

Then the week-old anger came again and filled him up. His mother, Kate, would have a pot of potatoes on boil, but he did not think of his own emptiness or Ola's. It was his mother's fault that his father was missing. The old man had sacrificed himself to make up for her lie. He had risked his life to care for the sick, offering his works of mercy to the Lord in the hope that He would forgive the selfishness of his wife.

"No, Father, we've none to spare," she had said.

Jim crossed himself with the shame of it. His mother had lied to Father Quinn, God on earth. She had the spares. She hid them under her bed and behind the coal shuttle. Some of the brown spuds were in her mending basket. They lay quietly under a piece of muslin alongside her small store of thread. She hoarded each one, aware of its dimensions.

His mother had planted potato eyes in February. In spring they had sprouted glory, each leaf promising a yield, but the drought of summer baked the vines brown, leaves curling inward for protection from the hot sun. Kate made her children carry water from the river for the potatoes. Jim, Tom, John, and Tade toted wooden buckets down the bank to the river's edge, raking their backsides on the steep knotty embank-

271

ment. Josephine and Katherine followed them, making it harder to return with the water, since the young sisters needed a push up the bluff.

When they returned with half-filled buckets, Kate would scour them with her eyes. "We'll never have the tates if you lads can't bring up the water." She would take off her apron and tie her coarse brown shoes very tight. "Jo, you'll watch Katherine and the baby until I get back. Keep inside." She would take Tom's bucket from his arm. "Your father will be needing you with the smithing. Go on with you. All of you. I'll be getting your share of the watering done."

Tom was oldest, so any shame for an unfinished labor fell to him. "Yes, ma'am." Tom would not eat much at supper after she stuck him with guilt by bringing twice as much water, hardly spilling a drop.

Not many of her potatoes grew large enough to eat, but still she worried constantly that the other boarders might snatch them while she tended her babies.

Her worry was a waste. She seemed not to notice her husband's pallor nor his "fetid breath," as she might have called it.

In the dream, Fowles pointed a long bony finger toward the underspread of the tree. Cottony lint covered the ground like a spun wool blanket. Jim stood in the cotton. From behind the tree, the blackness of night was eased by the touch of the moon. The trunk bark was gnarled in the torchlight, the leaves a dark lace dress above him.

Jim shoveled slowly, not wanting to disturb the old man. He was scratching the dirt, furrowing the shovelhead along the body, sweat sliding from his brow, dripping from his lobes like water from a spout, mixing with his tears that made mud dots on his old man's shirt. The feet were bare, the toes pointing upward. "You've stolen his shoes. Answer me, then." Anger singed his face and dried up his tears.

Jim imagined his mother peeking under the muslin, counting the potatoes, checking, lining them up, turning them so they would not rot. At the same time, his old man might be bleeding his guts onto a strange bed.

But his father was a blacksmith, one of the strongest men in the Pinch, his muscle swelling each time he raised the hammer to strike the anvil. Surely the man could survive anything.

Jim kept moving along the dark side of a tenement. No smoke came from the chimney. A small heap of ashes smoldered near the street. He stepped over piles of dung, scattering flies from the feast. They buzzed around his head, lighting on the tips of his ears, hitting his nose, flying into his eyelashes. They swarmed like an army over the mounds of garbage that spilled from the alleyway into the street. He swatted the air and slapped at the mosquitoes biting his arms. Gallinippers, he thought. Stinging ghost devils.

In the dream, he was moving his old man out of the fever patch and into the consecrated ground of Calvary Cemetery. Mr. Fowles was holding his dirty hat in front of his nose when Jim uncovered the head. Jim reached for the torch and brought it down into the grave. The firelight shone on the hands, turned upward as if to push away dirt from the face swollen in a scream. Jim crawled out of the grave, his fists balled in dirt. "You've buried a breathing man." Fowles stepped back, pushed by the glare of Jim's eyes. "You've buried him alive!" Jim raised the shovel above his head, the weight of it dragging him forward. He swung at the grave digger's head—cleaved it into a spitting black stream. Fowles sank to the ground, his eyes rolling back into his head, the dirty hat still in his hand.

. . .

Slop thrown from above splattered a yellow-brown wash over Jim's brogans, bits of it clinging to his nubby pants. He looked up to see a fat woman leaning over the upstairs porch railing of a tall brick house. She was holding a bucket. "Hey, watch it there!" he shouted.

"Watch it yourself, you dimwit!" Her heavy legs creaked the boards.

The corpse of a mule lay rotting in the street. Jim stuck his nose down in the front of his shirt, whiffing the small bag of asafetida that his mother had hung round his neck to protect him from the yellow fever. It rid his nostrils of the gangrenous odor, filling him instead with the smell of the noxious herbs. His father had refused to wear the bag she had made for him. "I won't be insulting the saints," he had said. The medals that he wore—Saint Christopher, Saint Joseph, The Blessed Virgin, Saint Patrick, Saint Aloysius—chinked when he walked.

Jim came to the front of the house and stood there. The rails had been stripped from the porch. The door was unhinged and leaned on the porch wall. The fear that had been hiding in the pit of his stomach crept over him like a growing vine. The house was buzzing like the flies. But his father could be waiting—he edged inside, the buzzing loud and constant.

A pattern of cracks spread over the walls like the spider webs hanging from the ceiling, mazes that seemed to move with the sound of the slow dizzying buzz. He was in the parlor, the greeting room. No human stirred on the first floor of the house. The shuffling, murmuring, buzzing, came from upstairs.

He took one step at a time pushing through the stink air that lingered at each step up the winding staircase. He slid his hand along the curved bannister that led to the landing, tightening his grip as went. He could hear a child crying low under the moaning, the sound an evil chorus, a miasma moving above him, coming down on him like a heavy black cloak. The "Dies Irae."

He reached the top and looked to the first door. It was high and heavy, hinting of grace that had long since left the house. He gagged on the stench. He wanted to turn and run, but held on to the railing.

The halls led off of the landing, then splintered into more halls, a labyrinth that confused and terrified him. His old man might be there behind the door carved with cornucopia or inside any one of the other rooms. His heart beat hard in his chest as the quiet footsteps behind him became deliberate.

"Stealing are you? Well, you can have anything you can find. Will a dead body do ya?" She cackled in crazy peals, the loose skin under her chin shaking, her eyes shut to slits. She walked toward him and grabbed his arm before he could wake from the fear. She was a wall of fat, her huge breasts vibrating with her hateful laughter as she shoved him into the room. And in the dim light, he saw rats gnaw the flesh of a face. They shrieked meanly at the intrusion, each clinging to a place on the chest of the body covered in hardened black bile.

His heart pounded like a hammer as he tried to push past the crone, but her big body filled up the doorway. His scream stayed in his throat, a lump of silence that gave him hard courage. He fixed his arms as though carrying a log for ramming and ran toward her, his elbow sticking her middlings where she lay hard down.

"Whah." She tried to roll. "The hell." The rats scampered to meet her as she tried to rise on her round knees.

He ran down the hall past the misery shut behind the doors. She kept shouting at the rats. He got to the front door, knocking it over onto the porch, her sound chasing him into the streets.

"Burning in hell you'll be . . . burning with me!"

275

He choked on his own sobs. It couldn't have been his own father dead in the rat filth. He had wanted to be the one to save the old man, before Tom or John. He ran through the muggy streets, only wanting news that the old man had been found by one of the others, alive. He tried to forget the slick black hair and the tiny cruel eyes of the rat gang.

He ran all the way to the bluff, slid down to the river and jumped in. He cried into the foam, washing himself in the brown water.

He kicked back to the water's edge and crawled on the mud like a snake. He lay there breathing hard, tasting mud. The hot sun beat down on him, his veins pulsing with the heat, his head throbbing. The crow flying above him cawed its knife sound.

His shoes, weighted by the water, sunk into the mud, the water lapping his ankles, dappling his skin through his black stockings. He could feel where the holes were. His hair stuck to his forehead, the clothes to his skin.

"Jim!" He heard the deep voice, the thud of footsteps. He turned his head and wiped mud from his eyes. The figure, dark in the sun streaks, lumbered toward him.

He got to his knees and stood up holding his chest, his heart beating like the old man striking the anvil. Tom's red face looked down on him.

He got hold of Jim's shoulder like a vise. "They've found the old man. He's dead. He took the fever when he was getting the O'Lanahans out to the camp. He was buried under a great tree." Tom bowed his head, unable to speak. He cleared his throat. "Come on now, Jim. Mother's been crazy looking for you. We're going out to the camp."

In silence, Jim and Tom climbed up the bluff and walked toward the boarding house. The cotton was coming down on them, a snowy eulogy floating through the growing darkness. Jim blew the lint from his sleeves.

Kate prepared for camp by storing her potatoes in a knap-sack. She hoarded them as before, keeping them under her skirts by day, sleeping with them at night. The musty smell of dirt stayed round her. Jim toted the sack of potatoes for his mother, but was unable to eat them.

Afterword

1922, *Jim Flanagan*

In 1918, George and I entered Notre Dame. For me, it was more of the Jesuits. The cold winters on the plains of Kansas had prepared me for the ice-covered landscape of South Bend, Indiana, but George entered the frigid region with only a vague understanding of either winter or the Jesuits. He suffered that first year with a string of physical illnesses and from the bone-chilling siege of his spirit, a consequence of higher learning. Books, as well as housing, were in short supply during these days. I made excuses, but George made the best of it. He eventually came to grips with the system and prospered both in Latin and in the study of literature. I stumbled on mathematics, stayed precariously on my feet, and finally found balance, though it was difficult to maintain over the next four years.

Holidays were spent in Memphis, where both of us attended rounds of parties that had begun with the signing of the armistice. It seemed as though the celebrations would never end, that the horrors of war, and the end of it, had increased our appetite for fun. Kathleen and Rose Kate were young ladies about town and, I must admit, had turned out to be quite attractive. Nellie, however, was the most beautiful girl in Memphis. She was enamored with the social scene and begged to be included. In truth, she looked even older than our sisters, although she was only fifteen. Mother and Dad always trusted me to guard my sisters at these functions, but I was busy being the life of the party. Oh, I danced with all of them, knocking off each one like an item on a checklist, but I wish now that I had lived up to the expectations of my parents. Nellie's life might have been altogether different.

I remember the night that Horace Lester first saw her. She was dancing with George, who was rounding out his obligations for the evening. Although the girls were attractive, they were like sisters to him also. He only had eyes for Mary Katherine Lanagan, so he was not sorry when Horace Lester cut in.

"George, it's my turn," said Lester. He slid his arm across Nellie's waist and swept her around the dance floor with the polished steps of a man trained in the art. His style and grace gave notice of how one should look while dancing. I felt inadequate after watching him and did not dance any more that night. She was lovely in his arms; her black hair shone, her green eyes playing with the light. I did not know it then, but as they danced he cast a spell on Nellie that caused her to forget every single thing she'd ever been taught.

Since I have always been a lightweight, my attention turned away from a duty that should have been constant—that being the guarding of my sister—and focused on Mary Leary, who had grown to be not only a saint, but pretty as well.

"Horace was married, Jim," Mary told me. "And divorced. He's the oldest man here."

I was busy watching her eyes—the bluest in the room—and paid little attention to what she was saying.

"I wasn't allowed to go to parties when I was Nellie's age," she persisted. "But she does look much older than fifteen. She looks even older than you." Her lips were full in a sensuous way that she was not, her blond hair like silk touching her shoulders.

I began to look forward to each party with an expectation that had been unknown to me. And to each party I was accompanied by Nellie, Kathleen, and Rose Kate. Kathleen fell in love with a bookworm, which surprised me. She suddenly took an interest in literature and asked all manner of questions, writing down the answers in preparation for the conversations that she planned with John McCrary, the reader.

George, who was usually modest, showed his scholarly bent with a propensity, instructing Kathleen not only in titles and authors, but also in literary terms, in themes, and in the elements of fiction. Kathleen's interest in the writing grew to the extent that she surpassed the bookworm in knowledge and began to find him boring. Her old concentration on manners was replaced by her enchantment with the English language, leading her to Joyce and Yeats and Lawrence in what became her quiet introspection, while I was still stuck on Dickens, Hardy, and other Victorian authors, who gave me no answers when I finally began to ask the questions.

The predicament for George was that while he read of things that led to an examination of life and particularly of religion, conflicts shot through him like arrows—but he never faltered in his loyalty to the Catholic Church even when he felt at odds with it. For him, it was like getting along with an unreasonable sister.

But while George studied God for answers, my mind was on the problems that I could see. One of them was the absinthe that Uncle Jim had sipped in his room at the Monteleone in New Orleans. I have often wished that he had finished it off, and that the Major had not carted it home. But my mother had asked that all of Uncle Jim's belongings that he had left in the hotel be brought to her—thinking that the bundle might contain a clue that could solve the mystery of the missing money. Uncle Jim's bundle held no such promise, just his dirty laundry and the absinthe, which became my father's nemesis. If Dad had a problem before this time, he kept it concealed. Or maybe I had just been too caught up in my own life to see his.

Absinthe was green liqueur containing oils of wormwood, anise, and other aromatics, the flavor reportedly that of bitter licorice. The sale of absinthe was prohibited even before prohibition because its continued use caused nervous derangement. *Artemisia absinthium*, the liquid substance of it was banned even in Turkey. I never tasted the absinthe, but its bitter flavor I know quite well.

My mother continued to dress the girls in the finest clothes money could buy. Mother was ill and walked down the stairs only once a day. Then she would sit in Mama Jo's green leather lounge chair and glow when the girls filed down for inspection.

My father, along with his brothers, had inherited the old saloon of my grandfather Emmett down on Main Street at Calhoun across from the Central Railroad Station. The saloon was a great wooden barn that had served its patrons well. After grandfather's death, my father and my uncles decided to tear down the old barn and, because of increased rail traffic, invest money in a new saloon and restaurant, which they called the Arcade. It was built in the modern Art Deco style. At the root of the enterprise was my mother's property, which she signed as collateral for the loan. Money then became tight in Memphis, as it was all over the country. My mother, the only one with any property, was sued when Dad's brothers could not pay their part. Left holding the bag.

My father was distraught and pleaded with his brothers for help. Rose Kate was with him when he called Uncle Patrick. "You can't get blood out of a turnip," was Uncle Pat's reply. Rose Kate fought to rally Dad's spirit, but as she later told me, "His face wilted. His will just seemed to float away."

His depression grew in length so that when Nellie left the Church proper, I think that the world was really over for him.

My mother was the love of his life, Nellie the brightest off-spring of it. Mother was dying of cancer; Nellie was dead to the Church, excommunicated for marrying a man who had prior commitments. And Dad's financial situation was grim.

George and I cooked beer in the kitchen with the assistance of both Moony and Distance in an attempt to change the atmosphere, an immature reaction vacant of any solid thought. Neither of them liked beer or the making of it, but were anxious to avoid the rest of the house, which had "soured" according to Distance. Viola was less than receptive to our intrusion of her kitchen. She was particularly disgruntled at our using her largest and best pot while the yeast did its work. She did not want anything to do with the project, and made us use the wood stove so that preparation of meals could continue uninterrupted on the gas range, even though no one was eating much. She did, however, help Moony wash the green bottles.

The sugar was expensive and scarce. It seems we were not the only men in town making the brew. We had to visit Walsh's as well as Mr. Bluestein's, MacAlexander's, and Mr. Ching's in order to come up with enough of it.

But nothing we did could lighten the heaviness of gloom that had come into the house. When Nellie ran off and married Horace Lester, the blackest of dreams came true. There was nothing so dark for a Catholic in those days as marrying a divorced person. Nellie was *excommunicatus*, but I felt no less love for her, not yielding to the grief of my parents and my sisters, whose hard slow steps sounded the death sentence, a one-way street for Nellie, an ending that I would not accept. My father shrank under the weight of his despair. For me these rules that the Church had set in stone began crumbling when the reality of life pounded at them.

She was shaking when she told me that she had traveled to Arkansas with Horace and was married to him in Marion by a justice of the peace, a skinny man with bitten nails, who hurried the words as though she were a sheep being herded to the pen.

"Nellie," I said. "Mother and Dad could have the marriage annulled." The look on her face, that of a woman who had accepted the guilt as well as the sentence, shut me up.

I knew then that she was caught in fate, an unforgiving wind that would blow her around in a never-ending circle of events over which she'd have no control.

It was left to me to present these facts to our parents, the prospect of the announcement a cold lump in my throat. But first I told George, thinking that he would know the right thing to say. He reply was, "Say it as quick as you can. And don't say more."

With the news, their faces struck expressions of mourning that would not wear off.

That day George and I spent a lot of time in the basement. The green bottles were kept in the darkest corner, away from the coal chute, the door, the vents, and the window. We worked under the yellow light of a single bulb that hung from a frayed cord. We had made a batch every two weeks and had drunk some of each one, keeping a record of the best results. George was in charge of the formula, making sure that the right amount of yeast was "presented" to each batch. I had told him that he was beginning to sound like Ted. I tried to let this project consume me, the tasting of it medicinal rather than scientific. But the distraction was only a fragment, one that was unable to lighten the weight of time.

Mother wasn't sitting in the parlor as usual when I went to tell her about the progress of the beer, a feeble attempt to take her mind from Nellie. I found her in the dining room instead. She had the table covered with silver and crystal. It was rounded up in four sections, each pile about equal in size. She had filled out a placecard for each pile, except one. She looked resignedly at her work. I saw my name on the pile that contained a silver pitcher with a frog on top.

"Mother," I said. "Why my name? On these things."

"One day," she said very slowly, "you will marry. I want you to have things that belonged to me."

"But you'll be needing them yourself." I knew that Mother was ill, but she would not put a name on it and I had not allowed myself to speculate on the possible consequences.

She smiled and wrapped her arms around my shoulders. Her face was soft on mine. "Keep your smile going, Jim. It sits well on your face."

Nellie's things sat there on the table without her name on a card, because Mother could not, in her faith, forgive the trespass. Nellie was Mother's sadness now, the one that had replaced Mama Jo.

Then it was that Dad parked his car in front of Spenser Sterler Funeral Home and blew his brains out. Dad, his blood splattered on the car windows like rain drops, his face a thousand pieces of bone and flesh, had excused himself from the earth, politely sparing my mother, my sisters, and myself from finding him blasted by the bullet that dismissed him from the pain of living.

The gun was Uncle Jim's and I had seen it in the glove compartment of the car the day before my father used it on himself. The barrel had looked like a black pointing finger, a chilling threat. I said nothing about the gun to him. I was afraid of it.

Often I have imagined myself lifting it out of the car, holding the cold steel in my sweaty palm and flinging it into the Gayoso Bayou, watching it sink, the profanity of it bubbling to the surface, a floating reminder of its absolute power and my own weakness and dissolution.

The insurance money that was paid to Mother after his death was used to settle the lawsuit, but we were forced to lease the old house and rent a smaller one. We would live on the difference and on the rent money gotten from Uncle Jim's property. I wondered if we would ever come back to this house. Mother was packed and waiting to die.

But it was the Major who I remember best in the days immediately following Dad's death. He helped me make the arrangements for the funeral, and then straighten out Dad's affairs. His confidence and demeanor were intact. Yet later, when these immediate concerns relaxed, sorrow for the loss of Dad drained him of his affectations. He had me sit with him in the parlor. He began a conversation several times without getting to the core of it. "Something to tell you," he murmured. "It's like this," he stammered.

"Yes sir," I said, wondering what had come over him. His loss of words was alarming.

Finally, he stiffened his neck and began again. "Jim, I once bet against your father," he confessed. "The river race. I wanted Jim Canaan to understand completely that Nate would never hold up under pressure. I underscored it with the bet." He shrank under the heaviness of guilt, but I let him continue, not telling him that Dad most likely knew it all along. "My prediction that he would not win was only that. I never thought he wouldn't finish."

Changing the subject, I asked his advice, hoping to bring him back to his size. I admired him for trying on humility, but didn't want him to wear it. "I told Mother that I would sell the farm that Uncle Jim left to me, but she won't hear of it. I was hoping that you would persuade her."

"She knows best. Your Uncle Jim wanted you to have the land. It fullfils his promise to his family. So be it."

"Uncle Jim was a mystery," I said.

His chest, rounded under the vest, began to swell as he sat quietly remembering. "Jim," he said, choosing his words carefully, "the abyss of the unknown begins with time clearly drawn. You will sort through these questions when time permits."

When Mother, Rose Kate, and Kathleen stood talking on the front porch waiting for Distance to come round and drive them to the rental house, Moggy ran from his resting place on the Morganstern porch, crossed the street, ran to our porch, and pawing the bottom step, barked and snapped at their sealskin coats. Mrs. Morganstern came over and swatted him "for his rudeness" and wished us all "a safe journey along the road of life."

After Mother and Rose Kate and Kathleen drove away from Second Street, George and I wandered around in the house. He had hardly left my side after Dad's death. We were staying the afternoon to pack up some more things and to throw away others that we no longer had room for.

George found a sword in the attic and came running down. I was walking around with Uncle Jim's shillelagh, wondering how he'd managed the weight of it. We ended up fighting a mock duel that went from the parlor to the kitchen and back again.

He helped me get the enormous portrait of Captain Culligan down from the wall. Mother's friend, Mrs. Sullivan, had invited the Captain for a visit until we could persuade one of his relatives to take him.

We lugged boxes of the girls' clothes, shoes, and old dolls down the stairs, lining the entry hall and crowding the parlor. The movers were coming in the morning. I carefully placed the plate painted with Mother's picture in a box of confetti and wrapped the clock in an old sheet, listening to its five muffled gongs.

In the breakfast room, we stood on chairs and took down the steins from the plate rail. George wanted the one with the blue goose on it. I took the one with the eagle and the one with the crowing cock. We packed some of the others that

were special—the one that said "You're at home with a
GUINNESS" and another with the word "EIRE"—but left
the plain ones for whoever might want them. Then, with a
look of resolve on his face, George picked up a solid white
stein and walked to the living room. I studied his footsteps,
followed, and watched him suddenly wind up his arm and
pitch the stein into the fireplace. He turned and smiled at me
as though I were the umpire and he'd gotten away with a spit-
ball. I went back and picked up a gray one and brought it into
the room. I looked at him. He returned my glance, his face
placid and firm.

"Ugly," he said, shaking his head at the stein.

I lifted it above my head, and, hurling it at the hearth,
laughed until the gaslight glowing beside the mantle
blurred.

"Now?" he asked.

"Okay," I said. Then he put out the light.

As we walked across the porch and down the steps for the
last time, the bottles of beer in the basement were exploding
one by one, the shattering glass the wildest of firecrackers.